Broken
The Divine, Book Three

M.R. Forbes

CHAPTER ONE

"*Landon.*"

The voice was a whisper, an ethereal suggestion that registered somewhere in the depths of my soul, a vaguely understood siren's call.

"*Landon.*"

A little stronger this time, almost loud enough for me to recognize the source. Almost loud enough for me to follow.

"*Landon.*"

I heard it. I knew it. Sarah. She was calling me. I tried to open my eyes, but they didn't respond. They refused my command. Was I being Commanded? No. She was calling me, asking for me, but not demanding.

"*Sarah?*" I responded finally.

"*Help me,*" came the reply.

Help her? I already had. As far as I knew, we were still laying on the old bed in the abandoned farmhouse where Dante had left us, not long before.

"*Josette?*" I called out for my angel, tried to focus and find her. I could feel my power, see the threads. They were still frayed from the damage the Beast

1

had done, and I wasn't sure they would ever repair. It was such a tangled mess, I couldn't feel Josette anywhere. I could see her there, but it was as though she had been torn apart. Time was the only thing that would put us back together. Time we didn't have.

"*Where are you?*" I shouted out, searching for her. Her presence was a nudge, a tap, a sleight of hand.

I saw a point of light, and it began to spread, expanding outward until it appeared to me as a doorway. The door was fresh, new oak, but its surface held deep claw marks. I had never seen this kind of doorway before, but I knew what it was. Josette had said that was how she had found me, when the demon Reyzl was about to end my life. She had come through it, and she had saved me. Now I would save her daughter, again.

"I'm coming," I said, feeling myself floating towards the doorway. There was nothing else in my vision, just an infinite blackness, and the oak doorway floating in the ether. As I approached, I could hear the sobbing behind it. I put my hand up to it, ran my fingers across the deep grooves the claw marks had created. A sharp pain, and I drew my hand back, blood running from a sharp splinter. I focused, and it vanished. The wound vanished. The door opened.

There was nothing beyond it. A white, impenetrable light. I knew it for what it was; a transport from my soul to Sarah's.

I didn't hesitate to step through. I was blinded for a moment by the light, and then I was there, and she was there. We were in her Source, the place where her demonic heritage and her angelic heritage combined and her power pooled. I expected it to be a calm place, a peaceful place, a place of meaning to her. Josette's was the room she had lived in as a child. Mine was all of Purgatory; something I hadn't understood before, but I now knew was the result of tapping into the Beast's power. Power that had been leaking out into the realm for thousands of years.

Broken

Instead, it was a place of contrasts and chaos.

It was large, larger than I could have expected from anyone who was still technically mortal. A forest that stretched out around me, a mixture of dense, green vegetation and the greyness of death and decay. Green vines snaked around rotted tree trunks, while dry, brittle branches threatened to snap and drop from otherwise healthy growth. The sky was both heavy and blue, with thick clouds racing unnaturally across a bright morning sky. In the distance, I could hear birds calling. In the distance, I could hear animals screaming.

I could also hear the sobbing, and I followed it into the foliage, stepping carefully past the corpses of squirrels and rabbits, and sending their living counterparts scurrying away. A blast of thunder shook the earth below me, and I heard a snarl from the trees to my left.

"*Landon*," came the cry, from up ahead. It was sharper now, more desperate. I scanned the trees for the source of the snarl, but couldn't see anything. I started running, not even noticing the thick mist that had begun to fill in around me.

My feet pounded the dirt even as the rain began to fall, and in moments the dry turf was a muddy mess. I had to strain to pull myself forward, to get my feet out of the muck and keep moving. Another snarl, this time on my right. She was calling to me for help, but there was something here. Something that wanted to stop me.

I saw a clearing through a copse of bramble, with a small, open pagoda resting in the center. I could see her through the vines, kneeling there, her head in her hands. I didn't hesitate, didn't slow. My body crashed into the vines, into the thorns, and they ripped and tore into me, doing their best to impede my rescue. For a second, I thought I was hooked, as I pressed into the bramble and it pulled back against me, gripping me tightly in a thousand fingers of sharp pain. I focused, strengthening my will, grunted and shoved forward. I could feel the thorns

3

release, and I stumbled out into the clearing, the blood running down into my eyes, down onto my hands, down to fall at my feet.

"Sarah," I said, approaching her, looking on her with bleary eyes. The rain soaked into me, mixing with the blood and diluting it, the effect causing my entire body to run red.

Her head lifted slowly. Here in her Source she had eyes, a striking red and gold that was muted in her pain. I could see them dilate when she began to focus on me. They were swollen from her sobs.

"Landon," she replied, her voice little more than a whisper. "You came for me."

I reached the edge of the pagoda, nearly under its stacked roof and out of the rain. The mist was flowing around my feet and rising, but the inside stayed dry and unaffected.

"I always will," I replied. I lifted my left foot, preparing it to take the final step onto the bamboo floor of the structure, to join Sarah in the comfort and safety of the structure.

Her eyes widened like a frightened doe, and I felt the presence beside me before I heard the snarl. Something slammed into my side, powerful and sharp. It dug into my flesh, deep into my lungs, before the force threw me away from Sarah.

I didn't cry out as I hit the wet, misty ground and slid through the mud, blood pouring from the wound. I succeeded in taking a haggard breath, but I could almost feel the air leaking out while my left lung deflated. I focused, willing myself to heal, reaching for a power I couldn't hold. This was Sarah's Source, not mine. I had no power here.

I heard it coming for me, splashing through the rain. I reached up and wiped my eyes, trying to get the water and blood out of them. I couldn't get a good look at my attacker through the distorted blur, but I could see they were right on top

4

of me. Desperate, I reached out, finding a tree branch at the tips of my fingers. I gathered my strength and heaved myself towards it, moving just enough to wrap my hand around its bulk. My assailant was in the air, pouncing towards me. I gripped the branch and swung it upwards.

The branch connected, and then shattered, scattering in hundreds of rotted pieces. My enemy was unharmed, and they landed on me, crushing down on my ribs and cracking them below the pressure. Now I cried out in pain, searching inward, begging for Josette or even Ulnyx to somehow find a way to save me. My words fell empty. They weren't there.

I heard another snarl, and felt a claw rip into my face, slashing deep wounds across my cheek. Another cry, but I got my hand up in time to block the opposing blow. I blinked desperately, trying to improve my sight, trying to get a look at my attacker. The water cleared from my eyes, and it was nearly enough to stop my defense.

It was Sarah.

My mind reeled, trying to figure out how Sarah could be crying in the pagoda, and straddling my chest beating the crap out of me at the same time. Had she lured me here to attack me? Was this just another one of the Beast's tricks? The pain in my lungs, the pain in my ribs, the pain in my face made it hard to think.

"Sarah," I squeaked, trying to get her attention, to reason with her. Her arm came down, and I blocked it. She used her other arm to bat mine away. Another blow, another gash in my face.

I blinked again, and I looked into her face. It was cold, so cold. An anger and fear so white hot that it had frozen. The rain dripped from her face, disguising her tears, but I could see them there on the edges of deep, dark, red-gold eyes. I started to raise my hands again to defend myself, but decided against it. I had no power here, no strength to defeat her. If she wanted to kill me, she could kill me. Fighting would only make it worse.

I took as deep of a breath as I could and let myself relax, feeling my body sink further into the muck. Sarah sat above me, her hate-filled eyes peering down. She snarled and wheezed, her breath coming out in chunks, her body convulsing from the effort.

"Get off of him," came the shout from behind her. Sarah shifted on me, turning her body to look back. At Sarah. What the hell was going on?

Sarah sat on top of me, her legs pressed down on my broken ribs, her claws raised above my face. Sarah walked towards her, sunlight trailing behind, the mist dissipating where she stepped. Her brown ringlets bounced with each footfall, silhouetting and framing her face, enhancing her calm, gentle, beautiful presence.

"I said get off," she repeated, her voice soft and forceful.

The other Sarah turned back and looked down at me again, her hate-filled eyes softening. Without a word, she slipped off of me and backed away, taking up position behind Sarah, who knelt down and put her hand against my forehead.

"I'm sorry, Landon," she said. Her eyes were still puffy from crying. "Please, help me."

There was a warmth from her hand on my head, and the pain vanished. The blood vanished. The rain and the mist and the thunder vanished. The hint of death and decay remained, but it had been subdued. Sarah had found the strength to resist.

"Help you?" I asked, shoving myself to my elbows, looking at the two Sarahs and trying to make sense of it. "You just helped me."

There was only sadness in her eyes. "For now," she replied. "I don't know how long I can control it."

"What is it?"

She looked back at the other Sarah, crouched behind her, claws planted in the dirt.

6

"She's me. The other part of me. My secret shame. I am a true diuscrucis, brother. The blood of the angel, Josette and the demon, Gervais courses through my mortal veins. The war out there is reflected in my soul, a war within myself. A fight for control. She is always with me, and I am always with her."

She reached back and put her hand on the other Sarah's head, gently stroking her hair.

"You fight?" I asked.

"Yes. Whenever I am asleep, we fight. It's not always physical. Sometimes, she haunts my dreams. Sometimes, I haunt hers. It is so hard to find peace, so hard to be normal. I've fought it for so long. My entire life I've fought it."

We all had our good sides, and our bad sides. Whether we just woke up grumpy one morning, had a bad day, or maybe something good happened. It wasn't so literal for most of us. Not that the two Sarahs were any more real - her soul was split, balanced as good and evil. As she had said, much like the outside world. All it would take is a push in one direction or another. Just one little shove.

"What can I do?" I asked.

I'd never imagined this was how she was living her life. She had never spoken to me of her inner turmoil, her struggle against her evil nature. Or was it a struggle against her good nature? One side of her was in control right now, but what about the scratches on the doorway to her Source?

She shook her head. "I can't be trusted," she said. "What happened with Rebecca, with the Beast. All of those people..." She took her hands away from the other Sarah, and used them to bury her face again, to let her soul cry out in pain for the lives she had taken.

I got to my feet and approached her, but she backed away.

"I don't want your pity. Not here," she said, taking a deep breath and catching herself. She looked up at me. "I want your help."

7

"Help to do what?" I asked. "I don't understand what you're looking for?"

"Just listen to me, brother," she said. "I was ready to kill myself for the Beast, to kill everyone for my release from this personal hell. He promised me when I died he could bring me back, the true, singular, balanced me. He promised that I would find peace, and that when he was done with this world he would leave me in charge, to do with it as I wished while he went to destroy something else. He told me I could bring them back, bring you back, if that was what I desired. All I had to do was serve him, by killing you and Charis, and then killing myself."

"He was lying to you," I said.

She shook her head. "I would have known if he were lying. He was not."

"Then why help me? Why help us escape?"

"You are hearing, but you are not listening. Balance, brother. When Rebecca brought me to Gervais, I became angry, so very angry. Not only for what he did to me, but what he did to my people." She reached back and grabbed the other Sarah by the arm, pulling her roughly to her feet. "This one here took control. She held out my fingers, and they became claws. She used them to carve out his eyes."

The other Sarah smiled. "He deserved it," she said, speaking at last.

I remembered what I had felt when I saw the underground city in ruins, its inhabitants scattered in a gory mess. I remembered Gervais' cold confidence when I had confronted him, his needling words and twisted jokes. He did deserve it.

"I cannot say if he deserved it," Sarah said. "This part of me says that he didn't. That no thing deserves to suffer, no matter what they have done."

"You fought me," the other Sarah said, looking at Sarah. "All of the time I could feel you trying to get back, to take control."

"Yes. Until I saw mother," she agreed. She looked at me. "I thought you had killed her, and taken her. I lost the will to fight against it when that happened. Why didn't you tell me?"

"I'm sorry," I said. "I wanted to tell you, but I was trying to protect you. I thought the truth would hurt more."

"The truth never hurts more," they both said at once. I had learned the hard way.

"I'm sorry," I said again.

"I know, brother," Sarah said. "That is why I called to you. That is why I need your help. She is able to kill, and have no remorse for doing so. She is able to be selfish, and have no regrets." Her eyes began to well with tears again. "I am not she, and I cannot bear the pair of the remorse, the agony of the regrets. I don't know how, and I fear in my weakness I will not be able to prevent her from taking over again. She would have just now, if you had not arrived when you did."

It was a chilling thought. What would have happened if she had woken up while I was still asleep? If she had found me there, unprotected? If she had found Charis there? What would she have done, knowing the Beast wanted us all dead?

I reached out for her again, but again she backed away. "No, brother. Please. I am not worthy to be touched. I'm not worthy to be loved."

I felt my own tears threatening at the statement. I looked at them both. "You aren't evil, Sarah. The Beast used you. He knew what would happen. He knew you would lose control." The Beast's thirst for destruction wasn't limited to the physical.

Another step. She backed away from me again. "You know what I did. How can you love me?"

My mind flashed back to the sight of the bodies, spread out on the steps of St. Patrick's, dead at her Command. The thought made me angry, and beyond sad. I had promised her I would protect her. I had promised her mother I would protect her, and keep her safe from the evil we all knew she possessed, though I had never imagined it would take such a form. I wasn't angry at her. I was angry at myself. I had let her down. I had ignored the problem when it had first arisen, and she had paid the price.

"It wasn't your fault," I said. "It was mine. I wasn't there for you. I promised I would protect you, and I broke my promise."

She stared at me, her eyes flaring in red and gold. The other Sarah watched me as well, and then leaped towards me with a snarl.

I was ready for it. I caught her wrist in my hand, twisted and pulled her, circling around behind her. I held her arms crossed over her body, and brought her in close, holding her tightly.

"It isn't your fault either," I whispered into her ear. "You didn't ask to be here. Neither of you asked to be like this. It was the pain of what Gervais did to you that caused this. If the Beast told him to have you, he surely told him how to break you. You deserve to be whole."

I spun her around, keeping my grip on her, and pulling her into me. She struggled for a moment, and then relaxed into my shoulder. Sarah approached us cautiously, afraid to be close to her counterpart. When she was close enough, I reached out and pulled her in.

"I do trust you," I said to them. "You aren't what you were made to be. You are what you make yourself." I kissed both of them on the top of their heads. "I'll help you. I have an idea."

CHAPTER TWO

I woke up to the crowing of a rooster somewhere outside of the farmhouse. When I opened my eyes, I saw that Sarah had shifted in the night, flopping away from me onto her stomach, where she was fast asleep. Four-thirty, I knew. I had been out for nearly twelve hours. Twelve hours that the Beast had been able to use to gain his strength.

"*Josette.*" I closed my eyes and reached out for her. I felt rested, but there was something there, a sense of wrongness that I couldn't place. I found her, but we were both still ragged.

"*Ulnyx.*" I tried calling out to the Were, but I didn't expect him to respond. He had shrunk away from me as much as he could after Lylyx had died and Charis had stolen his revenge, and right now I was nowhere near strong enough to force him out of hiding. I felt only a small drop of sympathy for him, knowing how he had resisted returning control of my body to me when the fight was already lost. He would have killed us both in his rage.

I slipped off the mattress as quietly as I could, and made my way out of the bedroom and into the bathroom. There was a cracked mirror hanging above a rusted out sink, which I used to confirm that I looked as horrible as I felt. I peered into the reflection, examining the remnants of the wound Sarah had made with Malize's sword. The heavenly light hadn't hurt the way the hellfire did, and it had healed pretty well externally, save for a smooth white line on my abdomen that I wasn't sure would ever fade. Instead, I felt the drain of it on the inside, as if it had burned away a part of me. The fact that I was healing so slowly, and still felt so tired only added to that belief. I evacuated the bathroom, creeping across the bedroom as quietly as I could, heading for the stairs.

Charis greeted me with a weary smile when I emerged into the small living room where I had left her. She was still sitting in the chair in front of the empty fireplace, her eyes bloodshot and puffy, her lips dry and cracked.

"You look like crap," she said.

"Speak for yourself," I replied. "Although, I do feel like I got run over. Malize's sword..."

She shook her head. "Malize's sword didn't do this," she said. "Heavenly light isn't like hellfire. It can only harm demons."

It figured that the angels wouldn't have anything that could harm one of their own. I wished I could have been more thankful for that, but the truth of it left me more concerned. "Then why do I feel so lousy?" I asked.

"You know why, signore" Dante said, walking in through the front door that I hadn't heard open. I was in worse shape than I had thought.

"The Beast?" I asked.

He nodded. He looked like he was faring much better than we were. At least one of us wasn't a total disaster. "Your power comes from Purgatory. This whole time I believed the power was part of mine, but as we've learned it belonged to the Beast. He pulled some of it back into his cage before I was able to stop it. He also siphoned some of it away from both of you when Sarah stabbed you." He looked around. "Where is she?"

"She's upstairs, sleeping," I said. I wasn't going to tell him what I had promised I would do for her. "She feels terrible."

He didn't show any emotion. "What she feels doesn't matter," he said. "She has to live, as do both of you, until we can trap the Beast once more."

His words made me bristle. "Doesn't matter?" I asked, raising my voice.

He raised a hand, and I was paralyzed. I didn't have the strength to fight it. "No, signore," he said. "It doesn't matter. What is done is done and the Beast is free in this world. There is no going backwards, so we must put our attention on that, and only on that. I am sorry if this is disturbing to you, but we must keep ourselves focused."

He released me, and I nodded. He really wasn't going to like what I had promised her, but there was nothing I could do about that right now.

"Okay," Charis said. "So, any ideas on how to trap something that it took the two most powerful angels years to figure out how to contain, and do it in a matter of weeks?"

Dante lowered his head. "I'm sorry to say, I do not know. I haven't had to work without Mr. Ross in quite some time. I know his assistance was in some cases a ruse, and in some cases to further his own ends, but it was helpful all the same. I haven't had time to determine how to gather the information we need."

He had a point. What the Beast had done, he had done for his own purpose, but it had been instrumental in helping us to create and maintain the balance. Without him, we were short on sources for this kind of information. I could picture him sitting in his cage, bathing in the power that had been released, laughing at us.

"What about Malize?" I asked Charis. "He helped us before, and he was the one who helped trap the Beast the first time."

"He can't leave the cave," she replied. "He is the forgotten for a reason."

"What reason?"

"I don't know. He didn't tell me."

I laughed. I couldn't help it. When everything seemed so impossible, it was the best thing I could think of to do. "I guess it doesn't matter why," I said. "We can at least ask him about what we should do."

I heard soft footsteps, and a creak from one of the step's wooden boards. All of our heads turned to Sarah. She approached us slowly, her empty eye sockets swollen and red, her hair a ratty nest, my shirt still wrapped around her wrist, and the thin dress the Beast had put her in stained with blood.

"We can put him in the Box," she said. "Put him in the Box, and lose it for all time."

I walked over to Sarah and wrapped my arms around her. "How are you feeling?" I asked.

"I'll survive," she said with a weak smile, returning my embrace. I let her go and turned back to Dante and Charis.

"What is this Box she is speaking of, signore?" Dante asked.

"Avriel's Box," Charis answered. "Rebecca let Abaddon and the archangel free, in order to use it to catch Landon." She smiled and looked at me. "It didn't work out very well."

Dante looked like he was going to feint. "You have Avriel's Box?" he asked.

"I have it," Charis said. "I left it with the Templars, back in Thailand."

It was another bit of news Dante wasn't prepared for. He swung around to face her, his face turning crimson with anger. He started to raise his hand, and then paused, staring at her. He pursed his lips, and his body slumped.

"Dante?" I asked.

He held his hand out towards me. "My feelings are as unimportant as the girl's," he said. He looked back up at Charis. "I am beginning to understand many

14

things. Why did you not heed my warning about the Templars?"

"Where would we be today if I had?" she asked.

Dante sighed. "Avriel's Box," he said. "That means the demon Abaddon is also loose." He stroked his chin and sighed again. "I never thought I would say it, but I think in this case, it's actually a good thing."

"Abaddon is nothing to be trifled with," Charis said. "Lucifer created him with the memory of the Beast, imbuing him with his own hunger for death and destruction."

"Yes," Dante replied, "but he is still a demon, and can be destroyed or returned to Hell."

"We know that Avriel is in the sewers beneath Paris, and the demon is there with him," I said. "So, we get rid of Abaddon, we grab Avriel, we take him to Thailand, and he shows us how to work the Box. It seems simple enough." Simple, like solving the Riemann hypothesis.

Dante laughed. "Do you know how to kill Abaddon, signore?" he asked.

"No," I replied.

"Neither did the seraphim. That is why they trapped him in the Box. Of all of them, only Avriel had the strength of will to even get close enough to strike, but what would he be striking? No one can pierce Abaddon's veil, to find the creature beneath it. He chose to trap him, and he was ensnared as well."

"I can Command the demon," Sarah said. "He will listen to me."

Dante turned back towards her. "Why would he listen to you, bambina?"

"Because it's our only choice," she replied.

Dante shook his head. "A choice that you force us to make," he said, shifting his attention to me. "How can you be sure you can trust her, signore? There is a reason the true diuscrucis were hunted."

Sarah looked at me, her expression blank while she waited for my reply. I understood Dante's concern, because I had seen the fears play out in Sarah's Source. We had come to an agreement though, one that I could only hope would help keep her opposing nature at bay.

"I trust her," I said. "That will have to be enough."

Dante's eyes bored into me, and he looked like he wanted to say something else, but again he let it go. "Very well," he said. "I will return to Purgatory and see if there is anything I can do from there. Remember, signore, your power is diminished. You must be more cautious than you are accustomed to."

"Wait a second," I said. "You're just going to leave us out here? We're in the middle of nowhere."

"Not true, signore," he said. "I dropped you off here because I knew this place was safe, but you are only a hundred miles or so from Florence. There is a demon transport rift there that Charis can use to get you back to Paris. I would take you, of course, but I've already caused too much damage to the equilibrium. To do much more would be a boon to the Beast."

He walked over to Sarah, who gazed at him with her Sight, her face remaining emotionless.

"You have a chance to do great things," he said. "Be strong, and believe in Landon. He is the anchor in the face of this oncoming storm."

A smile began to spread on Sarah's face, and she nodded. A moment later, the poet disappeared.

"Let me see your wrist," I said to Sarah, reaching out and gently unwrapping my shirt from it. It was crusty and stiff from all of the blood that had seeped into it and dried, and I tossed it off into the corner.

I had been expecting to be greeted with a deep gash and a lot of scabbing on a wound that was too straight and fine to knit back together with ease, but was pleased to discover that Malize's sword was as kind to mortals as it was to angels.

There was a familiar white line where the cut had been made, but otherwise the damage was healed.

"It's fine," Sarah said. "The only thing painful about it is the memory."

I knew what she meant. "It's still one less thing to worry about. The next order of business is to find some new threads. I'm not really feeling like going around shirtless, and you definitely can't go out in public like that."

Even if the dress hadn't been torn and bloodstained, it wasn't suitable. The material was just thick enough and long enough to qualify as clothing, leaving enough to the imagination to almost make it worse than nothing at all.

I hadn't heard Charis move, but suddenly she was next to me, holding out a crumpled mess of plaid. "I found these stashed away in the attic," she said. "They're old, and they smell like moth balls, but you can do what you want with them." Her eyes lowered to Sarah's feet. "I didn't find any shoes." She handed a flannel shirt to each of us.

Sarah took the shirt and uncrumpled it. "Thank you, thank you, thank you." she said, unlatching the buttons. "I can't get this thing off fast enough."

She pulled the dress over her head without warning, eager to replace it with the shirt. I turned my head away, trying to hide my embarrassment and drawing an amused smile from Charis. It did seem kind of silly to be ashamed by a little bit of flesh when we were faced with something so much worse. I took my own shirt and slipped it on.

Whoever they had belonged to must have been overweight, because they hung from both of us like a circus tent. I focused, forcing the cloth to shrink down to a more manageable size. Where before it had felt like I was drinking from a river, now the power fed into me like a stream. Charis must have noticed my look of concern, because she put her hand on my shoulder and squeezed it before using her own energy to convert Sarah's tent into a flannel dress. The end result actually looked kind of cute on her.

"There's a barn out back with a rusted old Fiat in it," Charis said. "The car won't start on it's own, but I'm sure we can change its mind. Dante said there's a rift in Florence. I hope I can reach Vilya by the time we get there, because I don't know how to work it without her."

I closed my eyes and called out to Josette again. I could see the frayed edges of our connection, and I knew she wouldn't be able to respond. Only time would heal the damage, and it was the one thing we couldn't spare any of. I reached into my pants pocket and pulled out my cellphone, happy to find the hardened device was still intact, unhappy to see that the battery was dead. Not that it was likely there would be any reception out here. Obi would have to wait.

"So, I guess we head for Florence," I said. I took Sarah's hands in mine. "We'll do it after we get the Box, okay?" I asked. "The Beast probably knows we have it, and if we've thought about putting him in it, I'm sure he's thought about it too."

She nodded. "I know," she said. "I can wait. I'm okay right now."

I could feel Charis' confusion, but there was no time to explain.

"Charis?" Sarah said, coming down off the last step and standing right in front of her. They were nearly the same height, but she looked so small. Did Rebecca forget that she was mortal, and needed to eat? Did she forget it herself?

"Yes?" Her expression was warm, sympathetic. It didn't have to be, after what Sarah had done to her. She didn't have the same history with her that I did. Then again, we had connected, so in some ways she did.

"I'm sorry," Sarah said, her voice creaking more softly than the wooden floorboards had. "For stabbing you. For everything."

Charis didn't say anything. She reached out and put her arms around her, holding her in a warm embrace. She looked up at me past her shoulder, and I felt a pang in my soul. I couldn't name it, or maybe didn't want to name it, but I couldn't ignore it either.

"We need to go," I said to them.

Charis gave Sarah one last squeeze and then straightened up. "The barn is out back, we can go out through the kitchen." She took Sarah's hand to lead the way. A soft tug, but she didn't move. That was when I noticed her gaze was transfixed.

I should have felt the change in my senses, noticed the new presence in my Sight. I should have at least paid attention to the spill of light that had been coming in through the open front door, and how it was suddenly blocked.

CHAPTER THREE

"Diuscrucis," the voice roared from the doorway.

I followed the long shadow from the floor to its caster. Way too late, I could See. An angel. A powerful angel. He wasn't alone. "Melody," I said. "Who's your friend?"

I couldn't see her behind the larger seraph's silhouette, but I knew she was there.

"Initiate Melody will remain silent," the angel said. "I brought her only as witness."

"Witness to what?" I asked.

The angel stepped into the room. He was a handsome one, with a square jaw and short blonde hair that was greying around the edges. He wore the toga-like sash that the seraphim sported to fly, and it revealed a warrior's body beneath, all muscle and grit. Melody trailed in behind him, her expression one of fear.

"My name is Callus," he said. "I was sent to speak to this one, after it was brought to my attention that one of the Canaan Blades had been found and activated. It belonged to one whose name we cannot recall, but we do know he was not the one who used it. Initiate Melody was very close to where it was sensed, and her Confession revealed your involvement. I required her as witness, so she might prove her innocence in this."

Charis and I stole a glance at each other. She had said that that archangels would know if Malize's sword had been used. Obviously, they hadn't wasted any time investigating. Still, I found it a little discomforting that Callus had forced Melody to Confess. It was more than that, though. He had forced her to Confess, and he was still more concerned with a sword than he was with the Beast.

There was no sense beating around the bush. "Are you a servant of the Beast?" I asked him. He could attack, or he could tell the truth. He could try to lie, but then he would be revealing the truth.

Callus looked at me as if I had just spat in his face. "Are you suggesting that I am disloyal to my Lord?" he asked, getting right into my face. I could feel his warm breath on my temple, and see the veins in his neck pulsing.

"You didn't answer the question," Charis said.

There was another way to find out if he was a servant. Angels weren't allowed to initiate violence.

His head spun towards her, and his eyes narrowed. A smile grew slowly along his face. I peeked over at Melody. She was still standing in the doorway, and she looked like she would have been super happy to be anywhere else.

"What do you think?" he asked. "Spare me your words, and follow your heart, Templar."

Charis stared at him, her eyes locking onto his. Her body tensed up, her hands balling into fists, and then she relaxed. "He's no servant," she said.

"Then why such an interest in a sword?" I asked. "When the Beast is freed to this world."

He backed away, and motioned for Melody to join him. "The Beast is a myth," he said. "A story told by those who are lacking in more productive pursuits. The sword is real."

"I tried to tell him," Melody started to say.

"Silence, Initiate," Callus snapped. "You may speak when I ask it of you."

Angel or not, Callus was a jerk. It was an all too common theme with the seraphim elite. "I hate to break it to you, my friend," I said. "The Beast is real, and the door to his cage is hanging open."

"I am not your friend, diuscrucis," he replied. "The only reason you live is because I am not strong enough to defeat two of you on my own, and they asked me to come only to parley."

I held back my laugh. He didn't know we'd been hamstrung. He didn't know he could probably cut us all down with barely a twitch. I felt Sarah shift next to me. Well, maybe not. I didn't know if she could Command an angel like Callus, but she had somehow managed to overpower Rebecca. It wasn't out of the realm of possibility.

"So, you don't believe me?" I asked.

"About the Beast?" He shook his head. "No."

It may have seemed like an inconsequential answer, but it brought our true plight into crisp focus. The Beast's power was growing, while ours had been diminished. Survival was going to be tricky enough, and near impossible if we couldn't hope to get the other Divine off our backs. The fact that the archangels didn't seem to think the Beast was a real thing was going to be trouble.

"You haven't noticed an uptick in fallen angels lately?" I asked.

"It has been noticed," he said. His eyes shifted, slicing into Sarah. It was the first time he had even acknowledged her standing there, but there was nothing warm about his expression. "Someone has been Commanding them. No demon can Command a seraph."

He knew what she was, and he knew what she had done. Was he trying to provoke an attack? For someone who believed he couldn't win, he wasn't being very smart.

"The sword," I said, trying to shift the conversation.

He smirked. "Do not think that I would not like anything more than to take your 'sister' and remove her head, as all creatures carrying the blood of Hell deserve," he said. "Do not think I wouldn't like to do the same to you. It is difficult enough to be in your presence, I pray that my Lord will give me strength to maintain my vows, and grant me eternal peace should you choose to defend your miserable wretch of a sibling."

He *was* trying to provoke me. He had said he didn't think he could win, and he had been telling the truth. Angels didn't play games, so what the hell was going on? Was he really just so filled with hate that he couldn't control himself?

I felt Sarah shivering next to me, and her hand clenched my arm and squeezed tightly enough that her nails broke my skin. This asshole was undoing everything I had worked to achieve.

"The sword?" I repeated, making sure my voice was calm and even. If Sarah made a move, I would need to be quick to stop her before she freed him to act. He might have been feeling he would martyr himself, but I knew what the real outcome would be.

"The Canaan Blades," he said, recognizing that I held the restraint to dismiss his jibes, "have been lost for many thousands of years. We've been searching for them, my brothers, sisters, and I since that time. I've been ordered to find out how you obtained it, and ask for its return."

"You're *asking* for it back?" I said.

He sighed. "As I said, I would prefer to rip it from your dead hand, but it has been made clear to me that retrieving the Blade is more important. There's a risk involved with attempting to destroy you, a risk the archangels are unwilling to take, but I would have been. Seeing as how you won't allow me to take that risk, however... yes, I am asking." He spat the words like he had taken in a mouthful of old coffee. I could tell that it killed him to say it.

"Why do you want it back so badly?" I asked.

"The Blade was one of three forged by the hand of the Lord, Himself in the light of Heaven," he said. "It bears properties that make it unsuitable to remain in this realm."

I had been stabbed with the sword. There was nothing special about pain and blood, but then, it was only supposed to work on full-blooded demons. "What kind of properties?"

He laughed. "I'm not about to tell you what makes the Blades special," he said. "It's bad enough you've somehow managed to acquire one, and even worse that you have used it. Now, will you Confess how you came to hold the Blade, and surrender it to me, or shall I return to report your refusal?"

I knew how badly he would love to tell the archangels that I had refused him. I looked at Melody. She was standing with her arms crossed, her eyes pointed at the floor. If I didn't give him something, he might cast the blame for it onto her. For all her brashness, she didn't seem like the fallen type.

"I can't tell you who we got it from. His name is not to be spoken or remembered by the seraphim," I said. "If that doesn't mean anything to you, ask your boss. I can tell you that Melody was there because she was assigned to work with Thomas, and that's it. It's not her fault he decided to do the right thing and forego Heaven in order to help me fight the Beast. The Beast you claim doesn't exist, who just so happens to be the one who has your sword. We lost it trying to escape from him."

Callus stared at me, his jaw clenching and softening while he attempted to control himself. "You lie, diuscrucis," he said at last. He tilted his head, and then smiled. "It seems I may not have to return to report you. Perhaps I will get my wish after all."

I focused on my Sight, sensing more angels approaching the farmhouse. There wasn't much they could do if I refused to fight.

"I will ask you one more time, diuscrucis. Surrender the Canaan Blade."

I held my hands out to the side. "I don't have it," I said.

Two of the angels reached the doorway, coming in behind Callus. One was old, with long white hair and a pristinely kept beard. The other was in the body of a ten-year old boy, with a mop of brown hair and a cherubic face.

"Callus?" the younger one asked.

"Eli. He will not surrender the Blade," Callus said. "He insists that the Beast is real, that it is free and that it has the sword."

"Truly?" Eli asked.

Callus nodded. "Have you ever heard anything so preposterous? You must have known he would refuse to turn it over, since you brought so many brothers with you."

Eli smiled. "Yes," he said. "We need to kill them all."

"It would be an honor, brother," Callus said, "but he cannot be provoked."

Eli looked at me, and smiled. A smile I knew, and would never forget, no matter whose face it appeared on. "I bet I can provoke him," he said, his eyes revealing only malicious intent.

Somehow, the Beast was inside Eli. Somehow, it had taken control of him. The angel hadn't fallen, which could only mean he was being controlled against his will. Or was he? What if the seraph had let the Beast in? Did it matter?

"Go ahead and try," I said, focusing, trying to pull as much power to me as I could.

The Beast took a deep breath. "Mmmm. I can smell it. I can feel it. Enjoy it

25

while you can, kid." He moved his attention to Sarah. "I understand you're a little confused, had a little case of cold feet, but the offer still stands."

I felt Sarah's grip on my arm tighten even more. I knew the Beast's words would be registering somewhere within her. I knew that there would be a battle raging in response. He had said he could provoke me, and it took all of my strength to resist.

"Sarah," the Beast said. "Think about it. The power, the freedom. No more being split in half." He was the destroyer, and he was trying to ruin her psyche.

"Eli?" Callus asked. "What are you doing?"

The Beast didn't answer. He kept looking at Sarah, and spilling his garbage. "You will be a goddess in my universe," he said. "I'll be the only thing above you."

The way he said it, I could feel myself losing control. My body started to quiver in anger.

"Eli?" Callus asked again. "Melody? Where are you going?"

I had been so focused on the Beast that I hadn't noticed Melody backing away, reaching the door where the other angel waited. Was he a servant, or just an unwitting ally? I had no way to know.

"Come on, Sarah," the Beast shouted. "Forget about them. You were born to be their master."

"Eli," Callus said. "I don't..."

"He's the goddamned Beast, you idiot," Charis shouted, unable to hold back anymore.

Callus' eyes widened, as though he finally decided to believe; just in time for a cursed dagger to appear in Eli's hand, and disappear into his neck.

"I tried to do it your way," the Beast said, wrenching the dagger from the seraph. Callus dropped to the floor. "I don't like your way."

Broken

It all happened in a blur of instinct and emotion. The Beast, lunging for
Sarah, trying to grab her. Charis, lunging for the Beast, her own dagger in hand.
Melody, twisting away from the angel she was standing next to and narrowly avoiding
being skewered herself. It was all so fast, and at the same time so slow. Sarah was
already gripping my shoulder, so I pulled myself forward and turned, wrenching her
out of the Beast's path, while at the same time pulling a poker from its resting
spot next to the fireplace, and sending it hurtling into the angel that had
attacked Melody. It impaled the hand with the sword, forcing him to drop it. The
attack would cause him to fall, leaving her free to act at will.

The Beast's lunge struck only air, and he was just quick enough to regain his
balance and avoid Charis' dagger. He smiled again, that stupid, confident smile,
and brought the dagger around, cutting into her arm. She grunted and kicked out,
and the Beast flew backwards to slam into the wall.

I felt the rest of the angels on the move, two coming in from the kitchen,
two upstairs, and two more circling around to the front. Melody had dispatched her
opponent, so I started moving forward.

"No," Sarah said, pulling against me. "The kitchen. We need to get to the
car."

Not that a car could outrun a seraph, but it would offer some measure of
protection. I reversed course, beckoning with my eyes for Melody to follow.

"Yes, get to the car," the Beast laughed. He stood against the wall, the
dagger in his hand. "You think a car will save you? I found you here. I'll find you
anywhere you go. I'm only getting stronger, Landon. You can't stop me now, and I'm
only getting stronger. You might as well..."

His speech turned into a harsh gurgle when Charis' dagger pierced his throat
and pinned him to the wall. "See...you... in New York," he sputtered. His eyes
flashed pure white, and then returned to the seraphim gold. He'd abandoned ship.

27

Charis rushed over and pulled the blade out, taking the one the Beast had been holding, as well as the angel Callus' sword. I could hear the footsteps in the kitchen, and I could sense them in the rooms upstairs. We were getting boxed in.

The two from the kitchen appeared first. They didn't know the Beast had started it. They didn't know we should have been safe. They came in with the swords raised, anger in their eyes at the death of their friends. I tensed, ready to attack, as did Charis.

"Hold your attack," Sarah said to them. She had her hand raised, as if she was directing the Command forward. The two angels paused, and anger turned to confusion.

A breeze, and the two in the front had arrived. Sarah turned towards them. "Hold your attack," she said again. They too held up.

"Come on," I said, taking Sarah by the hand and leading her around the angels in the kitchen. Charis trailed behind.

"Melody, are you coming?" Charis asked, noticing the angel didn't follow.

She shook her head. "No. I'll stay and explain this to them. I don't know if they'll believe it, but I have to try." Footsteps on the stairs next to us. Melody stepped in front of them. "Gaius, Lucas, wait," she said.

"Landon," Sarah gasped. "Hurry, I can't hold this for long."

I had seen the anger. I didn't know if they would give Melody time to explain. I led us out the back at a run, towards a small old barn fifty feet behind the house. The doors swung open as we approached. The Fiat was going to be a tight fit, but it was better than nothing. I focused on the door to pull it open, and helped Sarah slip into the tiny back seat. Sweat was pouring from her forehead, and all of the muscles were bunched up and throbbing.

"You drive," I said to Charis, knowing she had years more experience then I did. I did my best Luke Duke impression, sliding across the hood to the passenger side and falling around into the seat.

"That's it," Sarah said, with a heaving sigh. Charis put her hand onto the starter and closed her eyes. A moment later, the two angels from the kitchen burst out the back of the house, with Melody trailing behind them.

"I don't want to kill them," I said. "The balance."

"I've almost got it," Charis replied. The angels were getting closer, and I could hear Melody shouting for them to wait. I doubted they would listen, especially after they had been Commanded by a true diuscrucis. It was a shame, but I could imagine the trouble Melody was going to be in over not trying to kill Sarah herself.

They were getting close, but Charis got the car running, the engine sputtering to life. She threw the car into gear and pulled out of the barn as fast as the machine would allow. The angels followed behind as we drove along the grass towards the front of the house. I was sure they would go airborne, but Melody finally managed to catch up, and she tackled them, pulling them down into a heap.

"I didn't even like her the first time we met," I said, looking up into the rearview mirror and watching the three angels rise. "I hope they don't punish her too badly."

Charis snorted. "I hope they try listening to her," she said, "but I'm not holding my breath."

I turned my head back to look at Sarah. She was laying across the seat, rubbing her temples. "Are you okay?" I asked.

"I hope so," she replied.

CHAPTER FOUR

I turned and checked behind us again, scanning the sky for any sign of the angels. The fact that we'd been on the road for fifteen minutes and hadn't caught sight of them was the best news we'd had. I didn't know if Melody had convinced them on the topic of the Beast, but she had at least gotten them off our tail.

"I should take the wheel," I said. I checked in on Sarah before turning my attention to Charis. She had fallen asleep with her hands still on her head. She looked peaceful for the moment, at least.

"You're sweet, Landon," she replied. "I don't mind driving."

A simple prefix, but it registered. Could the timing have been any worse? "I'm sure you don't, but priority number one is to get you back in touch with your evil side. We're stuck traveling like mortals until you do, and I'm willing to bet the odds of us making it from here to New York in a jet without being torn from the sky are only slightly above zero."

Charis rolled the car to a stop, right in the middle of the road. Not that it mattered, there was nothing around us but pasture, and we hadn't seen another soul yet.

"You have a point," she said, pushing open the driver's side door. "Did I just hear you say New York?"

I swung open my own door and got out of the car. We both circled around the front, meeting at the hood. Charis still looked exhausted, and I was sure I did too, but it didn't take anything away from her beauty. I had a thought, and discarded it. It was bad timing for sure. I crossed on the outside, meeting her eyes on the way by, giving her a small smile. We finished the circuit and took our new places. I put the car back in drive and eased us forward.

"The Beast said 'see you in New York'," I said. "He's going after Obi."

"How can you be sure?" Charis asked. "He could have said that to distract you."

"He wasn't lying."

"Well, no; but he's not Divine. I don't think it works on him."

I peeked up into the rearview again, just to be sure. Nothing. "It probably doesn't," I agreed. "I'd rather be wrong and have Obi and maybe Izak with us, than be right and have one or both of them dead. We're at a huge disadvantage, because the Beast has an army of servants he can send to do his dirty work. We're what? Seven, including Dante?"

"If this is a pep talk, you're doing it wrong," Charis said. "I know you care about your friend, but it's a huge risk. Without Obi, we can still trap the Beast. Without the Box, we can't."

Her first comment made me smirk, her second sunk my battleship. She was right, and there wasn't much getting around it. "Maybe we should split up," I suggested. "Divide and conquer."

Charis shook her head. "For one thing, you need Vilya to travel the rifts. For another, that could be playing right into the Beast's hands. It would certainly make things easier for him if he could separate us."

I took a deep breath and sighed. "I just hope Obi and Thomas got back with Izak. He's the safest harbor they've got. Considering our current situation, he's the safest harbor we could get too."

"Thailand, Landon," Charis said. "I'm sorry, but we need to get to Thailand."

"I know, I know." There was something else I needed to do in New York, but that would have to wait too.

We spent the next fifteen minutes riding in silence. Charis closed her eyes and tried to relax and rest, and to put back together the tattered strands of her connection to Vilya. I kept checking the mirror every twenty seconds or so, until I was satisfied the angels weren't going to pursue. Why would they? They had enough of a mess to clean up back at the farmhouse.

I was just beginning to settle into some kind of less alert state when I heard Sarah start gasping in the back seat. I reached up and pulled the mirror down so I could see her in it. The reflection yielded only her torso, but it was convulsing erratically, clenching and softening in chaos. Charis must have been sleeping, because she hadn't noticed. I pulled the car to a stop.

"Sarah," I whispered, turning around in the seat and leaning over so I could see her face. Her hair was caked to her face in a layer of sweat, and her hands had dug into the cushioning so hard they had broken through the cracked leather surface. "Sarah," I said again.

"No," she said softly. "That can't be. That can't be how it ends."

I realized not all of the moisture was sweat. She was tearful, pleading with something I couldn't see. I didn't understand how her ability to see the future worked. I didn't know if it was ever accurate, or just a glimpse of some of the possible threads. I didn't even know if anything she was seeing was the truth, or if it was her evil alternate haunting her dreams.

"Sarah," I said again, a little more forcefully.

32

It didn't wake her, but it did wake Charis. Her eyes snapped open and she spun around in the seat, joining me in my vigil.

"Sarah," she said, her voice a gentle coo.

"No. I don't want to do it," Sarah cried. "I don't want to. It doesn't have to be this way. Please."

Charis and I looked at each other. "We have to wake her gently," I said, maneuvering back around and pushing open the car door. Charis followed me around to the driver's side, where I shoved the seat forward so I could get to Sarah.

"No. No. No. Show me something else," Sarah whimpered. She released her grip on the cushions and started punching herself in the chest. "Show me something else."

"She's going to hurt herself," Charis said.

I reached in and put my hand on her shoulder. As soon as I touched her, her entire body shot out stiff straight in a major convulsion, and then toppled back to the seat. Her head twisted towards me.

"Get away!" she Commanded.

Her Commands had never worked on me before. She had tried a few times, most recently right before she'd been taken by her father. I understood what the power felt like, the pressure in my head, the compulsion in my soul. I'd always been strong enough to fight it. Until today.

Against my will, I started backing up. Her face tracked me, and I could feel her forcing me further and further from the car, across the street and out into one of the fields. I closed my eyes and focused, pushing back against her, trying to resist. I couldn't do it. Not when she was so agitated.

"Please," I heard her cry out to Charis. "Please, leave me alone." Charis started backing up too. Sarah climbed out of the car.

In that moment, I felt nothing but sadness and pity. She stood there in front

33

of the car in her flannel dress, her hair stuck to her face, her expression one of pure misery. She held her hands down to the side and put her head towards the ground.

"Sarah, please let me go," I said, mustering the energy to speak. "I can help you."

"I saw it," she said. "I saw it." She dropped to her knees, burying her face in her hands.

"Saw what?" I heard Charis ask.

"I saw it," she repeated.

"Sarah," I said. "Let me go. Let me help you."

The compulsion dropped. She had let me go. I ran over to her, sliding on the ground to embrace her. I held her there for a few minutes while she sobbed out her fears, and then let her go.

"Landon," she said. "I'm sorry." She looked up at Charis. "I'm sorry."

"What happened?" I asked.

She used her sleeve to wipe away some of the moisture from her face. "You know that I see... ahead. Things that haven't happened yet. They aren't always things that will happen, but are usually things that do happen. Except... they're blurry. Like shadows of the future, or a silhouette of what's to come. I saw you defeat the archfiend in New York, but I never saw mother's sacrifice to you. I want so much to speak to her."

"Sarah, I..."

"No, it's okay. I know you can't right now. I know what the Beast did to you. I can See the change in you, the way your power has shifted. I can See mother, and the demon in there too, but they are so scattered right now. You need to sleep, for days maybe, but there isn't any time."

I hadn't expected her to be able to See in such detail. My own Sight was an

34

overall understanding of what different Divine souls looked like, and it presented itself in temperature and emotion. She had to be getting deeper, or maybe higher resolution, like a camera with more megapixels.

"So you saw the future?" I asked.

She nodded. "Yes. I felt so strongly about helping the Beast. I was sure it would happen. So much of it did, but not all. Like you said, it's a potential future, and the choices we make can change it at any time. You helped me make a different choice, a better choice." She smiled weakly.

"I'm glad I could help," I said, "but I don't understand. What did you see that was upsetting you so much, that you were able to Command both of us?"

She turned her face back towards the pavement. "It was so real," she said. "So much more... I don't know... true? I felt like it would happen, no matter what choice I made. That it was the future that would come to pass."

"What did you see?"

She put her hand on my shoulder. "I don't know if I should tell you," she said. "I'm so afraid of it happening. I can't imagine anything worse. What if telling you makes it happen?"

There was no way to know. "What if not telling me makes it happen?" I replied. "If I know what it is, maybe we can work to prevent it."

Her chest was heaving, her heartbeat ratcheting up with the anxiety of the situation. She squeezed my arm tighter and took a few deep breaths, trying to calm herself.

"Sarah," I said. "It's okay. You don't have to tell me. You'll know if it's happening the way you saw. You'll be able to make the choice."

She bit her lower lip and nodded. "It is my choice, isn't it?" she asked.

"Yes," I said. "Always."

She took a few more deep breaths. "We need to get to Florence," she said. She turned to Charis. "You aren't as damaged as Landon. Maybe because there's only one in there with you. You'll still need rest."

Charis smiled. "I'll rest," she said. "Let's get to Florence."

I got to my feet, and helped Sarah to hers. Charis started circling back around to the passenger side.

"Hop in, kiddo," I said, waving her into the back seat. She leaned forward and wrapped her arms around me, pulling me down towards her.

"Brother," she whispered in my ear. "I didn't want her to hear. To hear what I saw." Her breathing was ragged, her fear of the vision obvious.

"I saw her die," she said. "I saw you die. I killed you."

CHAPTER FIVE

The rest of the drive to Florence was tough, with Sarah's final words to me before we had regained our journey rattling around in my head. She was sure she was going to kill both Charis and me. She was more certain of it than she had been of helping the Beast. It wasn't that she wanted to, or even felt compelled to, but she truly believed that she would. Did that mean the Beast was going to win? She had been concerned that telling me would cause bad things to happen, and maybe it could. If I allowed the information to seep into my psyche and convince me not to try as hard, not to fight as hard, could that be how I wound up dead?

Shadows. That was the future that she saw. In the moments we had before getting back into the car, I had asked her how she did it. She said she didn't know, only that I was dust, and Charis was dust, and our blood was on her hands. It would have bothered me more, but I was resisting the urge to believe, knowing full well we had already altered one of her perceived futures. There was nothing to suggest we couldn't do it again.

I was glad Charis had taken the opportunity to go back to resting. She didn't notice my sweaty palms, or my sure-to-be-distracted expression. She rested in the seat next to me, her head lolled to the right, a thin line of drool running out of the corner of her mouth and onto her chin. There was something so normal about it, so perfect and yet surreal. Wouldn't it be so much better if we were sitting on a couch somewhere, watching a crappy movie? How much would I want to kiss her when she woke?

The thought was troubling, and getting harder to shake with each soft breath that escaped her, with each gentle effort to try to pull the spittle back in. We had shared everything in the cave, when she had connected her soul with mine. I knew everything about her, and she knew everything about me. How could I not feel something for someone who I had known for over two hundred years? I was there for every fault, every weakness, every evil deed. I had also seen her strength, her goodness, and her ferociously loyal love. So, she had been the one who had killed me. She had also brought me back to life. It was balance.

I cast one more glance her way, admiring the shape of her face, and then checked in on Sarah. She was in the back seat, head down, her breathing even. She hadn't said anything since we had gotten in the car, and I didn't expect her to. She had a greater burden to bear than I did.

Florence was an Italian city, which meant that it just kind of snuck up on you. Nestled along the Arno river, it didn't appear in the distance as some great metropolis, but rather just appeared at the end of an endless string of farms and pastures, from a vast quantity of wheat and grass to the hustle and bustle of one of the most famous medieval centers. I'd never been here before, and driving through the streets, looking around at the architecture and history, I was more amazed than someone in my position should have been. Wasn't being Divine more amazing than sculpted stone? I wasn't so sure.

I pulled us up to the curb of the San Gallo Palace Hotel, pushing my focus to glamour the car and its riders as a trio of wealthy tourists. I couldn't actually

38

change our clothes, but I pushed the image of finery and gold accoutrements. It was enough to fool a mortal. The vehicle took its last breath and died as I eased it to a stop, and the attendant came over and opened my door.

"Good morning, signore," I said, finding a bit of joy in being able to use Dante's line.

"Good morning," he replied. "Can I take your luggage?"

I smiled. "No luggage, my friend," I said. "We just flew in for the weekend. We're going to do some shopping to take care of our necessities."

He returned the grin. "Excellent, sir," he said, laughing. "I'm sure your wife and daughter will be very pleased."

"I'm sure they will," I agreed. "Honey," I shouted to Charis. "It's time to wake up now. We're here."

Her eyes opened and she sat up, using her wrist to wipe the drool from her chin. Sarah had heard me too, and she lifted her head to see where we were.

"Welcome to Florence," I said to them. The attendant helped Charis from the car, and I took Sarah's hand to pull her from the back. "Don't worry," I whispered to her. She bit her lip and nodded.

"Please head on inside, sir," the attendant said. "I will take care of your car."

I reached out and took Charis' hand as she came around the Fiat, and led my two girls inside. How I wished we really were on a shopping spree vacation. It was easy to picture Charis as my wife, and even though Sarah called me 'brother', I already felt like more of a father to her.

"Name?" The clerk asked when I approached the front desk. He was an older man with a ring of white hair around a bald top, a pair of wire-rimmed glasses on the end of his nose, and a decades old suit on his meek frame. At least he kept it ironed. I reached into my pants pocket, feeling around the cellphone, and pulled out a Taylor, Inc. corporate credit card. Seeing it in my hand forced me to remember Rachel, and I felt a twang of guilt and regret as I handed it over to him.

"I don't have a reservation, signore," I said. "If you have a room, I can pay."

He took the card. "Of course, sir," he replied. He started typing into the computer. "I will still need a name."

"Taylor," I replied. "Justin Taylor."

The clerk typed it in. I took a peek outside, seeing that the attendant was still struggling to get the car started. Charis noticed, following my gaze and then looking back at me with an amused lifted eyebrow.

"What?" I asked.

"Nothing," she replied, her voice hinting at her mirth.

"I'm sorry sir," the clerk said. "It seems your card is being declined. Might you have another?"

That was fast. I hadn't expected a company as large as Rachel's to be organized enough to cut me off in a matter of hours. There had to be someone else involved on that front. I took the card back from him and dug around in my pocket.

"Excuse me a moment," I said. I turned to Sarah. "Do you mind?" I asked. "It's okay if you don't want to, if it makes it harder to resist her."

"I don't mind," she replied. "We have a need."

I thought she was going to Command the clerk to give us a key, but she didn't. Instead, she walked outside and started talking to the attendant, still sitting in the Fiat. He smiled at her, and then reached into his pocket and handed her his wallet. She kissed his cheek, and came back inside.

"It's better to use a card," she said, handing me a credit card. "It will make it easier when we check out."

I was a little concerned about the ease of her deviousness, but she had told me she was okay. I handed the card to the clerk, glamouring it to look similar to the one I had already tried to give him. He took it without suspicion and ran it through.

"I've put you in a room with two queen beds, if that is okay with you sir," the clerk said, handing me two key-cards. "Room 314."

"It's fine," I replied.

"The stairs are over there," he said, pointing. "My apologies, but it is an old hotel, so we don't have an elevator."

"It's no trouble," I said. "Come, my lovelies."

Sarah giggled at the term, and took my hand. Charis walked beside us. We climbed the steps and made our way into the room.

It was pretty standard hotel fare, two queen beds, a desk, a television, and a bathroom. It didn't stand out in any way, but that was fine with me.

"So, we're here," Sarah said. "Now what?"

They both looked at me.

"I'm going to go out and see if I can get a battery for my phone. Failing that, an internet cafe. I need to reach Obi, make sure he's okay, and warn him about the Beast. You two are going to stay here. Charis, you need to rest. We're dead in the water without Vilya. Sarah, you keep her safe."

"You.. You're trusting me to keep her safe?" Sarah asked.

I was about to reply, but Charis took care of it for me. "It doesn't matter if he trusts you," she said. "I do." It was well done.

"But I don't deserve it. After what I did."

"Nonsense. You aren't the only one who's done something they wished they hadn't. We need you, Sarah. I need you to watch over me. You can keep anyone, mortal or Divine from hurting us until you can wake me. I know you can."

"Okay," Sarah said. "I'll wake you if I See anyone coming."

"I know," Charis replied. She walked over to me, and surprised me by leaning up and putting her forehead against mine. "You be careful."

I pressed my head forward against hers. "I appreciate your concern. I'll be fine."

She swung her head around to kiss me on the cheek, handed me one of the cursed daggers, and backed away. The warmth of her lips on my face sent a shiver through my spine.

"I'll be back soon," I said, sticking the blade in my belt, and then turning and heading out the door.

The attendant had enlisted a bellhop to assist him in moving the Fiat out of the way, and was in the process of pushing it off to wherever they kept the cars when I reached the front desk and got the clerk's attention.

"Excuse me, signore," I said. "Where can I find a store that sells phone batteries?"

"Of course, sir," he said. "You'll want to head to Home Away, on Via Chiara. Go south to Viale Spartaco to Piazza dell'Indipendenza, and turn left when you get to Via Chiara. Simple. Would you like a map?"

A map sounded good. "Yes, please." He went in the back and retrieved a map, opened it up, and circled the hotel and the store. "Thank you, signore," I said.

I dropped the glamour as I exited the hotel, and walked past the attendants pushing the car without being noticed. Divine weren't seen by the Sleeping, unless they wanted to be.

It was a fifteen minute walk from the hotel to the store. I kept my focus on my Sight, but I didn't push it very far, trying to conserve energy. There were no Divine on the streets I was walking, or in the surrounding buildings, or on the nearby rooftops. The quiet only left me more time to think, and my mind kept flipping chaotically between Sarah, Charis, and the Beast. One to save, one to match, and one to kill. I remembered Sarah's words again. 'Three brother, there are always three,' she had said. The patterns were everywhere. The balance was everywhere.

It was then, almost out of nowhere, that I thought of Rebecca. I remembered her first writhing in pain at the point of what I'd learned was a Canaan Blade, whatever that meant. I remembered her next in the janitorial closet of the Statue of Liberty, where she had first both frightened and fascinated me. It hadn't been an accident, I knew now. Ross had dumped me right into her hands, so she could look after and guide me to the destiny he had designed. Everything she had said, everything she had done had been false. Not a lie, exactly, because I knew the feelings she had developed for me had been as real as she could understand them to be. Then she brought me to the Beast so he could kill me and take back his power. Sacrifice was a part of love, but wasn't it supposed to be the other way around? Was a demon even capable of understanding that?

I was at Home Away before I knew it. It wasn't a surprise to me that it turned out to be a store specializing in helping foreigners get connected to their loved ones through electronic devices. The clerk approached as soon as I entered.

"Can I help you, sir?" he asked. He was young, maybe the age I had been when I had died. He was tall and lanky, with a spread of curly brown hair and a stylish pair of red glasses.

I reached into my pocket and took out my phone. "I just need a battery for this," I said.

He looked at it and nodded. "The S3," he said. "That's a popular phone. We have replacement batteries behind the counter." He led me over, and dug around in a drawer behind him until he found it. "We do an exchange service here. Just give me your battery, and you can take this one. The price is one euro."

I unsnapped the back of the phone and took out the battery, handing it to him. He gave me the replacement and I slipped it in. I snapped the cover on and hit the power button, thankful when it began booting. Then I grabbed the attendant's credit card and gave it to the kid. He ran it through, and it was done.

"Thanks," I said, taking back the card and heading back out into the street. The phone was almost ready to go, and there was a restaurant with outdoor seating nearby. I made my way across the road, the traffic flowing smoothly around me, and claimed a spot at the cafe. I leaned back in the chair and stuck my legs up on the table, ignoring the looks I was getting from the other patrons.

The phone rang four times before Obi picked it up.

"Where the hell have you been, man?" he shouted into the phone. "It's like World War 'D' over here."

I dropped my legs and stood up. "What do you mean?" I asked, finding the panic button in record time.

"I mean total Divine chaos," he said. "Demons and angels fighting together, hunting down any Divine they can find, and taking out whoever or whatever gets in their way. The angels are outnumbered, and without an archfiend, the demons are disorganized. We've been lucky, because most of it has been isolated to more private locations so far, but I think it's only going to get worse."

It was only going to get worse. The Beast's warning. He had started his destruction in New York, because that's where the factions were weakest, thanks to me. I was the one who had taken out the archfiend, dismembered the ruling vampire family, and caused the angel sanctuary to be decimated. I was the one who had created the balance in that war, and unwittingly designed a complete imbalance in the other. It was exactly what the Beast had said he needed me for, and I hadn't let him down.

I hadn't felt any of it. The balance hadn't moved, at least not enough to create that empty pit in my soul. If the angels were fighting on the side of the

44

Beast, they would fall. Unless they were only fighting demons. The Beast had said he needed the balance to keep his enemies from growing too strong. It made sense that he would order them to be careful about who they went up against.

"Is Izak with you?" I asked, hopeful.

"Yeah, man. He's the only reason Thomas and I are still alive. Seriously, what the hell is going on?"

I let out a held breath. If Izak was with Obi, he was as safe as he could be. "It's a long story," I said. "The important part is that the Beast is out of his cage, and he's consolidating his power. The Divine on the rampage are his followers. They're going to be doing their best to wipe all Divine out of existence, and then enslave humanity."

There was a pause. "Sounds like just another day at the office," he said.

"Yeah, but don't worry. Charis and I have a plan."

He chuckled. "Don't worry? You wouldn't be saying that if you were here. Did you find Sarah?"

"I found Sarah."

"You don't sound that thrilled."

"She was the one who set the Beast free. I'm trying to help her, but between you and me, I'm not sure if I can count on her." It was a tough thought. One that I hadn't wanted to confront, but was hard to avoid. "She told me she was having visions that she was going to kill Charis and me."

Obi breathed heavily into the phone. "I don't know what to say. Stay alert, I guess."

"The Beast took some of my power. I can still focus, but I don't have the mojo I used to. I have to trust her, even though it could cost everything, because we can't do this without her." She had already used her ability to Command to bail us out twice. We were going to live or die by Sarah's mental state. That one was

45

tough too. "Obi, do me a favor?" I asked.

"What do you need, boss?" he replied.

"There's a church near the Belmont, Our Blessed Lady Mary. The priest there, can you go and check on him? Make sure he's safe?"

"Sure, man," he said. "But why?"

"Just do it for me? I'll owe you one."

He laughed again. "You already owe me a hundred or something."

"Yeah. Think of how awesome it'll be when I pay you back." I gave him a few seconds to stop laughing. "Can you turn the phone over to Thomas?"

"Yeah, one sec," he replied. I hear the muffled sounds of the phone changing hands.

"Landon," Thomas said. "It is good to hear that you are well."

"For the moment," I said. "I wanted to ask you; have you ever heard of the Canaan Blades?"

Silence. A breath. Another. "Why do you ask?" he said, nervous.

"I was visited by an angel named Callus. He said that the sword Malize gave to Charis was one of three Canaan Blades. He wanted it back, but we lost it trying to escape from the Beast."

More silence. "The Beast is free?"

"Yes, and no. It's complicated. Thomas, I need you to talk a little faster. We're kind of rushed on time."

The angel sucked in some air, and sighed it out. "Okay," he said. "Callus is an Inquisitor, a seraphim detective, if you will. His job is to track down lost relics and artifacts, and retrieve them to either assist in the war against Hell, or return them to Heaven so they can't be misused. I saw Charis' sword... if I had known it was one of the Blades, I wouldn't have let you take it to the Beast. Who is this Malize? I've never heard that name, and I know the names of all of the elder seraph."

"Charis called him the Forgotten. She doesn't know why he's called that, but obviously its because nobody remembers he ever existed. Anyway, it's not important. What is important is how desperate the good guys were to get it back, and if it, or the other two Blades can help us against the Beast."

"I don't know if they can help you," Thomas said. "All I know of them is that they were created during what were known on Earth as the Dark Ages. Three swords, gifted to three seraph, to be used against a collective of archfiends who were massing an army around the mortal fighting, sewing even more discord and furor into the region. The angels brought the swords to bear against enormous odds, and emerged victorious. The balance began to swing heavily towards the Lord."

I had seen the sword do its work. It had burned so bright the archvampire Cho hadn't stood a chance in its glare. "Something happened to keep it from tipping," I said.

"Yes," Thomas agreed. "The Swords of Gehenna. You can guess their purpose."

The exact opposite of the Canaan Blades, for sure. Even without Charis and I, the two sides had managed to keep some kind of balance pretty well on their own. "So what happened?"

"I don't know. I don't think anyone does. The angels who were in charge of the Blades were killed, and they were lost. Which could have caused the downfall of Heaven, except the archfiends who held the Swords of Gehenna were killed as well."

It was hard to believe, especially since all of this had happened before any diuscrucis had walked the Earth. Who else would have taken them from both sides? "So somebody took all of the weapons. Why?"

"A good question. What's even more curious is that whoever took them, never used them. As you've found, their power is such that they're very noticeable when activated."

Somehow, Malize had gotten his hands on one. Even though he couldn't leave the Cave, and they hadn't been created until a thousand years plus since Jesus had been buried. Even though he would have fallen if he had killed an archangel to get it. Was Charis wrong about Malize? And, where were the other swords?

"So, what do they do that makes them so special?" Besides only being capable of destroying pure demons. The Beast must not have known what the sword was either, or he wouldn't have let Sarah use it to try to end us. And he called himself a god.

"I don't know," Thomas said. "That history is not kept in the open. Still, it doesn't comfort me to know the Beast has one."

Even angels had their secrets. "Me neither," I replied. "But at least he can only kill demons with it." Demons like Rebecca. "Thanks Thomas. I've got to get going. Remind Obi to do what I asked, and tell Izak that Sarah is safe. We'll be back in New York in a day or two. Stay safe."

"I'll tell them. You stay safe as well, my friend," he said. "By the way, how did you get Callus off your back?"

The question was posed with a thread of anxiety. Thomas may have signed up to join my little club, but that didn't mean he was comfortable with the idea of dead angels in my wake. I wish I could have given him better news.

"The Beast killed him," I said. "I've got to go." I hung up, feeling just a little bit dirtier than I had before the call.

CHAPTER SIX

I started walking back up towards the hotel, my mind churning through what Thomas had told me. Who would have had the power to kill angels and demons holding a set of the most powerful weapons ever made?

It would have been a vacation to be hunting down a more complete history of the things. I could almost see myself sitting on a beach somewhere with a laptop, cruising the internet for any tidbits of data I could dredge up, Charis in the lounge chair next to me. In my imagination, she was wearing a little red two piece, her toned flesh glistening in the sun, her hair laying damp around her shoulders. She pulled her sunglasses down her nose and looked at me, her eyes inviting, and then rose out of the chair and sprinted for the water, pulling off the shreds of fabric as she went.

"*Landon.*"

The knock from Sarah shook me out of my daydream, shoving me back into reality and leaving me a little bit breathless. Where had that little fantasy even come from?

"*Sarah, are you okay?*" I asked, glad that she was still able to keep an eye

49

on me.

"*For now,*" she replied. "*I've been watching over Charis, standing by the window. I saw a messenger demon pass by a few minutes ago, and now it's back, sitting on the roof of the building across the street, staring at me.*"

That wasn't a good sign. Whether it was the Beast, or just the local demonic overlord, the messenger demon would keep an eye on the prey while a more powerful contingent moved in. There was no doubt they would be picking up Charis' signal, the only question was how they would be receiving it.

"*I'll be there right away,*" I said. I focused, pushing power to my legs, and started running. I could still tear up the pavement, but the noticeable reduction in output nagged at me with every stride.

"*We'll be waiting,*" Sarah said. "*I'm going to wake Charis.*"

I felt her presence vanish from my mind, and I tried to push harder to pick up the pace. It couldn't be more than a few minutes to the hotel.

I put all of my energy into the run, and turned all of my attention to the thrill of it. The pumping blood, the wind on my face, the feeling of my muscles thrumming beneath the skin. It was raw pleasure, a twist of freedom I hadn't experienced in some time, maybe even since I had been mortal. It was short-lived.

There was no warning. I was so focused on the visceral joy of the chase that I never Saw the were charge out of the alley, leap, and grab me, throwing me violently into a second alley directly across from his origin. He landed on his feet, while I tumbled and rolled along the pavement, scraping up my meager clothes and feeling the bite of stone in my skin. I cursed at the pain, and came to a stop.

"Diuscrucis," he said. "We were told you would be here."

My body began to knit itself, and I stumbled to my feet. My assailant was keeping his distance, blocking off the only way out of the alley. He had hit me in his demon form, but had since shifted back. He was tall and muscular, with a huge

50

jaw and a bald head.

"Who told you?" I asked. I already knew the answer.

"A friend of yours," he said. "He told us where to find you and your friends.
He said you weren't feeling quite yourself."

"He must have been exaggerating, if you think you can take me alone," I said,
grabbing the dagger at my belt and holding it out, crouched into one of Josette's
favorite guard positions.

"Look up, diuscrucis," he replied. "I'm not alone."

I looked up, and I could see the throng of weres standing above me, edging
the buildings on either side of the alley. I hadn't Seen them. I still couldn't See
them. They were far enough away to avoid detection, but close enough to leap
without killing themselves.

"He offered to promote me if I captured you alive," he said. "I would never
have tried it, but he told me to test you out. We've been following you from the
rooftops since you left your hotel. I was sure you would have known we were there."

I should have known they were there. "You and your pack aren't acting alone.
Who's commanding you?"

"Myzl is leading the attack. He's probably meeting with your friends right
about now."

Myzl. I knew the name. A fiend without a home, he didn't seek out the kind of
power that most demons hungered for. His desires were much more physical. I could
only imagine what the Beast had promised him, and I could only imagine how he would
handle Charis and Sarah if given a chance.

I looked up at the weres surrounding me again. There were at least a dozen of
them starting back, ready to pounce if I tried to run. Of course, I didn't have a
choice but to try something. If I let them take me, I was as good as dead anyway.
It was all just a matter of timing.

I dropped the dagger and put up my hands. "Fine. You've got me," I said. "You should know, Myzl is working for the Beast."

"Who?" he asked.

"You don't know who the Beast is?" I said.

"I know there's an old legend about it," he replied. "I'm not stupid enough to believe that it's real, especially coming from you."

I couldn't help but laugh. The angels hadn't believed me, why would the demons? It had been such a long time, neither side could conceive of the fact that their oldest stories were true. "If the Beast wins, you're going to die," I said. "We're all going to die."

The bald were smiled. "There is no Beast," he growled, turning his attention to the rooftops. "Come and get him."

The rest of his pack leapt from the buildings, landing gracefully in the alley. Two of them grabbed my arms while the others loitered around them.

"Take him to the rift," Baldie said.

They started to move me forward, and I let them. The other weres formed up around me, leading me to where Baldie was standing at the end of the alley. It was a lost cause to try to get away from them while they had me boxed in. Once we got out into the streets, it was a different story.

"You're going to regret not believing me," I said. Baldie stood right in front of me, leading us out of the alley. The mortals had subconsciously fled the scene, something in their mind telling them to stay away from the area.

"I'm going to regret not gagging you," he replied with a snarling laugh. I heard a couple of throaty chuckles behind me. It was time to go.

I focused, pushing my will, demanding my body to become stronger, and then using the strength to stomp on the feet of the weres who were holding me. I felt their bones pulverize beneath my feet, their weight shifting as they recoiled in pain. The change in their balance was what I had been after, and I pulled them forward, throwing them into the weres in front of me. Four of the five fell together in a heap, leaving only Baldie between me and the open road.

"Going somewhere?" he asked, lashing out at me with hands elongated into claws. "Not if I can help it."

I took the blow on the cheek and let the force of the attack carry me to the side, away from the weres that had been behind me. I rolled onto the ground and hopped to my feet, ducking under a follow-up attack from him. The others were regaining their footing, shifting to their demon forms. I was running out of time. I wanted to go north, and north was clear. All I had to do was get the furry monkey off my back.

He tried to hit me again, and I sidestepped, twisting and planting my elbow in his jaw. I heard the crack of it breaking, and he crumbled to the pavement. At least my muscle memory had retained some of Josette's ninja moves. The coast was clear, and I propelled myself forward, legs pumping.

The weres gave chase. I could hear them growling, their sharp claws scraping the cement. I started to push harder, but I knew it would be a waste. Even pumping myself up, two legs were no match for four. Where the hell was Ulnyx when I needed him? In there somewhere, I knew, torn to pieces and licking his wounds. I reached out with my Sight, and ducked below a heavy tackle, sliding along the ground, then rising up and turning east. The weres turned with me, chasing me along a narrow street. I could see people up ahead, our battle shifting locales too quickly for them to evacuate.

Cursing, I saw a fire escape up ahead, and I coiled my legs and jumped for it. It was fifteen feet up, and I hit the metal hard, feeling my ribs cracking on the impact. The weres didn't slow, and I turned and lashed out with my foot, catching one in the snout and sending him careening back to the ground. I pulled myself upwards, ascending towards the rooftop.

The fire escape shook when the weres started landing on it, led by Baldie. Even in his demon form, there was a patch of fur missing from the top of his head. I could have laughed, if I had any strength to spare. Instead, I stopped, twisting around on the metal structure and putting my hands below my body, focusing on the iron, willing it to rust and crumble, pushing the corrosion along its length to where it was bolted into the stone. Baldie was getting close. I could see his yellow eyes looking up at me. I could feel the heavy stench of his labored breathing.

I smiled and waved when the fire escape lost its grip on the building, and the whole group of them went down with it.

It was a temporary victory, I knew. They would heal from the wounds, and be looking for a way back up to where I was. My body began to feel sluggish, but I pushed ahead, climbing the fire escape ten stories up to the rooftop. I could see the way north to the San Gallo Hotel. I resumed the run.

I sent my focus outward, capturing the heat of the demon army in front of me, and the growing heat of the weres gaining behind and below me. I reached the edge of each building and leaped, willing myself to the other side, fighting against fatigue to reach my destination. I Saw the grunts coming, their wings carrying them from nearby buildings on an interception course. I didn't slow, catching the arm of one mid-air and throwing it into another, lashing out with feet and hands to send the lesser demons scattering.

I hit the next rooftop and tripped, sprawling forwards and getting right back up, ducking under a claw and grabbing it on the way by, pulling the grunt from the sky. Without a blade or Ulnyx's strength I couldn't kill them, but it was enough to get me through their lines. One more jump, and the shorter hotel was right in front of me. I could See Charis now, and Sarah. They were backed into the corner of our room, a white hot beacon standing over them, flanked by a pair of fallen angels. It had to be Myzl.

Nobody was moving. Charis was in front of Sarah, and I knew she was trying to protect her. Why wasn't she Commanding the angels? I knew she had the power. Something must have happened. There was no time to stop and consider. There were vampires on the ground, and the weres had split up. The grunts still circled in the air, coming towards me more cautiously now. My feet were approaching the edge of the building, and I gathered myself for the jump.

Time seemed to slow as my feet left the ground, my body launched forward, angling towards the window of the corner room in the hotel. I pushed the air in front of me, shattering the glass before I hit it, collecting the shards and pulling them back out into the open atmosphere. Some of them dug into my body, but more of them flew by, implanting themselves into a pair of grunts who hadn't been cautious enough. I crashed into the room, the momentum carrying me forward into the drywall and through to the next room. I Saw Myzl and Charis both turn to look in my direction, right before I made my grand entrance by smashing through the wall and coming to a stop on my back behind the demon and his cronies.

I knew I should say something witty, but I was too tired and in too much pain. I groaned and tried to get to my feet, but was gripped by the angels within seconds. They pulled me to my feet, and I got my first look at Myzl.

"Hello, Landon," he said. He was handsome, middle-aged, with a neatly cut mane of salted red hair and a crisply groomed goatee. His smile was perfect and white, and his red eyes hypnotic. He was wearing a simple black suit with a black tie, and I could see the runes running up his wrists.

I looked at Charis. Her eyes were wide, and she was frozen like she was in shock. Sarah was on the ground behind her, head buried in her hands, whimpering.

"Do you surrender?" I asked. It was stupid, but it was all I had.

55

Myzl laughed. "Do you?" he replied.

I strained against the grip of the angels. One was male, the other was female. They both had short black hair and similar features. "What do you think?"

"I think I'll have to convince you, like I convinced them," he said. He held his hand out, and then he was gone.

"Landon," Rebecca said. She was standing in front of me, blood staining the front of the dress she had been wearing in the Beast's prison. "You let me die. You could have saved me. How could you do that?"

I knew it wasn't Rebecca, didn't I? It seemed so real. My mind felt muddled by the vision, by the power. "I'm sorry," I said, the words falling out unbidden. My head caught fire, and I felt the guilt and fear begin working its way up my spine.

"Sorry?" she asked. "I would have done anything for you, if you had only asked. I would have stopped following the Beast for you. I would have been on your side forever. We could have been together. Friends, lovers, anything you wanted."

My thoughts lost cohesion, and I dropped to the ground. "I'm sorry," I repeated. I felt the wetness of my tears. "Please, forgive me." My hands were up, and I was on my knees, begging her.

"I can't," she said. "You let me die. You gave me to the Beast."

I was tired. So tired. I fell forward, still in supplication. Rebecca stood over me, and the blood from the wound in her heart dripped down into my hair. "I'm sorry," I whispered. The floor was spinning, and I knew I was going to lose consciousness.

"*Hey, meat.*" The voice resonated in my faltering mind, echoing into a vast emptiness.

"*Ulnyx?*"

"*How did you like that bathing suit?*" he asked. "*Charis. Man, is she hot or what? Oh, and when she took it off? Wooo-Eeee! Too bad she killed that asshole vampire. I think I'm going to kill her."*

I felt the Great Were flooding into my mind, his power eating into my soul. *"What are you doing?"* I asked, my voice barely more than a croak.

"I've been waiting," he said. *"Waiting for you to be weak. Waiting for you to be spent. Waiting to take over. Your soul is mine, meat."*

I felt the power growing, felt him pushing me out of my own body, my soul sinking behind his own. I tried to focus, to fight it, but he was right. I was too weak. I had lost too much to hold him back, and I didn't have Josette to help keep him at bay. *"Ulnyx, wait. You don't understand."*

"I understand enough," he growled back. *"Lylyx is dead because of you, and her killer because of that bitch of yours. I'm going to get my payback, and then I'm going to go have some fun. You've been driving too long, meat."*

"The Beast," I said. His power was overwhelming me, pushing me further and further down. I felt like a ghost in a machine. Was this how he had lived since I had absorbed him, observing and waiting for a chance to surface?

"The Beast can suck it," he replied. *"Let him destroy the world, what do I care? I'll party while it burns, and I'll laugh when he comes around to destroy me. I'll laugh in that stupid bearded mug of his."*

I wanted to say more, but he cut me off. I pushed my thoughts forward to speak, but a vice clamped down on me, creating an insane pressure in my head. *"Keep it shut, meat,"* he said. *"I've got work to do."*

I felt my body moving. I saw it through my eyes. First, the floor. Then, the demon Myzl's feet. He was kneeling in front of me, his hand still out, trying to control me with his power. He didn't know I wasn't in charge anymore. He didn't know the new power he was dealing with. I felt my hand grow and change into a claw. My mouth emitted a harsh, guttural growl, and it lashed out, ripping the hand right off the archfiend.

He stumbled back, crying out in pain. Ulnyx lunged, grabbing the demon by the throat and twisting, snapping his head off his shoulders like it was nothing more than the top of a dandelion. He roared, turning towards the angels, catching their swords on enlarging, toughening skin, grabbing each by the head and smashing them together. They shattered like watermelons.

"God damn it feels good," he shouted in his deep, rocky voice.

The archfiend was dead, his hold on Charis broken. "Landon?" she asked, her voice tentative. Ulnyx turned to face her.

"Not quite," he said. "But if you want to leave a message before you die, I'll pass it on to him."

She gasped and whipped her sword up, too slow. Ulnyx caught her wrist and twisted, breaking it and making her drop the blade.

I tried to cry out, to ask the Were to stop. I tried to focus and force it. I tried to find Josette. It was like sitting in the front row of a movie theater, watching the nightmare unfold on the screen. I was powerless to stop him.

"I don't want to kill you too fast," Ulnyx said to her. "I didn't get to take my revenge on the vamp, so you'll have to do instead."

"Unlyx, wait," Charis said. The Were had finished shifting, and he crouched, packed tightly into the small room.

"For what?" he asked. "Are you going to undead the vampire so I can have a turn? One thing. One freaking thing in my entire life that meant anything to me. One thing that filled the blackness of my soul. I'm a demon. I'm evil. Deal with it." He reared back to lash her with his claws.

"No," Sarah Commanded, ducking out from behind Charis. "Stop."

I felt her power resonate through my hijacked soul. The Were was strong, and he fought against it. "You can't stop me, little girl," he said.

58

"I can," she replied. "Go back to your hiding place, dog."

The word infuriated him, but his fury cost him his concentration. The power shook inside of me, vibrating every molecule of my essence. I could feel him weakening below the Commands.

"No," he said again. He tried to bring his arm forward, to slash Charis. He couldn't.

"Give Landon his body back."

The pressure was intense. My existence shook violently, and I felt my body shudder.

"No," he said one last time, turning and leaping.

He crashed through the outer wall of the room and dropped to the ground below, ripping into the smaller weres on the ground. They scattered in front of him, and he bounded away, out into the city. I could feel my body working, my blood pumping, the raw power of the Were coursing through it. I didn't know where he was going, or what I was going to do to stop him. He knew the score, and he didn't care. What the hell was I going to do now?

CHAPTER SEVEN

We raced through the city, headed north. I don't know if Ulnyx knew where he was taking us. I doubted that he cared. Away was sure to be good enough. Away from Sarah, the only one who could stop him from ripping Charis apart.

"Ulnyx!" I tried to shout to the Were, to get his attention, to slow his escape. I could feel his power surrounding mine, the strands of his energy wrapped tightly around my own, holding it the way I had held his. Ever since Charis had killed Cho, he had hidden, hoping for a time when I wouldn't be able to stop him from taking over. He hadn't been wrenched loose by the Beast like Charis had been. Instead, he had seemed so small to Sarah because that was his design. He couldn't have known the Beast would weaken me so much, could he? It had been a perfect storm that had brought him into power. How long might he have had to wait without it?

If he could hear me, he was ignoring me. He wasn't giving me a chance to ask him if he was a servant of the Beast, or to find out the whole of his game. We ran at a breakneck pace, out of the city limits and onto a one land country road, twisting westerly into the hills. I wish I could have enjoyed the scenery more, because the landscape around us was beautiful. Instead, I had to figure out some way to get Ulnyx to stop acting out of the pain of his loss, and start listening to whatever type of reason I could pass on to him.

"*Where are we going?*" I asked him, focusing my energy and digging into his own. "*Damn it, Ulnyx! At least tell me that.*"

"*I'm going to find some nice country folk,*" he replied, finally answering me. I wished he hadn't. "*I want a farmer's daughter.*"

"*Ulnyx, don't,*" I said. "*Slow down, and let's talk about this.*"

His laughter boomed around me. "*You want to talk, meat?*" he asked. "*You never wanted to talk when I was the one in the sidecar. You never asked me what I wanted. Why the hell should I care what you want?*"

Why? I had no idea. I had nothing to offer. Nothing to give him in exchange for my freedom. He had my body, he was free to roam the world. Why would he ever give that back? If I was lucky, maybe one day Charis and Sarah could catch up to him, and she could talk him into relinquishing control.

"*I know you cared for her,*" I said. "*I know you wanted to kill Cho. I was there, Unlyx. He was kicking your ass.*"

He stopped running, skidding to a halt and standing in the center of the roadway. "*You think I don't know that?*" he roared. "*She was my mate, Landon. I couldn't even avenge her death! For all of my strength, all of my power, and even with your help, I couldn't kill that piece of crap!*"

That's what was really eating at him. "*So killing Charis is going to change that somehow? He wasn't just an archvampire. He had drank Rebecca's blood, my blood from the Holy Grail. The only reason Charis was able to defeat him is because she was using a freaking vorpal blade.*"

He started trotting forward again, but I could feel some of the fire and anger burning away from him. "*It doesn't matter,*" he said. "*She's gone, and I'm horny.*"

"*I've seen your memories,*" I said. "*I know the truth. You've done a lot of messed up crap, and you've hurt a lot of people, but I know what it's all about.*"

"*I'm a demon, meat. Remember? Just because I've been stuck inside you, doesn't mean I've turned into a wuss like you.*"

I flashed through the memories. The violent, angry, vile memories. He had murdered, he had tortured, he had raped. He had eaten the flesh of man while they were still alive, laughing as they screamed in pain and horror. He had ripped the teeth from a vampire one by one, feeding each back to their owner, forcing him to swallow them. He had done much worse than that. If my body was my own, I could have retched.

Yet, he also had the capacity to love. He had the ability to desire offspring, so badly that it had been this simple truth that had been his greatest undoing, driving him to so much of his violence. He was able to care about Rolix, enough that he felt such fury towards the Templar who had killed him. He was a demon, and his potential for destruction and lack of remorse over the agony of others was undeniable. So was his sense of loyalty, and of duty, and of pain and loss and love. He needed that spark of life, that connection to the Creator to survive, just like all of Lucifer's earthly creations did. It was that spark that made him more than just a machine of death and chaos.

"*You aren't all evil,*" I said. There was a time that I believed he was. That was when I had only seen the memories, but I'd since experienced them. The debilitating waves of history had brought me to a deeper understanding of both of my companions. "*You loved Lylyx.*"

I felt the wave of sadness crash through him. "*I did,*" he replied. "*I could never give her what she wanted, because I was too weak. She died to save me, because I was too weak. When a Divine dies, there is no afterlife. No Heaven. No Hell. No something more. She's gone... like, gone, gone. There's nothing else for* me, meat. *Nothing but the anger, and the hate, and the desire. It's all I have, and it's all I am."*

There was nothing to say. How could I possibly respond to that? I felt the pain myself, a sharp stab in my soul, and Rebecca's face rounded into my memory. No something more. My inability to save her weighed on me. I knew it shouldn't, she had been an enemy, but there was something there I just couldn't shake. I shifted my thoughts to Rachel, and to Zeek. Where were they now? They had been mortal, their longevity provided by their allegiance. Did they go to Heaven, or Hell? Would I see them again?

Ulnyx continued trotting for another hour or so, until he came to a high stone wall. He raised our nose to the air and took in a deep breath. It smelled like tomato sauce. *"Do you think they have a daughter?"* he asked, gathering himself and leaping the barrier with ease.

"You're really going to do this?" I asked.

"Why not?"

I was going to tell him not to, because it was evil. I almost made myself laugh. Instead, I said nothing.

We could smell them as we moved in closer. The musty, musky, dirty smell of the man who had spent the day out in the fields we now stalked through, tending tomatoes and herbs, caring for cows and pigs and goats. The sweeter, softer smell of his wife, who had made him fresh pasta and bread, and smelled like the kitchen she spent her days in. The flowery, youthful, evanescent scent of their daughter, fresh and clean out of the shower, ready for their meal together. Ulnyx had found what he was looking for, and he was going to do it, unless I could figure out some way to stop him.

He shifted back to human form, and crept through the fields. He didn't bother trying to conceal our approach, because they couldn't have seen us anyway. We reached the house, and we made our way right up to the kitchen window and peered in.

The family was there, sitting down at a small wooden table, enjoying their fare. The parents were middle-aged, with wild, greying black hair, their faces creased in reaction to their lives. They talked and laughed, touching one another lovingly as each told a story, or they shared a moment from their past and relived it with their offspring. She was no more than fifteen, with long, black hair and a freshness that I could feel stirred the desire in the Were's dark soul. She was smiling and happy, wrapped up in the joy and love of her family.

"*She's just a kid,*" I said. "*She doesn't deserve this.*"

"*Shut up, meat,*" he replied. I felt his power clamp down on my own, inhibiting me from speaking to him.

Ulnyx circled back around to the front door of the small home, and then reached out and twisted the knob. The door groaned slightly as it swung open. They felt so safe, they didn't even bother to lock it.

"Did you hear the door?" I heard the wife say.

"Probably just the wind," her husband replied.

Ulnyx slipped into the house, into a small living room with an old couch and a rocking chair, a fireplace and a shelf filled with books. We walked directly across it towards the kitchen, a creepy grin spreading across our face, our heart gaining speed with the imminency of our conquest. I could feel our libido thrumming and eager for the taste of young flesh.

"Is someone there?" the man asked, after we stepped on a creaky floorboard. It was that sound, that question, that propelled the Were into action.

He swept into the room, a figure out of their nightmares, reaching out and lifting the girl from her seat, holding her from behind. The girl's mother screamed, and the father rose to his feet, his kitchen knife clutched like he could

64

cut someone with it.

"Hello, child," Ulnyx whispered into the girl's ear. "Such a beautiful creature. I have something special for you."

The girl shivered in his arms, tears rolling down her face. The smell of her urine overwhelmed the other kitchen scents.

"Let go of her," her father demanded.

"Or what?" Ulnyx growled. "Are you going to butter me?"

The farmer's arm shook as he stepped forward, the knife shaking wildly from side to side. Ulnyx let out a soft laugh, and his hand shot forward, grabbing the man's wrist and twisting. I heard the crack, and the knife dropped to the ground.

"Let her go!" The girl's mother hadn't been stationary. She had grabbed a pan from somewhere, and it came screaming towards the back of our head. It hit us hard, and even managed to force Ulnyx to take a step forward to rebalance us. He growled and reached back, taking the woman by the neck.

"That wasn't smart," he said, pulling her towards him. He brought her right up to his face and took a deep breath. "I smell the sickly sweetness running down your leg. I was only interested in your child, but you may hold some entertainment value as well."

"Wait, please!" The husband was coming towards us again, his hand hanging limp. "I'll give you whatever you want."

"I already have what I want," Ulnyx snapped. "Now, be a good boy, and clear the table for me. As you can see, I have my hands full."

The man hesitated until Ulnyx tightened his grip on his wife's neck. "If you're agreeable, I might leave them alive," he said.

The man nodded and obeyed, using both hands to push the food from the table, despite the amount of pain it caused. Once it was clear, Ulnyx pulled the mother over to it, turning her towards him. "The end of the world is coming," he said. "Is it wrong for me to want some simple pleasures before it does?"

I closed myself off from him then, the way he had done to me. I retreated, pulling my soul in as tightly as I could, separating myself with every ounce of effort. I didn't want to witness what he was going to do. It would be enough that it was my face they would see.

As I retreated, I pushed one last time, sending one final message to the monster I was trapped with.

"I hate you," I said, letting go of my external senses, watching the world fade away even as the Were pushed the woman onto the table and tore away at her clothes. I couldn't cry here, but the pain was no less real, and no less intense.

Despite my best efforts, I could still hear the outside world as whispers in my disembodied consciousness. I could hear the crying of the girl, the pleading of the mother, and the heavy breathing of the Were. I could feel the racing heartbeat, the feral pleasure of conquest. A heartbeat passed, and then another, and then another. I waited for Ulnyx to act, to finish removing the woman's clothes, to ravish her in front of her family. I don't know why, but he had paused.

"Damn it," he cursed, tilting his head up and howling in rage. "What the hell did you do to me?" He looked at the woman. "Get up," he ordered. She rushed to comply.

He pulled the girl in front of him, looking her over. Her eyes were red with tears, and the demon just stared at her. Another heartbeat, and then another. He growled under his breath, and then turned and ran out the door, shifting as he cleared the house.

"*Landon, you son of a bitch*," he said, his soul reaching for me. "*What the hell did you do?*"

I let myself respond to his call, climbing back up from the depths I had sunk to. "*I didn't do anything*," I said.

"*Bull*," he shouted. "*You did something to me. Fruit ripe for plucking, and I couldn't do it.*"

We trampled through the fields, a full spring towards nothing in particular. We leaped over the wall and flew down the road, as though running faster would fix whatever Ulnyx thought was broken.

"*Impotent?*" I asked. Despite my predicament, I was finding enjoyment in his failure.

"*No,*" he said. "*I just couldn't do it. The crying, the pain, the fear. I used to relish in it. Looking at those pathetic mortals, all I felt was... was...*"

"*Pity?*" I asked.

He growled. "*Guilty,*" he said. "*That I shouldn't take advantage of them because they're so weak. I almost... almost...*"

"*Cried?*"

"*Cared,*" he said. He leaped over another wall, landing next to a large oak tree. He shifted, and sat down against it. "*You've made me weak.*"

"*I disagree,*" I said. "*It's easy to take advantage of the weak. It takes strength to walk away.*"

He was silent for a few minutes, in consideration of what I had said.

"*I don't know what you did, but I hate it,*" he said at last.

I laughed. "*I'm afraid there's no cure.*"

He was silent again. We turned and looked up at the sky, dotted with thousands of stars I could never have seen in Manhattan.

"*Ulnyx,*" I said, after a few minutes had passed.

"*What do you want, meat?*" he replied.

"*Give me back my body,*" I said. "*Please.*"

He didn't say anything.

"*You don't really want the world to burn,*" I said. "*There's no place for you*

67

*if it does, and like you said, there's no something more. Lylyx didn't sacrifice
herself for that."*

Silence.

"None of this would have happened if it weren't for the Beast," I continued.
*"I wouldn't even be here if it weren't for him. I'd probably still be guarding old
stuff at the Museum of Natural History, and you'd be out killing and not feeling
bad about it. If you want to get revenge on somebody, let's get revenge on him."*

He didn't say anything, but I felt the shift in his power. It was subtle, but
I focused and pushed forward, finding the resistance gone. My power sunk in and
around his, re-establishing the connection. I turned my head, in control of it once
more. Then I wiggled my fingers and toes. I could feel Ulnyx churning below me, and
I reached out for his power, watching my hand elongate into the Were's massive
claws. Next, I focused on the strands tying my soul to Josette's. They were still
ragged, but I could see that they were healing. Being in the background must have
sped the process.

"Thank you," I said to him.

"I didn't do it for you," he replied. *"I did it because I can't do eve
rything myself, as much as I wish I could. Don't think this makes us friends."*

"I can't do everything myself either," I said.

He'd never admit it, but he'd just shown that despite himself, we were
friends.

CHAPTER EIGHT

I was only sitting under the tree for an hour before Charis and Sarah pulled up in the rear of a taxi. I don't know if Sarah could track me while I was subverted by Ulnyx, but I had been sure she would find me once he had submitted. Even so, they approached slowly, Charis holding Callus' sword ready, and Sarah staying a few feet behind her.

"You won't need that," I said. "If you didn't already know, I'm back to my old self again."

Charis turned the blade face down and planted it in the dirt. "That's good to hear. How did you overcome him?"

I shook my head. "I didn't," I said. "We had a little talk, and he realized there was a bigger fish we could fry."

"So he doesn't want to kill me anymore?" she asked.

"*I'm still thinking about it*," Ulnyx said, his voice echoing across my mind.

"Not at the moment," I replied.

She walked over and dropped down on the ground next to me, sharing the tree. Sarah joined her on the other side. "I'm sorry, brother," she said. "He was too

69

strong for me."

"I know you tried." I turned my head to look at Charis. "I take it the party fell apart once Myzl lost his head?"

She smiled. "There were a couple of stragglers who didn't get it, but we took care of them. I have even better news." She closed her eyes, and when she opened them, they were a soft red.

"Good to see you again, metaphysically speaking." I said.

"She said she's glad to see you're still alive. She was worried about you."

"She was?"

It was faint, but a blush spread across her cheeks. "She knows you're important to me."

I felt my own face heating up. "Well, I guess we know what we have to do now."

"The taxi's waiting," Sarah said.

I leaned my head back against the tree, then reached out and out an arm around both of their shoulders, pulling them toward me. "Just give me a minute," I said, taking a deep breath. "I don't know if we'll have another chance to take a breather like this."

I closed my eyes, focusing on the weight of their heads pressed against me.

"*Touching*," Ulnyx said.

"*Shut up*," I replied. He responded with a laugh.

A few more minutes passed, and then I patted their arms. "Okay," I said. "It's time to go get the new cage."

We all got to our feet, and I followed Sarah through a gate not far from where Ulnyx had hopped the wall. The taxi was waiting outside, a green and black painted Volkswagen micro-van. It didn't have a driver.

"I persuaded him to give us the car," Sarah said.

"I can imagine," I replied. I went around to the passenger side, letting Charis take the wheel. Sarah climbed into the back.

"I hope it's not too late," Charis said. "We lost a lot of time chasing after you."

"I know," I said. "Ulnyx is a more willing participant in this fight now, so I think it will have been worth it."

"*You're damn right,*" the Were growled.

Charis hit the gas, accelerating forward, and then doing a quick three pointer to get us headed back towards Florence. We zoomed along the narrow country roads with abandon, and I was shocked by how far the Were had run.

We had gone about twenty miles when the verdant farmland began to convert to the dense habitation of the city, and within another fifteen minutes we passed by the San Gallo.

"Where is the rift, anyway?" I asked.

"The Pitti Palace," Charis replied. "Just across the river."

"I'm not familiar with it," I said.

"It was built in the fourteen hundreds," she explained. "It's been under the control of a bunch of European dignitaries and aristocracy, but now it's a museum. There's a room there, a room nobody goes in. That's why."

"Am I off base to assume that the palace was owned by an archfiend at some point?"

She glanced over at me and nodded. "Close. It was owned by a Turned, but he was really just the deed holder. The archfiend ran the place, until Myzl deposed him. He preferred to stay closer to the action on the other side of the river, but he still used the rift when he needed to travel."

Except now Myzl was gone. It was good riddance, especially since he had been a servant. Would another rise quickly to take his place, or would the Beast make his move here, the same as he was in New York?

We crossed the river, and approached the Pitti Palace. The street fed right up to the back of the structure, a massive three story brick building with plenty of arched windows and a few large wooden doors at ground level. I didn't need my Sight to recognize the gargoyles perched on the roof of the third floor, though it did come in handy to spot the fiend hanging out on the inside. Were they waiting for us?

"What do you think?" I asked Charis, pointing up at the demons. She leaned forward over the wheel to get a better look. There were six of them, spread across the roof.

"We don't have time to be subtle," she said. "If they're going to alert someone, we can be long gone before they get here. If they're going to attack, you can go furry and knock them down."

Go furry... I liked that. "Sarah, are you okay back there?" I asked, turning and looking back at her. She had been quiet the entire drive, and even now she seemed a little distracted.

"Huh? Yes, I'm fine," she said.

Charis slowed the car to a stop right outside one of the pairs of massive wooden doors. I looked up. We were too close to the wall to see the gargoyles, and they weren't registering in my senses either. That was a good sign.

"I've got the door," Charis said. A moment later, it started rattling, shaking against whatever locking mechanism was on the other side. There was a soft pop, and then the doors swung open.

We went through them, under the colonnades and out into the main courtyard. There was a door on the right that led to an art museum. Charis unlocked it, and I shorted the alarm system. How did the demons usually come in?

We skipped the art, and made our way through another locked door and up the large stairway to the second floor. I could still See the fiend, their signature motionless, sitting on a direct intercept course. We walked along the marble floors, our shoes clattering against the stone, our approach anything but silent. Every ten feet or so we passed by a large arched window, and I could look out and down onto the roadway where we had left the taxi. I checked on the fiend again. They had to be waiting for us.

"Who is it?" I asked Charis.

"The fiend? I don't know," she replied. "He isn't very powerful, whoever he is."

"I guess we'll find out soon enough."

We reached a very ordinary door. At least, it appeared ordinary, but I could make the sweeping curves of the demonic runes looping back from under the frame. The door was protected somehow. I focused, and tried to shove it open. It didn't budge.

"It's not the kind of lock you're used to," Charis said. Her eyes flared red, the frame of the door glowed for a second, and it swung open.

The room was lit by a single sconce of hellfire, flickering against the back wall. In the center was the rift, the circle of runes scratched right into the marble floor, giving off their own eerie glow. To the right of the rift was the fiend, a younger man in a denim jacket and blue jeans, thick wavy hair that fell to his shoulders, and a grin that was way too friendly. At least it wasn't the Beast.

"Diuscrucis," he said. "Hmm.. What is the plural of diuscrucis anyway? Diuscrucises? Diuscrucii? A bit of a quandry, that." His voice was odd, childlike yet deep, with a strange reverberation that made it feel like it was echoing. I couldn't help but smile.

"And you are?" I asked.

"You can call me Max," he said. "It's not my given name, but it's good

73

enough. A name is a label that speaks no words. Some say names have power, I say the ones who say that are stupid. No matter, that. I've been waiting for you."

"If names have no power, why not use your real one?" Sarah asked.

He chuckled. "Ahh, excellent question, young one. The answer is because these fat mounds of muscle we wag too easily cannot form the rich, elegant, beautiful enunciation of my true name."

"You're a fiend," she replied. "A human. Your name is human."

"Bah," he spat. "The name I was given on my mortal birth was merely a placeholder. No matter, that. I have been waiting for you."

"Clearly," Charis said. "How did you know we would be here?"

"The Beast told me," he said.

Charis drew her sword. Sarah backed up a step to give her space. I stayed completely still. "The Beast told you?" I asked. "So you're a servant?"

"Yes," he replied. "And, no. It's complicated."

"We're kind of in a hurry," I replied. "Either attack us, laugh at us, join us, or get out of the way."

"Ah-ha!" he shouted. "I should do all of the above, but probably not in that order. I have one purpose here, and one only. The Beast believes I am his servant, but I am not. I'm a spy."

"A spy for who?" I asked.

His teeth beamed in the light of the hellfire. "You'd never believe." He stepped forward, and Charis lifted her sword. "Hold, my dear. Hold your fury." He turned his hand over and slid back the sleeve of his jacket, showing his bare wrist. "There."

Charis and I looked down at it. "There's nothing there," she said.

He laughed, and then held up a finger. It grew into a sharp claw, which he used to slice the base of his arm. I had seen a lot, but I still felt a little

queasy as he grabbed the open wound and ripped it upward. Instead of blood, muscle,
and bone, there was a second layer of skin beneath. Scarred into his wrist was the
mark of the Templars.

"You?" Charis asked, her eyes wide.

"Indeed," he replied. "For many, many years. You might have thought there
were no demon Templars, but you thought wrong. I was secretly a Templar before I
died, but it had always been intended that I would become a spy. I refused a drink
from the Grail, and even refused the brand. I did some nasty deeds that I'm only
slightly proud of and was sent to the Pit. A few hundred years passed, and I earned
my way back. Yada, yada, yada, demon plus servant plus Templar equals spy. Of
course, I can't just leave my brand hanging out where the others can see, now can
I?"

"Your purpose?" I asked. The story was cool, but not very helpful.

"He's been broadcasting to his servants since you let him out. They know
about the Box, and he's already sent one of his most powerful minions to retrieve
it. If you were planning to walk through that rift intending to stop him, you may
want to reconsider."

It was bad news, but I wasn't surprised. We knew he would be after the Box,
and we had been way too slow getting to the rift. Still, the Box was guarded by the
Templars. Would it be that easy for the servants to overcome them?

"What would you suggest?" Charis asked.

"The Beast has sent a contingent of his servants to Paris, France. He's
spoken of enlisting the demon, Abaddon to his cause. It's rather humorous, because
none of his get wants to go near that one. Someone will though, soon enough, even
if the Beast has to possess him to do it."

"Damn it," I cursed. "Tell us something we don't know." We were losing,
badly.

He snapped his fingers and spun around, a weird combination of Kid Rock and Michael Jackson. "Did you know the Beast is convinced that you have the power to catch him in the Box, and hold him for all of eternity? He's afraid of you."

"The Beast is afraid of me?" I asked. It was a tough story to buy into. "He didn't seem too worried about us the last time I saw him." The grin crept back into my thoughts, chilling me. Still, he must have believed we could catch him, or he wouldn't be trying to get the Box in the first place.

"No," he said. "He's not afraid of you." He pointed at Charis. "He's not afraid of you." He shifted his finger to Sarah. "He's not afraid of you. Well, he's more afraid of you, but I don't know why, because you're just a little emo girl with bad genetics." He waved his hand around us. "He's afraid of all of you, together. The Three Musketeers."

Or the three diuscrucis. I looked back at Sarah. Always three.

"Why?" I asked. "How do we catch him, and keep him?"

Max shook his head. "I don't know," he said. "He hasn't said."

"How do you know he's afraid?" Sarah asked.

"Because he's desperate to catch you, and kill you. Because he's desperate to get the Box. The Beast's full power is a challenge to God. You should be nothing more than ants to be stepped on to him, yet he is putting most of his energy into trapping you. Yes, be careful diuscrusises. He is working to trap you."

I looked at Charis. "What do you want to do?" I asked.

"Thailand," she said. "The Templars can hold out for a long time against any demon who isn't Abaddon. We have plenty of safeguards in place."

"I was hoping you would say that," I replied. "Can you light us up?"

Charis' eyes flared, and she nodded, going over to the rift and kneeling in front of it.

"Are you coming?" I asked Max.

76

He shook his head. "You aren't listening. He seeks to trap you." He motioned to the rift. "This is just one of his designs."

I grabbed his wrist and looked at the Templar brand. "I've learned not to trust anyone who hasn't earned it," I said. "If you're right, then you'll have proven yourself, but until then, I can't risk believing you."

He laughed and clapped me on the back with his free hand. "Not as dumb as you look? Very well, old chap. I'll see you on the other side." He pulled his hand away and started for the door, bowing to Sarah on the way by.

"And I thought things couldn't get any weirder," she said, watching him go.

CHAPTER NINE

The runes around the rift began to flame, and Charis rose from her crouch. "I wasn't sure it would still be connected," she said.

"There's no reason for it not to be, if it's a trap," I replied. "Even if it isn't, the demons need a way back out too."

Charis nodded. We had two blessed swords, and she gave one to Sarah. "There may be too many for you to Command," she said, "and we might be too busy to protect you."

"At least we know they won't kill me," she said.

"Don't be too confident," I said. "Cho wasn't supposed to kill me either, and he nearly did."

"Sorry, Landon," Charis said, turning to me. "I don't have a sword for you."

I smiled and raised my hand, pulling in Ulnyx's eagerly given power. The hand grew and elongated into a nasty set of claws. "I don't need one."

"So that's it then," Charis said. "Landon, if this goes bad..." She trailed off, her eyes downcast.

"It won't," I said.

"If it does." She burst forward and put her lips to mine; a quick, desperate meeting of flesh that melted right through that mental barrier of attraction that I was trying to keep between us. If passion could be shared in a split-second, she had somehow managed it.

"Thanks," I said, feeling my face turning crimson. "If that's your idea of a pep talk, you're doing great."

She didn't say another word, pressing her lips together as if to hold onto the feeling for one final moment before we crowded through the portal.

One step in, one step out. We exited on the rooftop of the hotel in Thailand where I recovered from Sarah's attack, and where I had met the angel Malize. Coming through, the effect on my senses was staggering; a mixture of coolness and heat that nearly toppled me from the alien nature of it. I had expected demons to be crawling all over the place, but finding a number of angels gathered was a shock.

They were assembled on the roof, angels and devils, neither of them fighting the other. They stayed segregated though, the blue team on one side, the red team on the other, but both reacted as we came into view. Swords were drawn, claws and fangs bared. It was a small army of thirty or so, but there were no major demons, no archfiends, and not even any super-vampires.

Charis strode forward with confidence, holding her sword in front of her face, daring the enemy to attack.

"I don't know what the trap is," I said to Sarah as I started shifting, "but this *is* some kind of trap." It had to be. The Beast wasn't stupid enough to think a mixture of simple devils and angels would be enough to stop us. Even if we had lost some of our power, that wasn't the only tool we had in our belts.

There was a moment of total silence then. A complete calm. The sun was shining overhead, reducing the effectiveness of the devils even further, but did it strengthen the angels? The light glinted off Charis' sword, illuminating her face

79

in an ethereal glow. I could feel Ulnyx' bloodlust flooding into me, my thoughts turning more aggressive with each huffing breath. Sarah stayed behind me, sword raised. She had years of practice, she could handle these piss-ants.

The devils came first, rushing towards Charis in a mass of red-brown leathery muscle, fangs, and claws. As they reached her, the ground around them began to crumble, not decimated but enough to throw them off balance. She tore into them with the blessed sword, spinning in a tight circle, the blade a deadly extension of her exquisitely executed form. She was a whirling dervish, a tasmanian devil, and Edward Scissorhands all at once. I never had to move.

"Come on," I shouted at the angels, still standing on their side of the rooftop. "You're no children of God. You don't need to wait for us to make the first move. Come and fight."

The angels looked at one another. They didn't seem too keen on the idea of falling, even if they had chosen to serve the Beast.

"Pathetic," I spat. I could sense Ulnyx's glee at my rage. I had taken more of his power, let more of his soul leech through. I hadn't just gained his form.

One of the seraph stepped forward, a boy of no more than ten. His sword was huge, almost twice his height, but he held it with ease. "Why don't you go and get the Box," he said. His face dropped, and a grin spread across it. He was here.

"Why don't you send your little army of birds to get plucked?" I replied.

The Beast chuckled. "That would be a bit of a waste, don't you think?" he asked. "No, they'll wait right here, and you'll go down into the building to get Avriel's Box. I'll tell you right now that it's what I want you to do. That it's a trap, and you'll do it anyway. That's the problem with your kind. You just don't pay attention."

"Landon," Sarah said. "He's stalling. He wants to keep us up here, to buy more time for his archfiend to find the Box."

80

I let go of Ulnyx, reducing back to human form and turning to face her, and then glancing back at the angel being possessed by the Beast. Was she right? Or was he? How did he know we were here so fast? Unless he'd been waiting for us already, or unless Max was the trickster I had a feeling he'd be. What if Max was the Beast? Would I have been able to tell? What if Sarah was helping the Beast, and I didn't know it?

"Landon," she said, more insistently. "We're wasting time. I can See the archfiend, he's six floors down. There are others there, but they're dying."

"You see," the Beast said. "Listen to the girl. Walk right into my design, and do it willingly."

I looked over at Charis. She was still a dozen feet away, but her expression was pained. She wanted to go down. Sarah wanted to go down. The Beast wanted us to go down. Or was he lying? That power didn't extend to him. That his honesty was even questionable made the decision easier. I would trust Sarah, for better or for worse.

"Let's go," I said to her. We started running for the stairs, the Beast standing behind us, laughing. The laughter grew louder the closer we got, joined by the rest of the assembled angels. It was a disconcerting sound, hearing them augment the Beast with the same flat cackle. Was he possessing them all? I didn't slow to consider it. I pushed open the door to the stairs with a thought, and we charged downward, with Charis in the lead.

The stairwell was empty, but there were scrapes and scratches along the steps and railing, the inadvertent damage caused by the passing of a large force of demons. We dropped the first flight to the penthouse where I had recovered from my wounds. There was a pile of ash outside of the doorway, but the door had been torn aside and discarded, and the runes that had been protecting it had been scraped away by something powerful enough to withstand them. The archfiend.

"Where did you put the Box?" I asked Charis.

We ignored the penthouse, continuing down six floors to where Sarah could See the archfiend. I could feel the heat of the demon masses in my own senses, including one who was more powerful than the rest. It must have been him, but I wasn't sure. There was something not right about that one, like a picture that was hanging just slightly crooked.

"I gave it to Liam. He was second-in-command after Ezekiel. He should have put it in the safe room." She didn't turn back to speak, shouting over her shoulder.

"Which is down six floors?"

"Yes," she replied. "It's hidden behind a glamoured wall, and most demons won't be able to see it."

"What about an archfiend?"

"They shouldn't be, but we've never had a chance to test it. Nobody was supposed to know we were based here."

I saw her head shift slightly toward Sarah. It wasn't even an inch, but I knew what she was saying. I had been here, and Sarah had known I was here. She must have told Rebecca, who told the Beast, and now here we were. It sucked, but there was nothing we could do about it. Even though it had only happened a dozen hours or so ago, it had to be ancient history.

We reached the sixth floor down. The door had been decimated, burnt to nearly nothing by hellfire. Beyond it was a hallway, and there were signs of the passing battle everywhere. The walls were scored with sword marks, shotgun shot, and bullet holes. There were four dead Templars down near where a pair of twin doors used to rest, their heads lying distant from their bodies. The mortals among them didn't get the dignity of reducing to ash on their demise.

I watched Charis for a sign of emotion as we passed them, but she held it together, showing nothing. If I had been able to see her eyes, I was sure I would have found the smoldering rage, the gripping sadness, the eagerness for her revenge. I could See the demons in front of us, beyond the twin doors, beyond the doors that followed after that. I could hear fighting in the distance; the sound of claw against steel and the popping of gunfire.

"They've breached the safe room," Charis said. "The Box is in a secondary safe bolted into steel and runed against Divine. Somebody has to still be alive in there, protecting it."

"Why are they protecting the room, instead of retreating?" I asked. "They couldn't know the Beast would come after the Box."

"Do you think the Box is the only artifact we've recovered?" she replied. "Protocol is to protect the safe room at all costs."

What other artifacts might the Templars have stashed, that the Beast would love to get his mitts on? I didn't like the thought.

Beyond the twin doors was a large living area, with a spread of couches, a pool table, a couple of televisions, a card table, foosball and pinball. Most of it had been shattered and shredded, broken to pieces and scattered along with eight more Templars who hadn't been able to withstand the assault. Two had been burned to bones by hellfire, the others shredded by the demon horde. There was a fair share of demon dust here too, and it was clear they had put up a good fight. They had skill, but they didn't have numbers.

We rushed through the room, to a doorframe that had been twisted and burned almost beyond recognition. It was a misshapen portal, collapsing on itself and at the same time expanding, the weight of the building around it threatening to overthrow it at any moment. There had been a steel door attached to it once, and it had been coated in a thick layer of Templar scripture. That door was laying crushed on top of the remains of the pool table. Through the opening, I could see the backs of the demon forces, a group of harpies hissing while they waited for their turn at the front lines.

The sound of a shotgun firing overtook the hissing, followed by a howl and the body of a hellhound tumbling through the masses to land at our feet. That din was stepped on by the screaming gurgle of another Templar meeting their end.

"Hey," Charis shouted as we came up behind them. The back row turned in time to catch her blessed sword through their cheeks, and I could See the tide of the enemy turn as they realized they were being attacked from the rear. Within moments they were coming at us, reversing direction to take on the new threat. I could sense the archfiend there, held out of sight behind the army, near the front of the line. How could they be in front, yet there were Templars still fighting?

The harpies turned towards us. The three that had been sliced by Charis' blade began to smoke and collapsed, leaving the others to step over them. She used the obstacle to her advantage, kicking one of the bodies towards the rushing demons, tripping them up and stabbing them as they stumbled. I heard another gunshot, and then a cry.

"Hurry," the voice said from the far end of the room.

"We need to get up there," I said.

"Working on it," Charis replied over her shoulder, ducking under a claw and punching the attacker in the face. The demon flew back, knocking into a devil behind it.

"You're too slow," I said.

I took hold of Ulnyx's power, not shifting completely, but allowing it to flow through to my hands, transforming them. I focused, gathering my strength and springing forward over Charis' head, coming down towards a group of devils. I let the claws lead the way, clearing a path in front of me, hitting the ground and leaping into the air again before they could recover.

84

Broken

The safe room was big, much bigger than I had expected it to be. It had a low ceiling, but it was at least thirty feet wide and equally deep. The walls were made of steel, and there were small alcoves lining it where racks of weapons had once resided. I could see the mounts for daggers and swords, the racks for shotguns and handguns and magazines filled with silver bullets. There were other alcoves too, some holding bottles of holy water, others cans of food. It was everything a Templar would need to be sieged in for a few weeks at least, but it wasn't designed to be overrun.

It took four such leaps to get to the head of the class. I finally landed next to a scrawny, red-headed man in combat fatigues, holding a shotgun cradled in his arms, a magazine of shells snaking out of it. I had never seen a shotgun rigged like that before, but it allowed him to keep peppering the demons with holy water, preventing them from getting too close. Dead Templars lay on either side of him, their flesh turned black from the demons' poison. Behind him was a large painting of Joan of Arc. She had been a Templar too? I could only assume the secondary safe was sitting behind Saint Joan.

There was no time for pleasantries. I nodded to the ginger and turned around, looking for the archfiend. In my Sight, he was right in front of me, no more than ten feet away, a dark red mass of heat. To my eyes, there was nothing but harpies, hellhounds, and devils; a standard army, and outside of sheer volume a pretty pathetic one at that. There was no way this group had done the damage I had seen on the way in. The Beast had told us we were walking into a trap. I knew it was here, and yet I still couldn't find it.

"The archfiend?" I asked, hearing the blast of the shotgun and watching the front line of demons stumble back.

"He's right here," the redhead replied. I heard the gun clang onto the steel floor.

I didn't even have a chance to turn before the dagger was across my throat and he had me wrapped in a tight hold. He had grown, his voice had changed, and my Sight flared with the heat of him. He was powerful, so much more powerful than the fake signature he had somehow cast out into the mess of lesser demons. Worse, he was familiar.

I wasn't the only one who knew him. As soon as he was revealed I could feel it, like a change in air pressure that filled the entire room. All of the energy was stolen from it at once, and a mental coldness swept in; a raw, harsh void that caused the entirety of the Beast's army to fall, clutching at their heads to rid themselves of the emotion.

Standing in the back, her head jutted down and her arms at her sides was Sarah. Her empty eyes were drawn tight, and I could almost see the fury through the black shadows.

"Hello, my dear," Gervais said. "Did you miss your papa?"

CHAPTER TEN

Sarah didn't respond right away. She just stood there, her body language substituting for the fire that would have been in her eyes.

"Let him go," she whispered, a Command that drove the demons kneeling between them to try to duck their heads even lower.

I could feel the archfiend suck in some air, as if trying to capture the Command. "I'm sorry," he said. "Could you repeat that? I thought you tried to make me let Landon here go, but I'm not sure."

"Let him go," she repeated, a violently snapped growl.

Gervais' laughter was nauseating. "Your Commands won't work on me, daughter," he said. "Your toadie, Izak took care of that when he branded me and left me to be destroyed."

I didn't know what he meant, but I didn't like the sound of it. I squirmed against his grip, and he dug the dagger into my neck, deep enough to show me he could remove my head before I could escape him. The Beast had set the trap, and we had walked right into it, just as he had said we would. What choice did we have?

"If I kill him, you lose," Gervais said. "Not that you stand much of a chance to begin with."

"Then why not just do it?" Charis asked. "Cut off his head and end the game right now."

Gervais smiled. "Oh, I'd love to, after what he did to me." The knife point dug in a little deeper. "But there's something we need that is much more important than this one."

I looked at Sarah. Her body was trembling in anger at her inability to help me. She was the reason the Beast had brought us here. She was the prize. He had already gotten what he needed from Charis and I, but he had to kill Sarah, to take all of her Divine infused, mortal blood in order to gain his full power. He didn't even care about the Box; it was useless to us without her anyway.

If I could speak, I would have told Charis to get Sarah out of here, to run as fast as she could. There was no value to my existence if the Beast took Sarah; it would be a short existence after all. I looked at her and tried to express it in my gaze, and she looked back at me and it seemed as though she understood, but I could sense the reluctance to just give me away.

"Well, my dear?" Gervais asked. "Will you surrender to me, to save your friend? You never know, maybe he'll even find some way to save you. He's certainly proven himself to be quite resourceful."

Sarah's face grew wet with tears, her fists clenched, and I could almost feel the heat of her anger pouring from her body. She dropped her eyes to the ground, and then let it all go. "Yes," she whispered.

I had to do something. I tried to make eye contact with Charis, to beg her to take Sarah away, right now. She wouldn't look at me. She knew what she was supposed to do, and she wouldn't do it. Why? I felt my anger building, and I knew I had to do something.

"Just step over here then," Gervais said. "A simple trade. Landon for you, and then we will leave together, through the rift and then back to his prison."

Sarah's head nodded almost imperceptibly. This couldn't happen. I couldn't let it. If I was the bargaining chip, I only had value if I was alive.

I closed my eyes and focused, willing strength into my body. I knew Gervais would sense it, and I could feel his own power growing. He was expecting me to try to escape and throw his arm off. He didn't plan on me pulling forward to dig the dagger deeper into my neck, to try to sever my own head.

"No," he shouted as the blade bit into me. He couldn't fight back against my pull in time. The only thing he could do was let go, so he did.

I immediately began to fall. The weapon had gone deep, piercing my esophagus and nearly reaching my spine, leaving me only centimeters from reaching my goal. The blood poured from my neck, and I couldn't help but be reminded of Rebecca. She had done nearly the same thing to me, and now I had done it to myself. Was that balance?

Things seemed to slow down for me then. Gervais turned, reaching for the blade, to get hold of it before I could make another attempt at suicide. In the corner of my eye I saw Charis, her arm drawing back and then shooting forward, loosing her blessed sword towards the archfiend like a spear. At the same time, a glimpse of Sarah, running towards us, her fingernails impossibly stretched into daggers of their own.

It felt like ages, but it happened in less than a second. Gervais got a hold of the hilt of the weapon, and I felt the slick coldness of it being pulled from my neck. Charis' sword slammed into the archfiend, biting deep into him, entering his chest and piercing right through, forcing him back. Sarah leaped towards him, her hands raised high, her face as feral as any I had ever seen, and yet so familiar to me.

My body didn't reach the floor, smacking against the wall behind me. The dagger gone, it was already healing, and I managed to catch myself before I tumbled over completely. Gervais was run through by the sword, but it didn't seem to matter. He ignored the wound, catching Sarah as she flew towards him, spinning her around and pinning her against the painting, the weapon against her throat. There was stillness for a heartbeat, and then another. I watched the archfiend, waiting for his body to hiss and steam, waiting for even a trace of blood to bloom from the hole in his body. Neither happened.

"Stay still," Gervais said, holding Sarah. She struggled below his grip, so he whipped the butt of the weapon around, knocking it against her temple. He caught her unconscious form before she could collapse.

"You can't kill her," Charis said, approaching cautiously.

He turned, glancing at me, and then looking at her. He hefted Sarah over his shoulder. The sword was still lodged in his gut, but he didn't seem to notice, or care. "No," he said. "But you should be more worried about yourself."

A growl reminded us that we weren't the only ones in the room. With Sarah out of action, the demons had recovered, and now they launched themselves towards us.

"Farewell, mon ami," Gervais said, laughing. "Enjoy playing with your box."

Charis tried to grab him, but was intercepted by a hellhound. She stepped out of its lunge and punched it hard, knocking it to the ground. A devil took its place, and she ducked away from its claws and used her cursed dagger to remove its head. "He's getting away," she grunted.

My neck almost healed, I dove forward and took the shotgun up in my hands, squeezing the trigger. I had never fired a gun before, and the kick threw my aim, but the demons were so close it didn't matter. The front line fell back, sprayed with holy water. The monsters were parting around their master, and he had almost reached the front of the room.

I pulled the trigger again, and watched more demons scatter. Charis took up

90

position next to me, slicing at any of the demons who came too close. Wasn't this how the Templars at our feet had died?

"This is bull," I said, getting to my feet. I took the shotgun and threw it out, into the air over the demons, focusing and guiding it so it didn't hit the ceiling. The chain of shells trailed behind it, unspooling from the box they were piled in, extending like a ribbon.

I didn't need to tell Charis what to do. A moment later all of the shells burst, the holy water pellets raining down on the demons, diving into their skin. The mass cried out in pain, and I grabbed her hand and pulled her towards the exit.

"Wait," she said. "We need the Box."

"Not a good time," I replied. She stopped letting me lead her, and pulled back the other way.

"It doesn't matter if we get her back, if we don't have the Box. You go ahead, I'll catch up."

It was a lousy time for an argument. The demons would shake off the effects of the water any second. "Charis," I started to say.

"I can get back through this rabble," she insisted. "Go."

I didn't want to leave her. She hadn't left me. She took away my choice, grabbing me and throwing me towards the door with focused strength. I crashed through the demons, landing ten feet away.

"Go," she shouted.

I kicked and punched my way out of the scrum, reaching the exit. Gervais had dropped Callus' sword there, but he and Sarah were already gone. I picked it up and threw it back into the room, guiding it until it thunked into the wall next to the painting, and then turned and raced after them.

I could still See the archfiend, already on the stairs and climbing fast. There was no way I was going to catch them without a better route.

91

"*Try the windows,*" Ulnyx said, his voice permeating my desperation and finding its way into my mind.

The windows? I wasn't sure what he was getting at, but I let his voice lead me. I diverted to the far side of the room, where a wall of floor to ceiling glass awaited.

"*Let me drive,*" he said. "*You know I won't keep you.*"

He had already proven that. I gave my body up to him, feeling it shift, growing into the demonic monster that was the Great Were. We didn't even slow as we changed, and Ulnyx bunched us and lunged forward, leading with his claws. They cut deep into the thick glass, breaking the crystalline bonds and compromising the entire surface. Our body went next, and we crashed through, out into the air.

"*Push us back,*" he yelled.

I was so impressed with the feeling of running through the window I hadn't been paying attention. I focused, bringing a gust of air to shove us back against the building. We had lost a couple of stories, but Ulnyx made it up in a hurry, scrambling up the outer frame like Spiderman.

We raced up the side of the tower, but I could See Gervais was nearly to the rift. It was going to be way too close. I focused, giving us an extra boost from behind, and we reached the summit with one final shove that sent us out over the rooftop, a massive pounce that brought us directly in line with the fleeing archfiend. He Saw us coming. I knew he would, but it was enough to divert him from the rift. He turned and raised his hand, and all of the air around us vanished, leaving us choking. He ducked as we fell, tracking us with his hand, keeping us in the vacuum.

Ulnyx hit the ground and spun, ready for another go. "The angels," I said. We weren't the only ones on the roof. They charged towards us, all except the Beast, who watched with an intense gaze. I could swear I saw the hint of fear in those eyes, but I didn't have enough time to tell.

"It was a fine effort, Landon," Gervais shouted. He dropped his hand so he could resume his journey towards the rift, giving us back our air. Not that it mattered, we had our hands full.

Unlike the demons we had found in the safe room, these angels weren't some pity party meant to distract. They came on in an organized way, three at a time, encircling us. I knew this was standard procedure for taking on a Great Were, and I knew by their numbers if I didn't come up with something else they would win. I could only hope to hold out long enough for Charis to reach me. Giving her the sword had eased my concerns that she wouldn't make it.

I kept my Sight focused on Gervais while Ulnyx faced off against the angels. He would be gone within seconds, and I didn't see any way of stopping him. "No," I shouted, taking back control of my body from Ulnyx, roaring with anger and lashing out at the nearest seraph. My foot caught him in the chin, sending him flying backwards thirty feet or more. It didn't matter, I couldn't reach Gervais.

That was when it happened. Call it luck, call it destiny, call it the hand of God. Call it whatever you want. Gervais was no more than six feet from the rift, when it suddenly burst into flames. Not the typical soft burning hellfire on the runes that made up the circle, but a literal gout of heat and fire that filled the entire circumference and made it appear as though someone had unplugged a tunnel that led directly to the heart of the Pit itself. The hellfire launched up into the air one hundred feet or more, causing the archfiend to begin stumbling backwards, the angels to cry out in panic and begin beating their wings in an effort to escape, and that hint of fear on the Beast to grow into a full-blown worry.

A human figure stepped out of the flames.

Izak.

Gervais tried to shift Sarah so she would be between him and the demon, but

93

he came too fast, somehow managing to slam his fist into Gervais' face and at the same time catch Sarah before the archfiend could drop her. He laid her tenderly at his feet, and then looked up at his enemy.

"He isn't supposed to be here," I heard the Beast hiss.

I started running, not for Gervais or the Beast but for Sarah. I know Izak knew I was coming, and he stepped gingerly over her to put himself between her and her father.

"That might have hurt," Gervais said, recovering from the blow and straightening up. His nose was shattered on his face, but again there was no blood. "If I could feel pain."

He raised his hand, and I heard a groan from behind us. I turned to see that the now charred and somewhat melted radio tower the rift was located beneath had lost its base, corroded in an instant by the demon. It started teetering and then fell towards us, threatening to crush us all beneath it.

"What are you doing?" the Beast cried. "I need her alive!"

I needed us alive too. I focused, pushing my will against the tower, demanding it to stay up, or to fall any direction that wasn't this one. I felt the energy flowing, felt the strain of the demand as the universe countered my desires with its laws and rules and math. Still, I pushed. It wasn't enough.

I picked Sarah up, still focused, still trying. Her eyes opened the tiniest bit, but she was groggy.

"Izak," she whispered.

"He's here," I said. I looked at the tower. There was no way I could outrun it, no way I could stop it.

"He came," she said with a small smile. "He heard me."

I didn't have time to ask her what she had done. The tower was getting closer, and I pushed back, as hard as I could, feeling the strength draining from

94

me. I could have stopped it before the Beast had taken some of my blood.

Charis couldn't have picked a better time to get to the roof. She appeared out of the stairwell, her body covered in demon blood, her hair a mess. She saw the falling tower, she saw us under it, and she added her power to mine, pushing against it and forcing it away. Combined, we took control, moving it off the side of the building and letting it tumble to the ground below.

Izak hadn't even noticed the tower. He charged on Gervais, his hands lighting up in hellfire, his punches rocketing in at the archfiend. Gervais took the hits, letting them throw him backwards and burn him, getting back to his feet and laughing it off, taking the hits again. It only enraged the demon more, and he came on stronger. Gervais retreated away from him, reaching the edge of the rooftop. When he did, he gave Izak one last look, and jumped off the side. I don't care what he had done to not bleed or feel pain, nothing could survive that fall.

With Sarah safe and Gervais dealt with, I lowered her back to the ground and turned towards the Beast. He had been watching the fight, but now he noticed me coming.

"Do you surrender?" I asked as I approached.

I was sure he had the power to will someone to cease to be just by looking at them, when he had control of his full power. At least, that was how it seemed by the look he gave me.

"You think you've won?" he asked. "Just because you got lucky here? You think this trap, this Box, is the only play I have? You still don't get it, do you, kid? You still just don't understand what you're dealing with here. Enjoy your little victory. Go pop some Crystal, get wasted, and screw your women. Do it first, because I'll be doing it last. In the meantime, I'll give you a little better working sample on being a god. Keep your eyes open, kid. You might learn something."

He smiled again. That damn smile. A second later Callus' sword shaved the angel's head cleanly off his body, but I knew the Beast had already abandoned it.

"You have the Box?" I asked.

Charis nodded and patted a new pocket that had sprouted from her pants. "Right here," she said.

I went over to where Sarah was sitting. Izak had reached her first, and he had his arms around her, holding her so tightly it seemed she would suffocate.

"Izak," I said. "I've never been happier to see you."

The demon raised his hand in greeting without breaking the embrace.

"I don't want to rush the moment here, but we need to get moving. The Beast is pissed."

As if to back up my claim, I felt the ground below us shift, and heard a deep rumble.

"What the heck is that?" Charis asked.

I ran to the side of the building and looked down. It had to be a hundred stories at least, but I could see the dust forming around the base of the building. I could See Gervais standing there, his hands out, causing it.

"He's bringing down the whole building," I said in shock. The rumbling started to get louder, followed by the sound of the superstructure bending and cracking. "We really need to get out of here."

I turned and raced back towards Izak and Sarah. "Izak, we need to go, now," I shouted. "This building is coming down."

He scooped Sarah up like she was a little girl, and we ran for the rift. Everything began shaking around us, the ground lilting and swaying like we were on a boat.

"Light it up," I said, reaching out and taking Sarah from him. He crouched down and began scratching into the ground with his fingernail, leaving the runes

96

that would change the rift's destination. He poured his power into it then, and the runes flared up.

I heard a snap, and saw the rooftop behind us begin to disappear as the building collapsed from the south. Within seconds it would be gone, toppled onto who knows how many human souls, destroying who knows how many lives of those stuck inside of it. I could only hope the massive influx of Divine had driven most of the people from the area.

"Go," I shouted. I handed Sarah back to Izak as he stepped through, and then grabbed Charis. My left foot made it through fine, but my right began to slip as the matter beneath it started rushing away. What would happen if I was caught in between and the rift was destroyed? I pulled hard on Charis, using the force of her momentum smashing into me to get us both all the way through before we lost the world around us.

I didn't have a chance to get my bearings as we came through. I stumbled, the kinetic energy driving me off balance, knocking me onto my back with Charis on top of me. Our eyes met.

My first thought had something to do with timing. I discarded that one, and ditched the rest too. I leaned up and found her lips with my own, thanking her for not leaving me, thanking her for saving my life, and thanking her for staying alive. She didn't hesitate to respond in kind, and while it was a short moment, it was one I would never forget.

CHAPTER ELEVEN

"There's a smart-ass quip in here, somewhere. I just know it."

Obi's voice ripped me out of the moment I was having with Charis. She gave me a small smile and pulled away, rolling off and getting to her feet. Obi was standing over me, his face shining with the hugeness of his grin. He reached out and helped me to my feet.

"It's good to see you again, man," he said, clapping me on the back.

"You too," I replied. "Sarah."

I whipped around and sought her out. Izak had laid her on the floor, cradling her head on his lap. Her eyes were closed, and she was muttering under her breath. The demon stroked her hair, and looked up at me, pleading for me to do something.

"What's wrong with her?" Thomas joined Obi at my side.

"I don't know," I said, going over to her and kneeling down.

"I'll kill him. I'll kill him. I'll kill them all." She repeated it like a mantra, her head steady but her arms and legs spasming.

"Sarah," I said, trying to get her attention. She didn't respond. "Sarah." Nothing.

"His world? His world? No. Mine. My world." Her voice was jagged, her words crackling like flames. I said I didn't know the cause, but I *did* know. Her alter ego; the other half. The Beast had brought it out the first time by putting her in front of Gervais. He had used the archfiend to break her again, to summon that other Sarah that wanted the chaos of a destroyed world. He had done it with intent, to ensure that even if we had defeated his trap and rescued her, his loss wouldn't be total. Maybe it wouldn't even be a loss at all?

I looked around the room we had landed in. Stone walls with a layer of moss coating them near the top. Thick, moist air. A single wooden door across from us, with a crucifix hanging above it. There were some shelves on the opposite wall, boxes of old pamphlets, a neatly folded stack of black and white robes.

"We're in the basement of a church?" I asked, looking at Izak. "You put a demon rift in the basement of a church?"

Izak glanced up, his eyes telling me my question was the last thing he cared about right now. It was the first thing I cared about. I didn't even think it was possible.

"You told us to keep an eye on Father Tom," Thomas explained. "So we headed straight over. He knew what I was, or at least what I used to be. We started talking. 'Strange days, indeed,' he said, 'when the likes of you are falling to help the likes of him.'" Thomas did his best to mimic the Irish accent, failing pretty badly. "Anyway, he knew about St. Patrick's... about what had happened to the people there. I told him it was going to get worse, much worse, if he didn't help us help you, and that you had asked us to protect him. He wasn't happy about it, but he agreed to let us stay, and he let Izak come in as long as he kept to the basement. He's going to be really pissed about the rift."

I could hear him shouting at me in Gaelic already. "Izak," I said. "You need to destroy the rift. No traces, or we might lose the Father's help, and we need it right now more than anything." I reached down and put my arms under Sarah. "I'll take care of her," I told him. He looked worried, but he nodded.

"You guys wait here," I said. "We'll be back soon."

I picked her up, and carried her through the door to a narrow set of cement steps. I carried her carefully, whispering to her. "Just hang in there, Sarah," I said, wishing I had Josette with me to help. "It'll be okay."

"Kill them, kill them all. It's mine," she whimpered in response.

The top of the stairs fed out into a short hallway. I recognized the door to the Father's office right away, and brought Sarah towards it.

"You're back, eh?"

He was coming around the corner as I reached the office, as though he had known exactly when we would arrive. Not even Touched, but somehow he had an extrasensory perception of the Divine.

"Father," I said, bowing my head with respect. Our first meeting hadn't gone that well, and I had nearly choked the priest to death. I had gone out of my way to be reverent since then. It didn't matter whether or not I agreed with everything he did, he had earned it. I was just thankful I had learned to understand his brogue more clearly since then.

He saw Sarah spasming in my arms, and his eyes widened. "You brought her here?" he asked, his voice rising.

"Father, wait," I said.

"This is why you sent your boy-o's to protect me?"

I nodded. "She needs your help."

He shook his head. "She needs more than I can help her with. Do you know what could happen to me?"

"You aren't Divine," I replied. "As long as you ask Him to forgive you before you die, nothing will happen."

He huffed and sighed, and then came over and opened the door to his office. "Put her on the couch," he said.

When I had gone to Sarah's source, and fought her alter ego, I had promised both halves that I would help them become whole. There was only one way to do that, and that was to get them both to forgive themselves for what they were, and to come to some kind of agreement on who they wanted to be going forward. My bright idea to facilitate that had been to bring her to Father Tom so that she could confess to him, to earn forgiveness in the eyes of God. Maybe she really would be forgiven, or maybe it would all just be wind, but either way I hoped she could find some kind of comfort or closure in the act itself. She had hoped so too, expressing a strong desire to go ahead with the plan.

The problem now was that I hadn't planned on her being such a wreck when I brought her in. I didn't know if she would even be able to confess, her body currently home to a war that was raging between the split halves of her, her voice showing that the wrong side was winning.

"Sarah," I said, leaning in and whispering in her ear. "I know you can hear me. Father Tom is here. He came to hear your confession."

"Confession," she said. "Confess to what?"

"St. Patrick's," I said. "The Beast."

"The Beast," she repeated. "Yes. I remember. Kill the Beast. Take the world."

"Help the world," I said.

She laughed. "Help? There is no help for this world." She turned her head towards Father Tom. "Are you building an ark?" she asked, laughing.

Father Tom looked at me. "This is why they weren't allowed to survive," he said to me. "It isn't because of the evil. He forgives the evil. It's the madness. It always takes them in the end, makes them too unstable. You can't be split like this. You just can't. Doing them a service, He is."

101

It wasn't the time or the place to discuss motives. I moved up and put my face to his. "Do you know about the Beast, Father?"

"Revelations," he said. "Of course."

"Not that Beast. The real one. The one that Lucifer and another archangel imprisoned thousands of years ago, before Lucifer fell. You seem to know everything else, I thought maybe you'd know about that one."

He rubbed his chin. "The Bible isn't meant to be taken literally, is it?" he replied. "It's good to know what that bit is about. What of it?"

"He's coming," Sarah said. "He's coming to kill you, to kill me, to kill us all. But I'll get him first. It's my world. Mine."

"We set him free," I said. "If we don't stop him, the world is going to end, and not well."

"I knew you were trouble the first time I saw you," Father Tom said. "What does that have to do with her?"

I put my hand on Sarah's forehead, wiping away some of the sweat that was forming there. "The prison doesn't hold the Beast, but it still holds most of his power. With her, he can let it all out. Without her, we can't trap him again."

He looked from me, to Sarah, and back. "So the fate of the world rests on a mad diuscrucis?" he asked, furrowing his heavy brows. "Why did you have to pick my church?"

"Just help her," I said. "That's all I need you to do."

He took a deep breath, let out a huge sigh, and got up. He walked over to the back of his office, where his ornate copy of the bible rested. He was reverent in removing it, lifting it like a newborn, kissing it on the spine. He brought it back to the couch and kneeled down over Sarah. I noticed by the way he gazed on her, despite what she was, he felt the compassion that had already been my saving grace more than once. I had picked his church because it was the first one I had found, the one that had been closest to the Belmont. Was it coincidence, or luck? Was there even such a thing as either? With each passing hour, I was less sure.

"What is your name, child?" he asked, his voice tender.

"Name? You want to know my name? I'll kill you first, and bathe in your blood." She squirmed on the leather, and then settled. "Sarah," she squeaked.

"Lord, I kneel before You a humble servant. I beseech You to hear the confession of your child, Sarah, and forgive her sins. I ask that You guide her as a shepherd guides his flock, to the Light that is Your Light. Fill her with the Strength that is Your Strength, and the Hope that is the Hope You bring to all."

He opened the book to the center, where there was a fine velvet mark. He took his finger and ran it down the page, along a dense printing of words. He then placed his finger on Sarah's forehead, drawing the sign of the cross with the smudge of ink he had gathered.

"I would hear your confession, my child," he said.

I didn't See any power in the ink, or any power in his hand. Still, the action quieted Sarah completely. Her entire expression softened, and her breathing evened out.

"Forgive me, Father," she said at barely more than a whisper. "For I have sinned."

She took a deep breath, and her hand came up, seeking. I reached out and took it, and she gripped it as though she might fall away from the world at any moment.

"I am torn, Father," she said. "I have killed innocent people, defiled a holy place, and had impure thoughts. I have betrayed those who care for me, lied and stolen, and wished harm on others. I am split in half, for I love and hate in equal parts, and I cannot love more without hating more."

"Do you love Your Lord?" he asked. "Your Lord loves you, and He will forgive you. All you have to do is ask."

"How?" she said. Her empty eyes began welling with tears. "How can He forgive me?"

Father Tom placed a gentle hand on her shoulder. "It is not for me to understand how," he said. "Only to know that he does. All those who seek forgiveness are forgiven."

A small smile expanded on her face. "Please. Please forgive me." Her hand gripped mine so tightly, I thought it might break.

The Father raised his hand, making the sign of the cross. "In the name of the Father, and of the Son, and of the Holy Spirit, I absolve you of your sins."

Sarah's body fell limp as she let out an exhausted moan, reacting as if the weight of all existence had suddenly been lifted from her. In that moment, she looked as peaceful as I could ever remember. I felt the sudden pull of her hand in mine, and I lowered it, crossing it over her lightly undulating stomach. She was asleep.

Father Tom looked over at me. "We need to talk, laddie," he said. He got to his feet and returned his Bible to its pedestal, and then motioned me from the room. Once we were outside, he closed the door.

"I don't like that look," I said to him, seeing the pain in his eyes.

"God forgive me for what I just did," he said. "It will quiet her for a time, because she believes, but that belief will only take her so far. You can't confess away the madness."

"You're saying she can still turn evil?" I asked.

He shook his head. "She *is* evil, laddie. As evil as they come, when she's in that state of mind. She's also good. It's the curse of what she is, to be both sides of the same coin. She can be either at any moment, though most times she'll be equal parts of each, like you are. It isn't a disease you can cure, or a sin that can be forgiven. It just is. She'll find comfort in His forgiveness for a time, but if you think that it will hold out, I've got directions to a pot o' gold to sell you. Like I told you, sending her from this world to the next would be a kindness. It would be even better to do it now, when her path to Heaven is clear."

I had been holding out hope that allowing her to confess would settle that side of her, and give her the strength to fight against it. If Father Tom was right, I had been holding onto false hope, at least in the long term. No wonder he felt guilty. He had given Sarah the same false hope to hold onto; a rowboat in a maelstrom.

"*Josette, where are you?*" I said, calling out in my mind, wishing for her guidance. The priest was suggesting I kill Sarah, and I was starting to believe that it might really be the best thing I could do for her. Not that it mattered. She had to be alive. She had to help us fight the Beast. Somehow, regardless of anything else, I had to keep her sane until she did.

"You know I can't kill her," I said.

"Maybe not right now, while the Beast it out there. If you get him trapped, and I pray you do; you may only get one chance."

Trap the Beast, and then kill Sarah. I had sworn to protect her. Would that be breaking the promise, or keeping it? Or would she kill Charis and I first? That was the future she had seen, the one that I told her wouldn't happen. Would her murder be the only way to stop it?

CHAPTER TWELVE

I left Sarah with Father Tom, and made my way back down to the basement. The
Father had promised he would look after her for the time being, feeling confident
she wouldn't wake up an angry mess. My mind was flipping through an endless stream
of possibilities, switching channels until I ran the carousel back around and
repeated the circle again. In the end, it all came down to one simple truth. We had
the Box, and we had Sarah. What to do about her prophesied future, or my potential
future, could wait until we could be sure any of us had one to begin with.

When I reached the basement, I found Charis on her knees by the rift, helping
Izak by smoothing out the stone floor he had scratched the runes into. The demon
was looking tense, his eyes squinted almost closed, his mouth a straight line. When
he saw me, he got to his feet.

He came right up to me and leaned in close, looking into my eyes. For
Josette, I was sure, and I knew he was disappointed when he didn't find her.

"She's okay," I said. "We just got separated."

He scowled and raised his hands, mimicking Ulnyx, wondering how the Were was
present but the angel wasn't.

106

"It's a long story," I replied.

He shrugged, and tilted to look over my shoulder.

"She'll be okay too," I said. "She's sleeping."

He seemed satisfied with that.

"She called you, in your mind?" I asked.

He nodded.

"You knew where she was, just from that?"

He nodded again.

"How did you know the runes to connect the rifts?"

He stared at me.

I remembered who he was. "There's a master rune, isn't there?" I asked.

He nodded, his smile sly. If anyone would know it, he was the one.

"Does Gervais know it?"

He hesitated, but he nodded, and pointed to where the archfiend's brand used

to mar his skin.

"It's not your fault," I said. "What was with Gervais anyway? He took a

blessed sword in the gut, and didn't even seem to feel it." The archfiend had

always been powerful, but not bleeding had never been in his bag of tricks. Neither

was collapsing skyscrapers.

Izak tapped on his temple, and then his form changed as he shifted into a

Gervais doppelganger. He made a motion like he was stabbing himself, and then

flopped onto the floor, his eyes open. He got up and leaned in on where he had been

laying, miming his hand on Gervais' shoulder, emitting a stream of hellfire towards

the floor for effect.

"You think the Beast revived him?" I asked.

He held out his hand and shifted it back and forth. Not exactly. He made his

body stiff, and shambled around the room.

"A zombie?" Charis asked. She had finished smoothing out the floor, and was watching his charades.

Izak nodded and pointed at her.

"Not revived," I said. "Re-animated."

"Malize said the Beast used the defeated angels as his army, piecing them back together to make his soldiers," Charis said. "He must have put Gervais back together again."

Like a twisted Humpty Dumpty. "And given him a bit of his mojo," I said. "The tower, and the building. He decayed them until they fell apart."

"How do you kill something that isn't alive?" Charis asked.

"Cut off his head, I guess," I said. "Even if it doesn't shut him down, it'll make things difficult."

"Or burn him to ash," she suggested. "Let's see him reanimate dust."

Two thoughts, but only one I was going to voice. "If any of us fall, someone needs to make sure he can't use us," I said. "Either with fire, or decapitation."

Izak gave me the thumbs up. My attention turned to the other thought. Had the Beast done the same to Rebecca? Was he just waiting for the right moment to spring her on me? She had been almost whole the last time I had seen her, so it had to be possible, and I had to be ready for it.

"Where are Thomas and Obi?" I asked. I focused on my Sight, noting that neither were within range.

"I don't know," Charis said. "They must have left without saying anything."

I laughed. "Obi doesn't do anything without saying anything."

"Maybe I just didn't hear him. Anyway, they can both take care of themselves."

I wasn't so sure. They had said the Beast was laying siege to the city, and only Izak had been able to keep them safe. Why would they just go off on their own?

108

"How bad is it out there?" I asked the demon.

He shrugged again, and put his hand out flat. Whatever they were doing, they were being careful not to shift the balance. It was the quietest war I had never heard.

"Can I talk to you?" I asked Charis. We had some unfinished business, and my heart was telling me not to let it sit too long.

"Sure," she said with a smile.

I motioned for the door, glancing at Izak. He had stopped paying attention, settling down with his back against the wall, staring straight ahead.

"Izak," I said, getting his attention. "When we get back, can you teach Charis the rune?"

He looked at her, searching for something. He must have found it, because he nodded.

Charis and I started for the door. We had almost reached it when a shadow fell from the steps and spilled into the room. There were no footfalls to be heard, but someone was definitely coming. I focused my Sight, and took a few steps back.

"Signore," Dante said as he entered the basement. He was wearing his red velvet robes, his slight frame lost in their volume. "I have news."

The entrance had been uncharacteristically straightforward. It had to be important. "Good or bad?" I asked.

"Ah. That depends on who you ask." He pulled the hem of his robe wide, reaching under it with his other hand. "After I left you at the farmhouse, I made my way to the Library of Alexandria. Not the mortal one, of course, that one burned centuries ago. There is another in Purgatory, one that still contains vast troves of information, written down by those sent to my realm to earn their way. That's where I found it."

He located the target of his search, and slipped it from the robes. It was a small piece of torn parchment, not more than the size of a fist, the edges frayed and worn. He held it out in the palm of his right hand.

We gathered around him to look at it, Izak getting to his feet to join us. Burned into the papyrus was a pictogram of a pyramid.

"I don't get it," I said. "A pyramid?"

Dante laughed, excited. "Yes," he replied. "Do you know what this means?"

"Uh, no," I said.

"Dante," Charis said. "I don't want to question you, but how do you know this has anything to do with the Beast?"

He raised the index finger of his left hand, and then reached down and flipped it over. "This is why I am excited, signore," he said. "It is good news for us. Not so good news for the Beast."

The single bit of scripture burned into the corner of the small rag was familiar, even if I couldn't read it.

"How?" Charis asked, the word coming out as more of a gasp. The writing was Templar.

"It was more simple than you would think, and in this one case I believe Mr. Ross' betrayal served a more beneficial purpose. You see, as Lord of Purgatory, I have an innate knowledge of every bit of text stored in the Library. I'm like the Google of the Middle-Ages." He laughed at his joke. We didn't. "Anyway, Mr. Ross knew this, and so at some point prior to being released, he went to the library and destroyed anything there having to do with him. There wasn't much, I know, because I had taken a personal interest in the Beast before. Still, he made sure there was nothing."

"What about Avriel, and his Box?" I asked, interrupting.

He shook his head. "I'm sorry, signore. I am limited to knowledge that has been passed on by those sent to Purgatory. The Box is an angelic device, one that had been missing for thousands of years, though I am sure Mr. Ross knew where it was the entire time. In any case, the neutral have no experience with it."

It was disappointing, but not unexpected.

"Do not be too disappointed," Dante said, reading my body language. "I remembered when I saw you last, you mentioned the name Malize. It is one that I had never heard before, and one that I have been having difficulty remembering since. Still, after coming up with nothing on the Beast, I sought out anything that might refer to him. In all of the Library, there was one single piece of parchment with his name on it. When I found this, it was pressed between the pages of an illuminated copy of the Bible."

"Let me guess," I said. "Revelations?"

Dante nodded. "The facing page was an illustration of the artist's concept of the Beast, in this case a dragon. There is no other writing on the parchment, so I assume the script says 'Malize'. That I found it where I did could not be an accident."

I looked over at Charis, who looked as shocked as I felt. "If he can't leave the cave, how would this have gotten to Purgatory?" I asked her.

"Someone must have brought it from the cave," she replied. "Just don't ask me who."

"How many people know about it?" I asked.

"Not many," she said, "and none of them could enter. Only the Divine can go in."

"I believe we have enough mysteries to handle right now," Dante said. "How it got there is not so important. What is important is what it means. It is clearly a suggestion to seek answers in a pyramid."

I felt Izak tap me on the shoulder. When I turned towards him, he brought his hands together in a pyramid shape and brought them down, over and over again. Then he held his hands out to his sides.

"Izak's right," I said. "There are over a hundred pyramids in Egypt, and that's assuming he's referring to an Egyptian one. Oh, and that's only the ones that have been discovered. Don't get me wrong, it's great to get a hint, but time is one thing that isn't on our side."

Dante pursed his lips, but didn't say anything. Nobody said anything, until a few uncomfortable moments of silence had passed.

"It is what we have, signore," the poet said. "If we must, we will search every pyramid on this Earth, because what will happen if we do not is untenable."

"He's right," Charis said, putting her hand on my shoulder and squeezing.

I knew it was true, but that didn't make it any less frustrating. The pompous, arrogant, evil smile invaded my consciousness, leering at me. There was no way I was going to let the Beast win.

"I'm sorry," I said. "It's been a rough couple of days. We'll head to Egypt to see if we can find the path we're being led towards. I think we should make a pit-stop in Paris and get our hands on Avriel first. We have the Box, which means he's the Beast's most probable next target."

"Agreed," Charis said. "We need to reach him before he does."

Dante smiled. "Excellent," he said. "I will return to Purgatory to see if I can find anything to help you narrow your search. I'll let you know as soon as I find something of value. Here, take this." He handled the piece of papyrus like it was an infant, passing it carefully over to me.

With that he was gone, vanishing in the space between one moment of time and the next. The three of us stood together, saying nothing, until Izak broke it up by returning to his spot on the floor. I took the parchment and focused, finding the weakness and age in the structure, and putting it back together, strengthening it enough so that I could fold it up and stick it in my pocket. I could imagine Dante making his angry face at me for doing it.

Charis' hand was still on my shoulder, and she squeezed it again as she leaned up and in, her lips brushing against my ear. The move reminded me of when she had given me the Grail, and her warning. Even then, when I believed she was the enemy, her closeness had electrified me.

"You wanted to talk?" she asked. "In private?" Her breath was warm, and it smelled like cinnamon.

"I did," I said, reaching up and taking her hand, holding it in my own. I turned to face her, so I could look into her eyes. I could see the flames behind them, the red soul of the demon Vilya watching everything from her place within. I hadn't looked in a mirror lately, but I was sure my eyes were red these days too. I took a deep breath, my heart throbbing in my chest, every muscle feeling a charged ache from being near her. Privacy would be good. I leaned forward, tilting my head and placing it against hers. "But now I can't remember what I was going to say."

Our noses were almost touching. I could feel the heat from the blood running through her face, and smell the mixture of her breath and hair and skin with the heightened senses Ulnyx provided. It was intoxicating.

"You don't need to say anything," she replied. Her mouth was right there, her lips parted, inviting mine to join them. Never before in my life had I wanted anything else as much.

I pulled back. I regretted it right way, because I didn't know when I would get another chance, but I also knew it was what I had to do. She knew it too, because she didn't get mad, or embarrassed, or shy.

"You owe me," was all she said, and then she smiled. The ease of it made me smile too. "So I guess we're headed to France. You know where Avriel is?"

"I know where I left him," I replied. Hanging from a meat-hook, being tortured by one of the most powerful demons ever created. I wasn't thrilled about

113

the prospect of going back there. I had promised the angel I would end his misery,
and then reneged because it didn't suit me. I didn't regret that decision, I just
hated that I was going to have to take the consequences head-on. Being Divine
didn't take away every level of my human cowardice. This would be a lot easier if
Josette were around to help me talk to him.

Charis let go of my hand. "We should get a move on then," she said.

I nodded, but hesitated. "*Josette*." I called out for her, focusing and
reaching for the frayed ends of our connection, trying to pull them together, to
smooth them out. Chaos raced along the trail, my mind pulled in so many directions.
Avriel, the Beast, Gervais, Sarah, Rebecca. Why did it always come back to Rebecca?
Even when I let go and accepted my growing attachment to my counterpart?

"You saw what happened, between the angel and I?" I asked.

"You did what you had to do," she said.

"Tell that to Avriel. You needed Vilya back to get us through the rift. I
need Josette back if we're going to convince him to help us. He was called 'the
Just' for a reason."

"Landon, there isn't time," she said. "Especially if the Beast's next move is
to bring Abaddon under his sway. If he gets the demon on his side, and sends him
for Sarah..."

She didn't need to finish the sentence. I knew what would happen. Sarah would
try to Command him, and if she failed, she would be taken, and we would be
destroyed. Abaddon had caused Izak to run. She would fail.

"I'm close," I said. "I just need a chance to rest for a little while." It
was a lie. I had no idea how close I was, but the feeling that I needed Josette was
becoming more concrete in my soul. Or was it my backbone?

"Landon!" The shout came from the top of the steps. Obi. I tapped Charis'
eyes with my own, and we rushed up the stairs, Izak not far behind.

114

The first thing I noticed was the blood, running in a tight red line,
following the seam of the hallway's stone floor. My first thought was that Obi was
hurt, but it was wrong. The second thing I saw was the former marine, kneeling
close to the floor, cradling a woman in his arms. Thomas was standing behind him, a
nasty gash in his cheek. The second thought was confusion, and the third anger. The
woman was Divine, an angel, Melody. Her toga-like dress was stained red along her
stomach, and her tucked wings hung limp behind her, the blood using them to run
down off her body to the floor, creating the line I had followed.

The fact that she was bleeding could only mean one thing. She had been
attacked by one of her own, with a blessed weapon. The fact that she still had her
wings, meant that her attackers had traded in theirs for a different set.

"There's holy water in the rectory," I said, running over and dropping to my
knees opposite Obi. "Thomas, go."

The angel looked dazed. He glanced down at me, and then turned and headed off
to get the healing agent.

"Melody," I said, my voice soft. "Can you hear me."

Her eyes were closed, but they fluttered open when I spoke to her. A small
smile made it onto her lips. "Landon," she said. "I came to... to warn you." Her
voice was broken and weak. The rectory wasn't far, but she was as close to gone as
I could imagine. Thomas wasn't going to make it.

I reached down to her stomach, finding the hole in her garment where the
sword had stabbed her. "You aren't going to die today," I said, closing my eyes to
focus on the wound. We needed to hear whatever she had to say, and I knew Obi had
the hots for her. Then there was the third reason to heal her. A selfish reason.

I had healed Josette once this way. It was the only other time I had even
tried it, but the action felt familiar as I concentrated on the wound, finding the
torn internals and willing them back together, knitting the muscle and tissue and

115

staunching the bleeding. I could hear activity around me, a subliminal understanding of speech and motion, but I didn't pay it any mind. I pushed my energy into her, feeling her flesh grow warm to the touch, and knowing that she would live.

My eyes opened, and I pulled back my hand. I was weak, but not weak enough. The selfish reason. I wanted to pass out, to find the sleep that was the only thing that would put Josette and I back together again. It was denied to me, but at least I had saved her.

"What do you think you're doing, laddie?" Father Tom was leaning over me, yelling into my ear. Charis had a grip on his arm, trying to pull him away. Obi's face was stretched tight with concern, and Thomas was holding out a paper cup filled with holy water. "You have no right to touch the flesh of such a creature."

I flipped my gaze over to meet his, and didn't back down. I managed to maintain my calm as I spoke. "I just saved her life," I said.

"You did," Melody said, her voice quiet but strong. I looked away from Father Tom to check on her. Her eyes were open, staring up at me with a reverence and respect I didn't deserve. "Thank you."

"Melody," Obi said, leaning down over her. "I'm happy to see you, but can we meet under better circumstances next time?"

"Now what fun would that be?" she replied, reaching up and tapping his cheek.

"How are you feeling?" I asked.

"A little out of sorts, but I'll survive, thanks to you."

"Father Tom, do you have a bed, or another couch?" I knew the one in his office was already taken.

"She can swap with me," Sarah said. She had come up behind the priest, her face haggard but more relaxed than it had been since the day she had been taken. It was good to see, even knowing it wasn't going to last.

116

"Come on then," Father Tom said. "Clear a path. Carry her in, and be gentle boy-o."

Obi lifted Melody as he rose to his feet, and carried her easily past us and into the Father's office. The priest genuflected when they passed.

"I can't even begin to understand the Lord's plan for me in all of this," Father Tom whispered as we shuffled into the office behind them.

The Beast was loose, Abaddon was free, and angels were attacking angels. I wasn't convinced the Lord had any plan at all, or that His eyes were even open. Maybe there was some twist of fate involved, and maybe there wasn't. We were all here, now, and we knew what we had to do. "I'm the last person who can answer that for you, Father," I said," but I'm thankful for your hospitality."

Obi laid Melody on the couch, still warm and indented from where Sarah had been laying. Melody fluttered her wings once and sunk into the leather, squeezing the former marine's hand before allowing him to withdraw.

"Okay," I said, resting with my back against the desk. "What the heck is going on?"

Melody turned her head so she could see me. A bead of moisture began to form under her eyes. "They don't believe in the Beast," she said. "They don't believe he's real."

My eyes shifted to the splotch of red on her stomach. "They attacked you," I pointed out. "You're saying they weren't servants?"

She shrugged. "I don't know if those blokes were servants or not. After you fled the farmhouse, I had a little chat with the two you left eating dirt." She smirked. "They dragged me back to Heaven, and brought me before Kassie."

"She's the Head Inquisitor," Thomas said, before I could ask.

"Kassie forced me to Confess, again. She was anything but gentle. I told her everything I knew about you, from the first time we had met in the airport." She shifted her gaze to Izak. "They made me tell them who he is. They're scared, knowing he's with you. They thought he was out of play."

Izak's grin was priceless. He might have softened up since meeting Josette, but he took delight in his reputation.

"They said I was sullied, and would need Cleansing."

I heard Thomas gasp behind me. "Cleansing?"

"When Confession isn't enough," Thomas said. "It's an... interesting ... form of torture. It's supposed to purge impurities from your soul. The Inquisitors created it as a way to get information without being cast out for cruelty."

Heaven got more interesting with every bit I learned. Even with all of their black and white rules, there was still room for a lot of grey, and it didn't sound pleasant at all.

"The details aren't important," Melody said. "Kassie ordered me to be Cleansed. My interactions with you, and your demon, and my..." She paused and looked at Obi. "My growing affection for your sidekick supposedly poisoned me."

"Man, why do I have to be the sidekick?" Obi asked. "I'm bigger than you. And smarter."

"Let's see you turn into a fourteen foot tall beast monster," I replied.

"Boys, can we focus?" Charis said, her tight smile betraying her amusement. I still thought levity was the best cure for tension, and I could always rely on Obi to instigate.

"So you escaped?" I asked.

"They were bringing me to the Cleansing chamber. I used a move Obi taught me, getting free and making a run for it. I was almost away, but Kassie managed to head me off. We fought. I lost."

"But you didn't fall," Sarah said.

"I didn't use my weapon against her. I knew what it would mean. I never expected her to stab me, but she was furious."

"So she fell?"

Melody shook her head. "Inquisitors have extra leeway, as long as their motives are pure. She didn't stab me out of malice, but because she thought I was a threat to all of the seraphim. She'll have to answer to an archangel, and likely Confess to be sure her actions were appropriate, but it isn't an automatic out. Anyway, Obi had given me a cell. I called him, found out where he was, and came to him."

"That's why you went outside?" I asked. He nodded. "So, you came to warn me. About what?"

"Kassie," she said. "The Inquisitors are convinced you have a Canaan Blade, and they're going to come down on you hard to get it. They may even get Gabriel involved. Like I said, they don't believe the Beast is real."

"Don't they know they've got demons and angels right outside of this church attacking both sides?"

"Landon," Thomas said. "The angels are only attacking demons. They may be helping the demon servants locate targets, but it's business as usual as far as Heaven knows."

I took a deep breath, and kicked my foot back against the desk, hearing the wood crack behind the force. Father Tom winced at the sound, and I immediately felt guilty. "Bad to worse," I said. "What the hell is so important about those swords?"

"I told you everything I know," Thomas replied. "I wish I could tell you more."

"I know," I said. I brought my hands up, resting my head in them. I needed time to think, to rest, to take a breath and escape from being me for a minute or two. The Beast, Abaddon, Gervais, Sarah, Inquisitors, Avriel, Josette. It was too much to deal with at one time.

"*Just kill 'em all*," Ulnyx said, choosing the wrong time to make his opinion known.

"*Shut up*," I replied, ignoring the resulting laughter.

"Landon?" Obi asked. "You okay, man?"

I hesitated. "No. I'm not." I dropped my hands and stared down at the floor. "I didn't sign up for this."

Charis was at my side in a second, her arm draped around my shoulders. "It's okay," she said. "None of us did. Not like this. Take a look around for a second though. An angel, a demon, a priest, a fallen angel, a mortal, a pure diuscrucis, me. We're a motley bunch, but we represent every facet of what God created, either directly or indirectly." She swung around in front of me, putting her hand under my chin, lifting my head to meet my eyes with hers. "You brought us together. You. We're all on your side first and foremost, regardless of our personal reasons. There is nothing out there that could have planned for that, or planned to go up against that. Maybe you can't do it on your own, but you don't have to."

It was a good speech. A little cheesy, but effective. I smiled at her and nodded. "You're right," I said. "Thank you all for being here."

"Anytime, man," Obi said, speaking for all of them.

"So now what?" Sarah asked.

I looked at her, and then at Melody. "Now it's time for a nap," I said.

CHAPTER THIRTEEN

I kicked everyone out of the office, except for Melody, Charis, and Sarah.
Obi protested the loudest, but he was still evicted. My motivation might have been
dubious, but the fact is that I believed I needed Josette back, and that was
enough. Charis was right in that I had brought a disparate and diverse group
together by following my path without question, so it only made sense to keep going
with the flow, rather than rushing against the tide.

"Are you ready?" I asked Melody. I had taken her spot on the couch, and she
and Sarah were kneeling over me, next to one another. Charis was standing behind my
head. She didn't have to be there, but I had wanted her nearby.

"Are you sure about this?" she asked.

"Yeah," I said. "It's tough having Ulnyx in here without anyone to help keep
him quiet."

"*You're getting on my nerves,*" the Great Were said in response. "*We don't
need the White Princess back.*"

"*Didn't I tell you to shut up?*" I replied.

My hope was that Josette would help me deal with Avriel, and maybe even the

Inquisitors. If she knew anything about the Canaan Blades, that would be an extra special bonus. I figured we could fix the connection if I were sleeping, the same way Charis had with Vilya, but that was going to take some time. My new plan was to have Melody and Sarah Calm me, together, and hopefully put me into a state of being that sped up the process.

"Just don't ask me anything personal," I said to Melody.

"Like the color of your knickers?" she laughed.

"I'm not wearing knickers," I lied.

"Naughty, naughty."

I closed my eyes and breathed in, a deep breath that caught the smell of Charis standing behind me. The warm cinnamon of her was comforting, and I focused on pulling apart every molecule of it.

"Tell me about Josette," Melody said. I felt the pressure of her Calming words, my mind reflexively trying to defend against it. I doubled my efforts to capture Charis' essence. I hadn't been sure Melody would be strong enough to Calm me, which is why I had Sarah standing by.

"Yes, Landon," she said. "Tell me about mother. Tell me about how you met, and what she means to you."

The words started flowing without thought or effort. It wasn't that I even recognized when the Calm began to take hold. First it hadn't, and then it had. "The Apple Store, of all things," I said. "I was trying to keep a low profile, to get some information and figure out what I was supposed to do. She saw me, and I saw her, and I don't know... it didn't start that well, but there was just something about her. We were always meant to meet, I think. We were always meant to be friends, or something..."

I knew I was still talking, somewhere in the back of my mind. I knew words were still coming out, because I caught a phrase every now and then, "plain, but pretty", "fun and exciting", "taught me so much". The world was dark behind my closed eyes, dark and comfortable and calm. It was peaceful in a way I hadn't experienced in years, and that peacefulness picked up the world I was in, and carried it away. Or maybe it carried me away, from the trouble and the worry to somewhere else, another life, another existence, I don't know. The important thing was that I was there, and he was there, and *she* was there.

I couldn't see her, but I could feel her. The same feeling she had left at the Belmont, that first time. The indelible sense of her, that she was present, and had been present. It was something I hadn't gotten from any other angel I had met, and I had met quite a few.

"I guess we should find her," Ulnyx said.

We were standing on a white marble floor, surrounded by marble posts from which hung huge swatches of white gossamer fabric that shifted and billowed in a soft breeze. The sky was bright and blue above us, and everything about the place reminded me of her.

The fabric was translucent, and looking through the surrounding weaves revealed more posts and more cloth; a maze of silk. I turned to Ulnyx. The Were was out of place here, with his destroyed blue jeans and 'F*ck Good' t-shirt. A thought, and he was in a tux.

"Have some respect," I said. A half-smile was his only reply. "Josette."

I called out to her. The sound of my voice echoed into the sky, and reverberated through the maze, but there was no reply. I shouldn't have expected this to be easy.

"We can just cut through the cloth," Ulnyx said, his hand growing out into his weapon of choice.

I was inclined to agree, but it ran counter to the metaphor. "No. Try to think peaceful."

He laughed. "Me? Should I sit in lotus position and start ohm-ing?"

"Just follow me."

I walked past the first opening in the posts, and turned right, following the fabric twenty yards and then making a left. Every few seconds, I called out for Josette again.

"Do you think she knows we're here?" Ulnyx asked.

"I don't even know where here is," I said. "But I hope so."

The where was the interesting part. Was this her Source? Was it mine? What had being Calm tag-teamed done to me? I focused, trying to lift myself into the sky, a test to see if we were in Purgatory. Nothing happened.

"Landon."

The voice came from around the corner, and I could see the shape of the speaker through the fabric.

"Sarah," I said. "What are you doing here?"

"I felt you calling," she replied. "So I came."

She was wearing a modest white dress that covered her shoulders and fell to her ankles. Her hair was put up like she was headed to a wedding, and her red-gold eyes sparkled in the light.

"She's here," I said. "I just don't know where."

"I know. I can feel her too. We'll find her together."

"Hey, don't forget about me, hot stuff," Ulnyx said.

We started walking again, threading through the posts, plotting a course through the maze. It didn't take long for me to discover that even when I intentionally made a square, we never wound up back in the same place.

"Do you know where we are?" I asked Sarah while we walked.

"Your soul," she replied. "It reflects your emotions and your feelings. You're at peace, but conflicted. Why are you conflicted, brother?"

I wasn't having that conversation here, or now. "You don't know?"

"What I told you... about killing you?" she asked.

"Yes," I replied. It was part, but not all.

She smiled, her entire face brightening. "It doesn't have to happen, and it won't happen. I know you'll protect me."

I kept myself focused on the path ahead. Protect her by killing her?

There was no way to measure how much time passed. It seemed like hours, and I would have lost hope, except I could feel Josette slowly growing closer. I understood the maze to be my conflict, and maybe Josette would help me come to some kind of resolution. In order to smooth the edges, to reconnect with her wounded soul, I had to accept whatever would come to be.

The marble floors and walls of white cloth slowly began to fade away, replaced with a thick layer of low green grass forming the shore of a small lake. A thin fall of water tumbled from the spring sky, splashing gently into the pool and kicking up an invisible mist that tickled my face. It was in the pool, floating face up, her arms crossed over her chest, that I found her.

I know right away she wasn't dead, only resting. Waiting.

"Stay here," I said to Sarah and Ulnyx, deliberate in my fully-clothed entry to the lake, calm as I waded in to retrieve her. The water was only waist deep when I reached her. Her eyes were closed, and her breathing was steady. I put my arms under her and lifted, the water streaming from her white dress as it emerged into the warm air. "Josette," I whispered. "Can you hear me?"

She smiled before she opened her eyes. "Landon. I knew you would come. It's been lonely here, but I've tried to stay centered."

I leaned down and kissed her forehead. "Of course you did," I said. "Sarah is with me."

Her eyes beamed. "She is here? Now?"

125

I nodded, but took a serious tone. "We're in a lot of trouble," I said. "Sarah most of all."

It didn't quell her spirit. "We will overcome," was all she said.

I carried her to the shore, and lowered her to her feet. Sarah rushed over, wrapping her arms around the angel with the fierceness reserved for mother and child.

"I'm so happy to see you," she cried.

"As am I," Josette replied. "I'm proud of you Sarah, for turning away from the destruction of the Beast."

It didn't seem possible, but she dug her head deeper into her mother's shoulder. "Thank you," she said. "Thank you for being here, for giving yourself up for me. For sending Landon."

Ulnyx approached them, falling into a deep bow. "Princess," he said, his voice half a snarl.

"Monster," she replied. They both smiled.

Sarah broke her embrace, and mother and daughter stood face to face, just looking at one another.

"I never imagined I would get to hold you again," Josette said. "To see you here, to look on you." She glanced over at me. "I didn't know what waited, when I gave up my soul to you."

"I didn't think I would ever know you at all," Sarah said. "Izak told me about you, about how gentle and good you are, and how I should be proud to be like you. I want to keep making you proud."

"You will," Josette said.

Her faith drove a knife into my chest. You can't stop the madness. Only delay it. I decided not to tell Josette what the Father had said. Not yet. She deserved this moment.

"What of the Beast?" she asked me.

"He is gathering his power," I said. "He's still trying to get Sarah, because he can't juice up enough to take Heaven and Hell without maxing out his levels. He already made one grab for her. He..."

"Sent father to take me," Sarah interrupted.

"Gervais is alive?" Josette asked, her shock evident.

"No," I said. "The Beast brought him back. He's not living."

"More like a puppet without strings," Ulnyx said.

"But we retrieved Avriel's Box, and Dante found a clue left by the angel Malize."

"Who?"

"The angel Malize. You were there, in the cave with Charis and me. Do you remember?"

She shook her head. "I remember the cave. I don't recall an angel."

The Forgotten. "It doesn't matter," I said. "We need to go back to Paris and rescue Avriel from Abaddon. I don't think I'm at the top of his friends list, so I was hoping you would be able to reach him."

She sighed. "Landon, you made a promise to him, and then broke it. You put him back to be cruelly tortured by the demon."

"I know," I said. "I didn't know I would need him again."

She sighed again. "Listen to yourself, brother. This is not only about what you need or don't need in any given moment."

It stung, but I deserved it. "I didn't have a choice."

"There is always a choice. You took the easy path, because it was easy. It is fitting that you aren't finding it so easy now."

I couldn't disagree. "So you won't help me?"

"I will help you," she replied. "My advice is to be respectful, and

127

apologetic. Sincerely apologetic. Avriel is known for his sense of justice, and he is a faithful hand of the Lord. He will forgive, if you are true."

"She told you," Ulnyx said.

"Shut up."

"I know every moment is precious," Josette said. "Still, I would be grateful for a few minutes to spend with my daughter."

I would never deny her that, even if the world was collapsing around us. "Come on Ullie," I said. I could sense him bristle at the nickname.

We wandered away from them, going to sit by the lake.

"What do you think she's saying to her?" Ulnyx asked.

"I don't know."

"You going to tell her that her kid's psycho?"

"You're one to talk," I replied.

"Look, meat, I may not be the nicest guy around, but at least I'm stable."

I looked out at the waterfall, pouring from the sky. "I don't think it'll help. Not now anyway. With any luck, having her mother around will keep her on the golden path until we can get the Beast in the Box. We can worry about her prognosis after that."

"I'm not looking forward to it," he said.

"If it means we stopped the Beast, I'll take what I can get," I replied. They were words spoken, but not words that sat well. Sarah was two inches from coming apart at the seams, and I was going to have to watch helplessly while it happened.

We were sitting silent when Sarah and Josette approached. They were holding hands, and Sarah looked more content than I could ever remember seeing her. Enjoy the moment, anyway. It was the only thing I could do.

"We're ready," Sarah said. "Let's go catch a Beast."

I closed my eyes, and tried to will myself awake. It didn't happen. "Somebody needs to wake me up," I said.

"It's nice to see you so calm, brother," Sarah replied. "Even if it is forced." She squeezed Josette's hand one last time, and vanished. A moment later, the earth around us began quaking, knocking us to our knees.

"See you around, meat," Ulnyx said.

The world darkened and disappeared.

CHAPTER FOURTEEN

"Well, what do you think?"

We were all gathered in Father Tom's office, all except Izak. The priest was sitting behind his desk, looking worried, while the rest of us took up the extra chairs and sofa. I had only been out for about an hour, but it was long enough to be concerned that Kassie and the Inquisitors would pop in at any moment. Kassie and the Inquisitors. I pictured angels playing electric guitars.

Obi turned the papyrus over and looked at the script on the back. "I don't know, man," he said. "I'm not that clean on my egyptian antiquities, and I don't know that much about pyramids. This drawing looks like a standard triangle with a few lines so you know its more than just a triangle."

I reached out to take it back. "Don't worry about it. I figured I'd ask."

He didn't hand it back over right away. He turned it over to the pyramid side again and stared at it. "You know, I do remember reading something not too long ago, about the Great Pyramid. There's this guy... I can't remember his name. Hamas or something. Anyway, he claimed that there's a secret chamber inside. I read about it online somewhere. I know, that's probably not that helpful." Obi handed the papyrus back.

"I'll take what I can get right now," I said. "It may sound like a long shot, but what else do we have? We'll start with the Great Pyramid."

I put the fragment back in my pocket, and set myself to deliver the news.

"I need you to stay behind," I said, bracing for impact.

"Aww, come on, man," Obi complained. "You need me, and I'm sick of getting left behind. Heck, I just gave you your only lead. I should be there to see if it pans out."

"Someone has to stay here and keep Kassie off our tails." I said. "We can't fight both of these battles at the same time."

It wasn't my favorite approach either, because as resilient as the former marine was, I didn't think he could stand up to the seraph. What I *did* think he could do was get creative, and keep her dashing at shadows while we tried to reach Avriel. I would have preferred to leave Izak with him, but now that he and Sarah had been reunited, he outright refused to leave her side.

I put my hand on his shoulder and leaned in. "You're the only one I can trust to do this."

"Look on the bright side," Melody said. "You get to spend more time with me."

"I don't think we'll have much time to ourselves while we're playing hide and seek with Miss Inquisition," he replied. He was upset, but there was nothing I could do about it.

"If the seraph shows up here, I'll be defrocked for sure," Father Tom said. "Harboring three diuscrucis, and a demon of all things. The sooner you all get out of my church, the better I'll feel."

"Obi?" I knew he would acquiesce. He always did, but it made him feel better to complain first.

"Yeah, okay, man," he said, after a silent pause. "So Kassie is going to be

131

following Melody, right? Because she thinks she's with you, or will lead her to you." He looked at the angel. "But are you with us?"

Melody's face contracted, and she looked torn. "I'm with you, Landon, as long as what you're doing is in line with the Lord's plan. The Lord trapped the Beast once, I don't think He intended for it to be free. I can't help that my brothers and sisters refuse to see the truth. It's easy to deny what we don't want to see."

It wasn't a full pledge of support, but I hadn't expected one. We'd still come a long way since our first meeting. "Thanks, Melody," I said.

"What are we waiting for?" Sarah asked. She was looking much better, having found a shower and a change of clothes in the short time since I had woken. She had lost the ringlets in her hair, choosing to contain the natural curl by pulling it back into a tight ponytail. The makeshift dress had been traded for a pair of jeans and a simple black pullover hoodie she'd found in a box awaiting pickup by Goodwill.

"Nothing," I replied. I swiveled my gaze around to Obi, to Melody, to Thomas, and to Father Tom. "Good luck, all of you. Stay safe."

Obi reached out, taking my hand in his and clasping it tight. "You too," he said, leaning in and clapping me on the back. "We'll keep you clear to do what you need to do."

"I know," I said. With that, I made for the door, Charis and Sarah following behind.

We headed down the hallway and back into the basement, where Izak was putting the finishing touches on a rebuilt transport rift. I felt kind of stupid for asking him to get rid of it, and then remake it, but I hadn't been thinking very clearly at the time. I could sense his anger when I had made the new request, but it had subsided when he had noticed the change in my eyes.

"How's it coming Izak?" I asked as we entered. He was crouched in front of the rift, his hands clasped together. The runes flared to life. "I never doubted."

"Father Tom is going to crap the rosary when he finds this thing," Sarah said.

I knew it, but there was nobody on this side who could take it apart. Besides that, I wasn't sure we wouldn't need it again. The best I could hope for was that he wouldn't turn us in to the Inquisitors as soon as he saw what we had done.

"Sounds painful," I said. I didn't even slow on the approach, hitting the edge of the circle, and stepping through.

I was surprised by my location when I came out the other side. I had just assumed that Gervais' personal rift would have been destroyed when the Beast had sent his servants after Lylyx and Izak, but on emerging I found myself walking down a gilded stone platform in an overdone neoclassical hodgepodge of artwork and furniture. My eyes immediately went to the four posted bed that served as the centerpiece of the room, and my breath caught on the memory that hung there in the stale air. It was a memory I had relived a hundred times or more.

Sarah came through next. It was her birth I was seeing, but not from my own eyes. Gervais had taken her from Josette, and thrown his sister out the window.

"*Landon.*" Josette's voice was a tonic to my whirring thoughts. "*Let the past stay there.*"

That was the trick, of course. I looked away, to the door at the far end of the room. It was hanging open. I focused my Sight. It told me the home was deserted, but in the back of my mind I half-expected Gervais, or maybe even Rebecca to come charging through.

"There's no way the Beast wouldn't expect us to come here," I said. I felt the energy of the rift subside as Izak came through and shut it down.

"Another trap?" Charis asked.

"Whatever it is, I guarantee it won't be as easy as going in, and getting

133

out." Unless he wanted us to just come in, and get out. I didn't know which scenario worried me more. "Izak, lead the way."

The demon gave me the thumbs up and took the front of the line, taking us away from the open door, towards the corner of the bedroom. There was a marble statue of the archfiend there, his face a diabolical grimace, his hands up over his head in victory. Izak waved a stiff arm, and the statue flew away, smashing against the right-hand wall.

Satisfied, he reached for the wall, his hand sinking through a glamour that I couldn't see beyond. He manipulated something, and then beckoned for us to wait. A few seconds later, he waved for us to follow, and he walked through the glamour.

We were in an elevator, with rich wood walls and plenty of gold inlays. Izak didn't press any of the buttons on the inside, but I could feel him reaching out with his power. The elevator began to sink.

"Is this an express?" I asked. He glanced over at me, but didn't respond.

"Why do you think the Beast wouldn't have set his goons here to wait for us? Gervais especially?"

I was surprised that Sarah was the one asking about her father, and so nonchalantly. "We know he had his heart set on convincing Abaddon to join him. If he has Abaddon, he can do whatever he wants with Avriel."

"Kill him?"

Or use him to bait another trap.

The elevator slowed to a stop, and the doors opened. Another glamour. We stepped through it, and I found myself in familiar surroundings.

Before, the machinery and computers had been whole. Before, there had been a gurney with a corpse on it. Before, Gervais had been hanging from a chain, left as a gift from Rebecca as incentive for me to join her cause; the Beast's cause. Now, the chain hung alone, and the rest of the lab had been torn apart, mangled, and

134

burned. Whatever Gervais had been researching, it was all gone.

"What was he researching?" Sarah asked. Izak stopped walking and turned to her. He frowned and shook his head.

"Okay," she said, dropping the subject.

I knew the way from here, so I took the lead. Out of the laboratory, past the torture room, to the cells where Josette lived during her pregnancy. It was here that Sarah stopped again, putting her face to the bars and looking in on the room. She didn't say anything. Her expression didn't even change. She just stared in until Izak took her arm and gently pulled her away.

Out of the prison and up the steps, down a hallway of rooms stocked with supplies, and into the small room where the rift between the Paris sewers and the Chateau sat. Still, there was no sign of any Divine, no suggestion of anyone mortal, immortal, or in-between. With each step I began to get more nervous, more concerned that we were being careless, reckless, thoughtless, and foolish. The doubt began to gnaw at me, picking its way into me and planting thorny seeds.

"This is a mistake," I said. Izak was bent over the rift, about to bring it to life. "It's too easy."

"What choice do we have?" Charis asked. "We need Avriel to help us with the box."

"Do we?" I was having second thoughts. "We're just assuming since he made the thing, he can work some kind of magic that will ensure it can contain the Beast. Maybe it already can? Or maybe, it never can?"

"Which is why we need to ask him," Charis said. "It's better to find out from a reliable source than to risk everything. Even if it feels like we're walking right into a trap. Again."

"It worked out okay last time," Sarah piped in. "The Beast thinks he's smarter than we are. He's arrogant. We can use that to our advantage."

I looked at her like she had two heads. This wasn't the Sarah that Gervais had turned into a whimpering mound of hurt. "It looks like I'm outvoted."

Izak had paused his work while we argued. Seeing it settled, he went back to the runes. Within moments, they flared up.

What happened then was nine seconds of pure chaos, so quick and so dirty that there was no time to even try to decipher it. The very moment the runes came to life, the room grew cold, so cold, and a shadow of a form appeared in the rift.

One second: Abaddon had come into the small room, so close to me that I could almost see the demon behind the shadows, a sharp, dark-fleshed, humanoid face with rich blood eyes obscured by the swirling darkness of his power.

Two seconds: Sarah started to scream, the words deep in pitch and tone at the slow-motion speed in which I remembered them. It wasn't a scream of fear, even though that was the effect of the vaporous tentacles that flowed out across the space. It was a scream of Command.

Three seconds: Izak dove towards Sarah, his hand getting a firm grip on her wrist, his body shifting and pivoting. Her words launched forward at the demon, and I felt her power as a wave of pressure on my soul.

Four seconds: I was close to it. I found my focus and fought back against the fear, pulling energy into me, cocking my fist back. The demon stood in its spot in front of the rift.

Five seconds: I heard the *snikt* of Charis' sword coming free of its scabbard on her back, as she prepared to face the demon. Maybe the fear subsided due to Sarah's command, or maybe I had just overcome it for just a moment, but it was enough for me to let the fist fly, shifting my weight and angle to I could pummel it from the side.

Six seconds: The blow struck Abaddon hard, making pure, solid contact with an actual creature of flesh and blood, and sending him toppling away from the rift.

Seven seconds: Izak had seen the attack, and he pulled Sarah, yanking her through the rift with him.

Eight seconds: I felt the breath fall out of me as Charis rushed me from behind, crashing into me and throwing us both through the circle.

Nine seconds: In the sewers of Paris, the fiend Izak, the demon once known as Mephistopheles, had already put his hand into the runes to shut the rift down. Hellfire crawled along him, and the smell of his burning flesh was overpowering. His face bore no sign of pain, though it must have been excruciating. Instead, he was deliberate and steady in his concentration, working to manually scratch away part of the still-burning circle to disable it.

Once it was done, he fell onto his back, clutching his forearm with his other hand. Smoke rose from the wound, and I could see that below where he held there was nothing but charred and useless flesh.

"Oh, no," Sarah said. "Izak." She bent over him, trying to offer comfort. He held out his good hand and pushed himself away.

"Izak," I said. I kept looking at the no longer identifiable mass of skin and bone at the end of his arm. I couldn't heal that.

He held his good hand out to me as well, and shook his head. His eyes squinted in pain, and he took a few deep breaths. Then he got to his feet, and motioned in the direction of the bone room.

"You are a serious badass," I said. He glanced over at me, and shrugged.

"*There is no way to heal that. Not ever,*" Josette said. "*That wound will fester and bring him pain for the rest of his eternity.*"

"*He's played with hellfire before,*" I replied.

"*He's never touched it. The fire he wields sits above the skin, too close to see, but it never touches.*"

I stared at the demon's back as he started walking down the corridor. Badass

137

indeed.

We hurried to catch up to him, my mind trying to sort out what had just happened, and what it meant. Abaddon had obviously been lying in wait for the rift to become active, which meant that either the Beast had been successful in his recruiting efforts, or the demon had just decided he'd had enough and wanted to catch the next, closest train out. The former seemed a lot more plausible.

It didn't take much of a stretch to assume that Ross had believed Abaddon would overwhelm us, especially in ambush, and get a hold on Sarah. As before, he had underestimated our own resilience. Or maybe just the square footage of the room Gervais kept his rift in. I doubt that he had considered Sarah's ability to at least confuse the demon with her Command, or the power of my right hook. I certainly hadn't.

There was one thing about it that was bothering me above everything else, and as we turned the corner and spilled out into the bone room, my fear was confirmed. The huge wooden crucifix was still foisted in the center of the room, but Avriel was gone.

"This can't be good," Sarah said, breaking a silence that stretched out too long.

I approached the cross, scanning the ground around it for any sign of dust that might be the remains of the seraph. The area around the structure was clean. He might have still been alive. He might have been in the hands of the Beast, being tortured anew by something worse than the worst demon around. I felt the guilt welling up again, and I had to close my eyes to force it back down. This is what we had come for? This is what Izak had given up his hand and would live in eternal pain for? I had felt this was a mistake, and I hated being proven right.

CHAPTER FIFTEEN

"Is he dead?" I asked. I wasn't asking anyone in particular, and I didn't expect a reply.

"Does it matter?" Charis kicked at the ground in front of the cross. "We're not going to get what we wanted this time."

"What if he tells the Beast how to disable the Box?" Sarah asked.

"There's nothing we can do about it, but I have a feeling it will take quite a bit to break him, after what he's been through with Abaddon." The guilt again.

I reached into my pocket and pulled out the folded up piece of papyrus. I held it up to the others. "This is all we've got now," I said. "This, and no nearby rift."

I didn't even ask Izak if he could make us a new one. The script that formed the rift circles was more intricate than I could even describe, which is why so few demons could create their own. Izak had reached in to save us without thinking, doing so with his dominant hand. His writing hand.

"Don't forget that Abaddon is topside," Charis said. "Not that I'm trying to make things worse, but we know he's in play for the Beast."

"Closest rift?" It was the only thing that mattered right now, unless we wanted to drive back to Gervais' chateau to challenge Abaddon. After barely getting away from him, I wasn't enamored with the idea.

"We can take the train from Paris to London," Charis suggested. "It isn't the closest by miles, but it's probably the fastest to get to. Izak, what do you think?"

The fiend hadn't moved since we came into the room. He just stood with a stoic expression, holding his mutilated hand across his chest. When Charis asked his opinion, he nodded once.

"Okay," I said. "That's our move. Let's go."

We traveled back through the sewers, along the path I had last seen at a full run while trying to escape Abaddon. The sewers were a cold, dark, empty place, more so now because the demon's dark existence had destroyed every manner of life it had encountered. Even the rats hadn't been safe from him, and a sewer without rats was an especially creepy thing.

I noted the dashes of Gervais' age-old blood when we passed them, Izak guiding us back in the reverse of the trail I had followed only a few days earlier. It would have suited me much better if we could still draw blood from the archfiend. It reminded me of a line I had heard in a movie once. "If it bleeds, we can kill it," they had said. What if it didn't bleed?

We didn't take the same route all the way back. We were eighty percent of the way there when Izak pulled us to the right, along a much smaller and more damp corridor with an odor that could have dropped a skunk. A few minutes later, we were slashing through ankle-deep muck, the source of which I was afraid to ask.

"This is the way out?" I asked the demon. He didn't turn around, or make any other motion. Just a simple nod. "This is how Gervais used to go out?" Another nod.

"*He hasn't used these tunnels in years,*" Josette said. "*Why would he wander*

140

through filth now that he is Lord of the City?" Her tone was sarcastic and mocking.

The stench-ridden passage finally ended at a ladder up to a covered exit. I took the lead, climbing the rungs and focusing to push the steel lid aside. I climbed out into a small alley, down which I could see the hum of Parisian urban life moving along at its normal flow. I bent down and held out my arm, taking Sarah's hand as she reached the summit, and doing the same for Charis. I held out my hand for Izak too, but the demon ignored it, emerging from the sewer on his own.

"I won't miss that," Sarah said. Neither would I. With a thought, I willed the fetid air away and hit us with a clean, fresh blast.

"Which way from here?"

I pulled out my cell, ready to hit it up for directions. I didn't need to. Izak glamoured himself, morphing into a tourist-type in a polo shirt, khaki shorts, knee high socks and sneakers, and walked out onto the street. We hurried to keep up, matching his ridiculous garb.

I'd thought he knew where we were going, and would lead us to the train station. Instead, he reached the street and raised his good hand to his mouth, spreading his lips and blowing in a sharp whistle. We caught up just as the cab pulled up along the curb.

"Where to?" the driver asked. He was mortal. Harmless.

"We need to catch the train from Paris to London," I said. I started digging into my pants pockets, searching for funds or something I could pass as funds. Charis tapped me on the shoulder, holding up her own credit card.

"You want Eurostar?" the driver leaned over and pushed the passenger side door open.

"Yes." I didn't know if that's what it was called, but I assumed he did. I opened the door for Charis and Sarah, giving Izak shotgun. The driver eased out onto the street.

141

I kept my Sight focused as we drove, a radar in search of any Divine that might even consider trying to get in the way. When I didn't sense anything, I pushed the focus, extending my reach out at least a mile or two from our position. At first, I considered that we were just in a slow spot, but we were in one of the oldest cities around, a place where even the architecture oozed Divine essence. Still, the further we traveled from the sewer, north through the city, the more uncomfortable I began to feel. There was nothing. At all. It was as if every Divine living or stationed in Paris had vanished. Or fled. Or died? Maybe they had learned what was lurking in the sewers below their feet?

"There are no Divine here," I whispered, leaning over Sarah so Charis could hear.

"None?" She was surprised. I had thought maybe she had been doing the same exercise.

"No. I've been a lot of places, but I've never felt such quiet before." Even in the Scottish Highlands there had been a Touched or a Turned keeping track of the locals, spreading the good works of God by tending to the homeless, or hustling them at cards.

"The Beast?"

It was possible. Gervais was the local archfiend, which meant he could have brought all of the nearby demons away from the city to wherever he wanted them. If the demons were gone, it made sense that angels would follow. But all of them?

"The calm before the storm," Sarah said, barely loud enough to hear. The uncomfortable feeling sprouted into a darker foreboding.

We reached the Eurostar station without incident, and without any hint of Divine anywhere close by. Charis paid the driver, and for the tickets for each of us on a train that was leaving in the next half-hour. By the time we made our way from the ticket office down to the tracks, it was already boarding. Getting the

first train out was a bit of luck, and I was thankful that just once today
something had gone our way.

It was a smooth flow to our seats in Business Premier, two by two facing one
another in the back of the car. I took up the aisle seat against the luggage closet
so I could watch everything happening in the car. Izak sat across with Sarah, and
his eyes stayed glued to the inter-car doors.

The quiet and ease of the departure should have helped us relax, but it only
served to make us more tense. It had been too easy to get from the sewers of Paris
to here. Too easy to escape from a location where the Beast *knew* we were going to
be, headed for one he hopefully didn't. Had he been *that* sure that Abaddon would
capture Sarah, and either catch or kill the rest of us? Would he be *that* foolish,
after we had fought our way out of his first trap? I didn't like it, and looking
around at the faces of my companions, I didn't need to ask them to know they didn't
either.

The trip time from Paris to London was a little over two hours. We were
fifteen minutes in when my cell began to ring. I pulled it from my pocket. Obi.

"What's the good word?" I asked, picking up.

"Hey man," Obi said. "We need to talk. Are you alone?" He sounded more tense
than I felt. His voice had a minor quake that betrayed his nervousness.

"No, why?" I glanced around the seats again. Sarah was staring out the
window, Izak was watching the rear doors, and Charis mumbling to herself under her
breath, talking to her demonic admirer.

"Get yourself alone," he said. "This news isn't good for mixed company." He
lowered his voice. "It's about Izak."

I raised an eyebrow, looked at the demon, and stood up. Sarah turned her head
and titled it questioningly.

"It's Obi," I said. "Nothing to worry about. I'm just going to take a walk

143

while we chat." Sarah was satisfied, so I started walking down the aisle. "What's going on?"

Silence.

"Obi?"

Nothing.

"Obi?" I said it a little louder. I was near the opposite end of the car.

"He can't hear you." The statement came from my left. I turned my head, and felt my heart rate jump. The teenager with the blue mohawk was smiling at me. "Have a seat." He patted the empty seat next to him.

I considered shouting for help, or trying to run, or something. There was no point. He had known where we were the entire time. He had known we had gotten away. How long he had been waiting, watching, and following, I couldn't know. I sat down.

"Not Obi?" I asked.

He chuckled. "I'm a god, kid. Changing my voice and sending it over cell frequencies is something even you could do, if you'd ever thought to try."

Which I hadn't, but it might come in handy in the future. "So, why the sit down? Decided to give up?"

I got a half-smile for that. "Truth be told, I came to gloat. You got the Box, but I've got its creator. Oh, and you already know about Abaddon. I am curious though. How did you get past him?"

"You came to gloat? Aren't gods above gloating?"

He leaned back in the seat. "I would say yes, but the thing is, I despise you. Always have. Any chance to rub salt in your wounds is a chance I'm going to take. Besides, you still see this thing as some kind of adventure or something, like you have a chance in Heaven or Hell of stopping me." He leaned forward, putting himself right in my face, and spoke with a quiet intensity. "I've told you before. You can't stop me, kid. My power's been growing faster than even I

expected. I guess I got a little more of that little nut's juice than I realized."
A laugh. "How's she been anyway? I hear those types can be hard to handle,
especially under pressure."

He wasn't just gloating, there was more to it. "She's fine," I said,
returning a smile of my own. "Better than ever, if you have to know." I lowered my
voice, mimicking his tone. "You think this is a done deal, that you've already won.
Maybe you have Avriel, but I'm pretty sure we can manage without him. It may all be
a game to you, and that's awesome. There's a reason the game gets played though.
Just because you think you know who's going to win, there's always the chance of an
upset."

His arrogant smile corroded, if only for an instant. Maybe he thought I
didn't notice, but I had. For all his loud talk, the reason he was here wasn't
because he wanted to tease me. It was because he was afraid. Afraid because we had
gotten past Abaddon, and evaded him yet again. Afraid because we were proving to be
more of a challenge than he had expected. Did he really even have Avriel captive?
My lie-spotting power didn't work on him, so there was no way to know.

"Not today, kid," he said, regaining his composure. "Not today." He pushed
back the sleeve of his suit jacket to take a look at his watch. "It's been nice
chatting with you, but I'm afraid it's time for me to collect what is mine, and be
on my way." He turned his head and leaned up, so he could see to the rear of the
train. "And there she is. So cute in that hoodie. Maybe I'll stuff her, make her
into a little trophy commemorating your abject failure. After I bleed her out, that
is."

The Beast stood up, still looking back. I followed his gaze to the rear of
Sarah's head, covered by the black hood of her sweatshirt.

"I don't want my prize getting hurt in the accident," he said. "I'll pick her
up after the fun."

I don't know what he did to her then, but I could see her head stiffen, and Charis look up. Whatever was going on, it caused her to jump to her feet. She looked past Sarah then and saw the Beast standing there, that wicked smile on his meat puppet's face.

"Better try to find something to hold onto," the Beast said. "She's not the worst choice, but I don't think she'll soften the impact much. See you soon." The body went slack and collapsed. Dead.

I was still trying to make the connection between the Beast sitting me down to talk and his foreshadowing of the train's impending doom when a bell began to ring from somewhere in the car, and a second later the change of the locomotive's momentum forced me to put a hand against the wall to stop my inequivalent deceleration. I glanced back to Charis, our eyes catching, and that's when it hit me. Stupid. I was so stupid.

I focused, throwing my Sight forward to the front of the train. We were in the fourth car, and there was nothing on the train. Past the train was another story. I nearly collapsed from the powerful heat that blasted my soul. The Beast was sly, and he'd duped me into useless banter while we'd sped headlong into his net.

Except the train was slowing, and the demonic assault group was too far away to force the train off its rails before we ground to a stop. I hadn't been the one to throw the emergency brake. Had Charis?

I dashed to the back of the train, ignoring the looks of the confused mortals who thought I was batty for even being out of my chair while the machine whined and shuddered to a stop. Reaching them, I saw the Beast had belted Sarah in tight.

"What's going on?" Charis asked.

"You didn't throw the emergency brake?"

"No!"

Someone had, but that would have to wait. "He was looking to crash the train," I said. "There's a serious ambush up ahead."

I grabbed the knife from behind Charis' back and focused, keeping my hand steady enough to slice through the straps of nylon that were holding Sarah in while the car vibrated and slowed.

"There's no way to escape it," Charis said. "We have to fight."

I could still See them up in front of the train, but they had started moving towards it. "Come on," I said. "We need to head them off, or they're going to rip all of these people apart."

I swung around, past the luggage racks to the train doors. It was trivial to push them open. Izak went first, jumping out and rolling to a stop. We were in the middle of farmland, so at least he had found some grass.

Sarah and Charis joined me at the doors. "I'll break our fall," she said. Izak would heal from any breaks or scrapes he had just suffered. Sarah wasn't so fortunate. I felt the pressure of Charis' power, and then she jumped from the train, floating parallel to the doors for an instant before they began to lose speed and lower gently to the ground. I saw Izak running past them, surpassing the velocity of the train and catching up as I threw myself out.

I didn't want to waste energy breaking my fall, so I hit pretty hard. First came the smell of the grass, and then it dug into my mouth and nose when I face-planted into it. The nose broke, and I was sure I felt a tooth pop free, and then I was rolling and tumbling, getting bruised but not feeling the agony of any more breakage on my way to a stop. I was healing before Izak helped me up with his good hand.

"You okay to fight?" I asked him. He gave me the finger, and we both ran.

Somewhere between one running step and another, I starting shifting, and my sprint became an awkward bipedal hop, and then a smooth and fast four-legged

147

sprint. Somewhere between the hop and the sprint, Izak had gotten his arms around my neck, and when I launched ahead at monster speed, he was along for the ride.

"*Hey Ullie,*" I said. "*Take the wheel.*"

The demon was hungry for the power, and he grabbed it without hesitation. Knowing he wouldn't use the opportunity against me made it easier to give it up to him, and giving it up made me a more effective force. I could concentrate on the Divine attack, while the Were took care of the physical.

"*Stop freakin' calling me Ullie,*" he growled, his finer control pushing us faster than I could manage. "*And tell Izak if he ever does this again I'm going to rip his throat out.*"

"*Like you could,*" I replied.

We blew past the front of the train, which had nearly stopped. The demon force was close enough to see now, a small army of the many-armed half-man, half-snake naga, a dozen trolls, an earth elemental, and a fallen angel Commanding them. It was the massive earth elemental that would have been the one to smash the train from its tracks, and the signal that there had to be a witch somewhere close. The rest had been brought in to keep us busy while the Beast picked up his prize. I didn't need to see the fallen angel's face, to see him smile, to know the Beast had taken over.

"The angel is the Beast," I growled to Izak through Ulnyx's toothy snout.

Our speed brought us yards closer in seconds, and now I could see his face. He wasn't smiling at all.

"Can you take the elemental?" I asked Izak.

He grunted and let go, hitting the ground on his feet and sliding impressively to a stop. The last thing I saw before pouncing onto a troll was the demon conjuring a sword of hellfire into his good hand. Heaven and Hell had good reason to worry about him.

Broken

The troll toppled to the ground under our weight, and before I knew it I had a huge chunk of it's throat in my jaws. We spat it out and dove away, just in time to avoid being crushed under a second troll's heavy iron mace. Ulnyx pounced on that one too, and I used my Sight to track a third about to flatten us. I focused on the mace handle, corroding and rusting the iron thousands of years in an instant.

We'd dropped two more of the trolls and were in the thick of it with the rest by the time Charis and Sarah reached us. Charis had Callus' sword in hand, and she charged towards the naga. They had more arms and more swords, but they couldn't make up for her speed and focus. Pebbles from the ground swirled tightly around her as she twisted into the reptilian mass. Most of them bounced harmlessly off the naga's scaly skin, but enough found their eyes, giving her the split-second she needed to break their defenses and put the blessed blade into their hearts.

I heard Sarah's voice shout out, and one of the demons turned on the others. It didn't survive long, but as soon as it had fallen, she Commanded another to take its place.

"*Ulnyx, get the angel*," I said. I had expected that once Sarah arrived the Beast would make to salvage the mess that had been made of his plan. We were fortunate that he was limited to the physical prowess offered by his host, but we were way too far away, the battle with the trolls pulling us across the farmland.

I needn't have worried.

I hadn't seen him do it, but somehow Izak had toppled the earth elemental and set it to melting, as he had with the monster at the airport. He'd already started moving towards Sarah, and he cut the fallen angel off on the way. There was a flash of heat as the Beast lashed out with cursed metal against the demon's blade of hellfire, and then the hellfire was gone and Izak was on the ground.

"*Ulnyx!*"

The Were finished ripping the throat from a troll, using its falling body as an anchor to spring from. Powerful legs coiled and launched, and we were off. The Beast was quickly approaching Sarah, his host running full speed towards her. She was concentrating too hard on controlling the naga, and didn't see him coming.

Charis did, and she broke off her attack, leaping back away from the demons and putting herself in front of Sarah, Callus' blade over her head, ready to attack or defend. Sarah saw what was happening now, her brow creasing while two of the naga slithered over and launched their assault against the Beast. He skewered them without slowing.

We pounded the grass, the Were stepping easily over Izak, still sprawled on the ground. We were closing the gap in record time, but the gap to Sarah was closing just as fast. Dark wings unfurled then, pushing through the black linen shirt the fallen angel was wearing, spreading wide into the air.

"No," I shouted. Charis was still standing between the Beast and Sarah, and she didn't disappoint. Her sword was a blur, whipping around, meeting his. The contact rang out across the countryside, then again, and again. She had gotten between them and put up a wall, slowing the Beast's assault.

It wasn't enough.

Charis swung her blade again, and the Beast caught it. He caught it with the angel's bare hand, the metal digging deep into the flesh. In an instant, it had disintegrated to nothing, the power running down the weapon's length and causing Charis to drop it with a cry of pain. A follow up blow, and Charis tumbled away.

Ulnyx's leap was strong and true. The Beast was only yards away, Sarah a few yards further ahead. We would get to him before he got to her.

At the last possible moment, he turned, bringing the sword up and lashing into us, the blade ripping through flesh and bone and muscle, the force nearly splitting us in half and throwing us away. We landed and slid, the grass finding

150

its way up into our nose again. The pain was intense, but I didn't care. It would heal. There was no one between Sarah and the Beast now. And he knew it.

He threw his sword away and approached her at a walk. She kept her eyes fixed to his, and stood still.

"Well, my dear," he said. "You're full of surprises. I had thought you'd be too much of an emotional wreck to have any kind of grip on reality, but here you are an effective member of Team D." He shot a look over at me, laying in the grass waiting for my body to be whole enough to rise. "This whole thing has been buckets of fun, but it's time you came with me, and fulfilled your destiny."

"No." A Command.

The Beast laughed. "You can't Command me. Why would you ever think you could?"

Sarah's eyes narrowed, her entire demeanor tight with intensity. "I don't need to Command you, asshole," she said. "Just your meat."

The Beast's eyes widened, and he tried to reach out and grab her. Every muscle moved in slow-motion, the possessed Divine's body caught in the middle of the opposing forces.

"Keep trying," Sarah said. "You aren't strong enough."

The Beast growled in frustration. "Don't be too certain," he said.

I wasn't too certain. Neither was Charis. She came up behind him and removed his head with a clean easy stroke of the cursed sword. The fallen angel dropped in two pieces, and both began to dissolve. The Beast had left the building.

I took my body back from Ulnyx and pushed myself upright. The hit had nearly severed my leg, but it had already made itself right again. I started running towards Sarah and Charis when I remembered the witch. Earth elementals weren't from Hell. They were created here. I sought her out with my Sight, feeling for the heat of her dark core. With their leader dead, the few surviving demons had begun to flee. She must have gone with them, because I couldn't pick her out.

"Well, that sucked," I said, reaching Charis and Sarah on the field. Izak joined us a few seconds later, none the worse for wear.

"I did it," Sarah said in a happy, singsong voice. "I really did it. We won!"

"Yeah, you did it." I gave her a hug, letting her enjoy her small victory. I wasn't going to tell her about the chill I was feeling. The dread of knowing the Beast was getting much stronger, much faster than even he had expected. The truth that she had taken him by surprise, and even then her Command had only slowed him. If Charis hadn't been there, she would be gone already.

We'd won the first three rounds because we'd been lucky. The Beast knew how to fight angels, and I knew from experience how predictable they could be. He was still learning how to fight us unpredictable, volatile, humans, and I had a feeling he was a fast learner.

Broken

CHAPTER SIXTEEN

We were back on the train. Shortly after re-embarking, the conductor had made an announcement that someone had pulled the emergency brake, but it had been a false alarm, and the culprit couldn't be found. We'd continue on to London as planned, though we would be fifteen minutes late. The convenience of it confounded me, and occupied my thoughts while we skated along.

Someone was helping us, but who? My first thought was of Max, but if he was in communication with the Beast it would have been hard for him to sneak unnoticed onto the train. Even if he had, and had just shown his true colors, why not hook up with us now? In any case, I would have Seen him. It had to be someone who could avoid detection. Maybe even a mortal? There had to be someone else with something to gain, who knew about the Beast, and had stuck their needle into just the right spot. I was grateful for them, but I would have felt better to be able to thank them in person.

We had settled back in to our original seats. Izak looked dour, surely unused to being tossed aside with as little effort as the Beast seemed to have needed. He wouldn't have taken the excuse, but I knew it was at least in part due to the loss of his hand. When he had met up with us outside the train, Sarah had hugged him with the jubilance of a groupie at a rock concert, but he had just stared straight ahead, unspeaking in words, gesture, or emotion. Sarah was too high to even notice, but I had, and Izak's worry was enough to put me even more on guard.

She was still smiling, the hood of her sweatshirt around her neck, her face almost glowing from her excitement. She had changed so much since we had been reunited with Josette. It was hard to resist the naive voice in my head that was telling me what Father Tom had said wasn't true, that it didn't have to be that way. I had listened to the naive voice for too long though, and it had never led me in a good direction.

Josette. She had been almost silent since I had woken up. Her presence was a constant familiar companion, and she had never been as outspoken as Ulnyx, but I knew there was something more to it.

"*Josette.*" I called out to her.

"*Yes, Landon.*" She responded right away.

"*Is everything okay?*"

She took more time to answer. "*If I tell you it is, I think you'll know I'm lying.*"

"*Sarah?*" It wasn't a lucky guess. I knew we would have to have this conversation, but I had expected I would be the one to initiate it.

"*I can feel what you feel. I can hear your thoughts. They are mumbles and whispers, and I don't understand them all, but I understand enough.*"

"*You didn't know?*"

She sighed, the action echoing in my soul. "*I've always known. Every angel knows, whether it is something they ever think about or not. What angel falls in love with a demon, after all? Yet, there she sits, and look at how beautiful she is. It doesn't matter how she came to be. She still is.*"

I glanced up at Sarah. She was looking out the window now, watching the countryside, but I could still see the edge of her smile.

"*I love her unconditionally. Yet, I know there can only be one true end for her. I had hoped to save her. I had hoped Izak could save her. A demon, a favorite of Lucifer himself, his heart softened and molded by love. I forgive her for releasing the Beast, but her complicity has shown me that Izak was not enough. Even you were not enough, and I can never be enough. The madness is in her, and there is no way to get it out.*"

"*She told me that she has seen herself killing me, and Charis. That it's the future she felt will come to pass, and she was terrified of it. Looking at her now, I can't believe it is the future she's still seeing.*" Except, what if it was? How was there any way to know her mind, when it was shifting like a sand dune?

There was a long silence. It sat uncomfortably, but I knew Josette well enough to know what it meant. She was deciding how to say something she didn't want to have to say.

"*I believe it is the future that will come to pass, if you let it.*"

"*You mean I'll have to stop her?*"

"*Yes.*"

I glanced over at Sarah again, trying to picture myself pushing a knife into her chest, or taking her head in the Were's massive paws and snapping her neck. I had to fight against the tears that threatened to fall.

"*How can I live with that?*" I asked. "*How can you? How could we together, and have you never resent me for doing it?*"

Another long silence. "*I don't know,*" she said at last.

Three words were never harder to hear. Josette had always trusted in God, and had always pointed to His will and plan whenever I questioned the path we had to walk. She had even invoked His name the last time the thought of killing Sarah had entered the conversation. Had meeting her daughter eroded her faith? Or had her love of something tangible and real, a part of her, a mother's love, grown stronger than her love for her Lord?

"*What if killing her was a kindness?*" I asked. It was something I had thought about at length. I had seen the way Gervais had broken her, just by his very presence. I had been inside of her soul, and witnessed the way she battled herself. Given a choice, would she really want to live that way?

"*Landon, I don't know.*" Her voice was soft and sad.

I didn't know if I could do it, either. Even as a kindness. I knew Charis could. She didn't have the connection to Sarah I did, even sharing my memories of her. I wanted more than anything for that to be good enough, but I had my own feelings getting in the way and turning the equation back on itself. Could I watch Charis kill her, and forgive her for it? Could I love her then?

The word came unbidden to my mind. Love? I snuck a glance over at her, leaned back in her seat, staring at the ceiling. My heart jumped just to look at her.

"What?" she asked, her eyes staying focused on the soft grey plastic above. She hadn't needed to see me, to know I was looking at her.

"Nothing," I said unconvincingly.

There was no doubt she had feelings for me too, but did they stretch as far into the horizon as my own? It seemed too soon, too fast for such a thought, but I knew everything about her, and she knew everything about me. There had been a connection since the first time I had set eyes on her, though at the time I couldn't begin to guess what it was. I had just thought she was insanely attractive. Now she was attractive, intelligent, cunning, loyal, smart... I could just keep rolling the adjectives all day. Which brought me back to love.

I had never been in love before. I thought I had cared for Rebecca, and a part of me did, but it wasn't love. More of an infatuation, with an unhealthy dose of lust thrown in. She was gorgeous, and dangerous, and she had been interested in me. Me? A washout ex-con security guard who couldn't be trusted with anything beyond old cups. She had saved my life when I had no idea what I was doing. I had an appreciation for what she gave me, but I knew now it wasn't love.

Charis had stayed behind to try to save me, and risked the entire future of the world to do it. I realized that if I were in her shoes, I would do the same thing. Seeing the world destroyed before letting someone be killed? If there wasn't some manner of love in there, I was hopeless.

"Seriously, Landon," Charis said. She turned her head now to look at me. "What?"

It must have been my expression. Her face turned red, and she smiled.

"You still owe me."

That was all she said.

CHAPTER SEVENTEEN

"I should have known the rift would be in the Tower of London." I held the

cab door open while Sarah and Charis slid into the back seat.

We had arrived in London without incident, and I had decided not to say

anything to Charis about the feelings that had been percolating during the trip.

After all, they had spent the remainder of the ride sparring with my agony over

Sarah's potential future and the fear of what one of us might have to do. Swimming

in that soup, there was just no way to be sure what my true emotions were for

anyone, and I wasn't about to go spouting such a powerful word to someone unless I

was completely sure I meant it, and could back it up full-time. Besides, we both

knew there was something there. Words could wait.

"Under the White Tower, to be specific," Charis confirmed. "There's a

basement, under the basement."

"Of course there is." I lowered my voice, so Izak wouldn't hear. "How many

demons can create their own rifts?"

"Very few on Earth. Maybe a dozen of the most powerful archfiends? Which is

why most of the circles are tucked away in old places." She whispered back, and I hoped Izak either couldn't hear, or wasn't paying attention. I had no doubt the loss of his hand was painful in more ways than one, whether he would ever show it or not. "I made the rift in Thailand, with Vilya's help, but it took me nearly a week. Reyzl knew the secrets, but even he would be hard pressed to draw one from scratch in less than a day or two. Izak's skill was amazing."

And now it was lost, at least temporarily. I expected if we survived, he would learn to do it with his other hand.

I focused on my Sight, pushing it out around us. I found some bit of comfort in catching the familiar waves of heat and coolness that reflected the Divine factions of the city. A vampire here, a Touched there. It seemed the Beast's war hadn't made it here yet, but I didn't expect it to last. He knew we were headed here, and I was sure he wasn't happy.

"Oy, Tower of London." The cabbie's shout broke me away from my thought.

I looked out the window. We were stopped in front of the main tourist entrance to the landmark. "Do you know who put it there?" I asked Charis.

"The rift? No. Maybe it was Izak."

The demon heard that, and he shook his head, then tapped it. He hadn't done it, but he knew who did.

Charis paid the driver, and we exited the cab. We all approached the tourist gate together. Sometimes, the most straightforward route was the best one. Charis paid for our entry, and four American tourists shuffled onto the grounds.

I focused on my Sight again, and cast my eyes out towards a throng of tourists. At the same time, one of the tourists turned their head and focused on me.

Charis noticed an instant later. "Do you know him?" she asked.

"*I don't know him,*" Josette said.

"No. I should go introduce myself."

160

Broken

We met halfway, the angel and me. He was tall, and strikingly handsome. His hair was cut short around a model's angled face, his polo and jeans hugging tight to his lean, muscled form. He hadn't hesitated to approach when he caught wind of me, and that told me a lot. Especially considering the company I was keeping.

"Diuscrucis," he said, putting a slight flourish in his bow. "My name is Adam."

"Not *the* Adam?" I asked. I had already met Mephistopheles, so I couldn't be too sure.

He laughed. "No. I was named after the first mortal." He looked over my shoulder to where the others waited. "Quite a crew of miscasts and misfits you've assembled."

"Desperate times," I replied. "Did you know I would be here, or is it just your lucky day?"

"All of Heaven knows you're here. We got a tip from one of our Touched that you were on the Eurostar, bound for London."

Except there hadn't been any Touched on the Eurostar. "If that's what you want to believe. You have to know I won't attack you."

"We do. Which is why we haven't assembled in force. In fact, it was decided that we should pass your whereabouts over to the Inquisitors. They're quite eager to catch up to you, and not bound as tightly to our laws."

I looked up, half-expecting Kassie to land on my head.

"I was charged with delivering the message to Kassie," Adam said. He started laughing. "I understand she's in New York, chasing after you."

Interesting. "So, what are you doing here, instead of there?"

"The Beast."

I could have laughed myself. "You believe?"

He shrugged. "I was there when they brought Melody in. She's pretty raw, but

161

she's a spunky one, and I believe in her faith. She was insistent that the Beast was real, that it was free, and that we needed to leave you alone, because you're the only one who can stop it." His eyes searched me. They were looking for truth there, for acknowledgement that what Melody had said was true.

"Do you believe her?"

"I don't not believe her," he said. "Which is why I'm here. I'd like to tag along with your motley crew."

"*A spy for the Inquisitors?*" I asked, sending the thought along to Josette.

"*It is possible,*" she replied.

"*Even better.*"

I turned my attention back to the seraph.

"What about delivering your message?"

"I promised that I would deliver it," he said. "I didn't say when."

Now I did laugh. The games of angels were always worth it. "You're okay with going through a rift?"

That was my test for him, to see how serious he was about following. Angels weren't forbidden from traveling the rifts, but they hated it.

"The idea doesn't please me, but I will do what I must. If what Melody says is the truth, she will need allies to convince the others." His face was serious and he put his hand out, resting it on my shoulder. "Whatever you think about Heaven, Diuscrucis, not all of us are so wrapped up in laws that we cannot see the storm for the clouds. Even Inquisitors."

His openness was unexpected, but refreshing. "So you are an Inquisitor?"

"Yes. I was up until recently referred to as a 'Tenth'. There are nine active Inquisitors at any one time, and many of us who wait to serve in that role. I became Ninth when Callus was killed. I was still being briefed when Melody was brought in, which is why I'm not with Kassie now."

"I didn't do that," I said. "The Beast did."

He removed his hand, and cast his eyes back to where the others waited again. "We shall see. She carries his sword."

"Desperate times," I said again. "I'm sure she'll trade with you, if you'd like. Anyway, I don't have your Blade. Charis did, but we lost it to the Beast. Sticking with us is probably your best chance at getting it back, and if you don't... it won't matter, because the Beast will be running the show."

"So you're saying I can join you?"

"Welcome aboard," I replied, holding out my hand. There was only a small hesitation before he took it and shook. "Whatever you think about me and my crew, Adam, we aren't against Heaven or Hell. We're for the billions of mortals that have populated this world, and who deserve to survive and thrive here regardless of what your master, or the other wants. The Beast, though... the Beast doesn't care about any of us. He wants to see all of us enslaved or destroyed. He doesn't have a side other than his own, and he has a lot of followers, both angelic and demonic. I need you to think about that, because you may need to fight and kill someone you thought you knew, before this is over." I saw an image of Rachel in my mind, slumped in her chair. I let the wave of sadness wash over me. "I have."

His look was that of startled fear, but he gave me a short nod.

"Let me introduce you to the club," I said, leading him back to where they waited. "Everybody, this is Adam. He's an Inquisitor. He asked to come along so we can prove the Beast is real."

I looked at Adam. His eyes were fixed on Izak's mangled hand. "I've heard you travel with the demon Mephistopheles." He turned to me, his startled fear enlarged to full-blown. "Whatever did this to him, I fear you won't have to work very hard to prove it."

Izak glared at him while Charis shook his hand. When Sarah approached, I could see the flush of her face, and smell the pheromones.

"I'm Sarah," she said, her voice shaky.

"A true diuscrucis," Adam said, giving her the same bow he had given me. "It's an honor."

I knew he was lying. She probably would have too, but she was too busy being a teenage girl in the face of an adonis. "Thank you," she squeaked.

"Adam," Charis said, unslinging Callus' blade. "I took this from your brethren's corpse in order to defend myself. I'd be happy to swap with you."

Adam seemed surprised. "Return it to me when you no longer need to defend yourself from the Beast," he said. He scored a lot of points for that one.

We made our way up into the White Tower with the other tourists. While we wasted a little too much time plodding ahead as part of the larger group, I considered what Adam had said. The Beast had told the angels where I was going. Why? What could he hope to gain by having them descend on us en masse, unless a decent number of them were sure to be servants, and he could possess one and snatch Sarah during the ensuing chaos? That was the point where my brain stuck. How many of God's army were even fighting for Him? Or maybe the Beast had known they would pass the buck to the Inquisitors, and they were the ones who were on his side?

I watched Adam walk alongside Charis. Had I taken him in too easily? Who was it that said to keep your friends close, and your enemies closer? Except, Callus hadn't been a servant, so there were holes in that theory too. Too many balls, again. There was nothing to do but go forward and hope for the best.

"He's so handsome," Sarah whispered.

It was undeniable. He was. So much so that even Sarah could See it. I didn't completely understand how she viewed the world, but it seemed to reflect pretty accurately. "If he didn't think we were useful, he'd be more than happy to stick that sword of his into your chest," I said. It was cold, but the last thing I needed was for Sarah to be hung up on a crush.

"So you say, but Melody likes Obi."

Ugh.

We broke off from the main tour when we hit the basement, following Charis to what the mortals probably saw as an unbroken part of the stone floor. What I saw was a block of cement with a loop of iron driven into it.

"Down here, I assume?" I said.

"Yep." Charis put her hand on the ring, and lifted the cement like it was made of foam.

Adam took it from her, and held it open. "Ladies first."

Charis gave him a polite smile, and moved to the opening, mounting a wooden ladder down. When she saw me looking at her, she rolled her eyes. I held back the tempting smirk, and ushered Sarah to the ladder.

"Thanks, Adam," Sarah said as she started climbing.

"Of course, my lady," he replied. Who was this guy?

Izak went down after Sarah, and I followed behind him. We all waited at the bottom while Adam maneuvered himself onto the ladder while holding up the stone door. It was an impressive feat of strength for a seraph.

One he reached the bottom, we approached the rift. It was older than many I had seen and been through, a ring of hewn stones with the runes etched along them, drawn on all sides of the rock.

"So, where in Egypt is this going to land us?" Sarah asked.

"You're going to love this," Charis said.

"Where?" she repeated.

Izak leaned in, using his good hand to draw new connecting runes, the master key.

I had Charis' memories, so I knew the answer. "Cairo. The Museum of Egyptian

Antiquities. They have a rift there that they pulled out of one of the tombs. They have no idea what it is, but they took it apart and put it back together with perfect precision. They've never told anyone about it, because the writing is clearly not hieroglyphic."

"The Egyptians had rifts?" Sarah asked.

"Remember, child, our kind predates the mortals' by many millenia," Adam said, "and the differences between what your historians believe and what is the truth can at times be pretty stark."

"You're saying the Egyptians weren't pagans?" I asked.

Adam shrugged. "I'm saying that they were worshipping the same God, though their understanding was not as complete as it is today. They saw different faces of the same surface. They also idolized those who were Awake, much unlike today's societies."

"Hold on," I said. "Pharoahs... Divine?"

He laughed. "Didn't you kill Reyzl? They weren't all Divine, but they always had our attention. I suppose the pyramids didn't hurt. I wish I had been around to see them when they were still covered in limestone."

Izak grunted, and I felt his power flare and feed into the stones. The rift was ready.

"Ladies first," Adam said again.

"Not this time," I said. "We don't know what's on the other side, and Sarah's too important to send through first."

"In that case, I'll go," he replied, and he did.

"Izak?"

The demon nodded and stepped into the rift.

"You don't like him, do you?" Sarah asked. She seemed disappointed. Or maybe that was because he had called her 'child'?

"I don't trust him. You shouldn't either." I motioned for both of them to wait, until Izak reappeared and gave us the thumbs up.

Stepping through the rift, we found ourselves in a massive underground warehouse lit by a million fluorescent lights. The smell of burning plastic lingered in the air, and looking down I saw that activating the circle had caused the wrapping the archaeologists had put over it to burn away. I was relieved that for once we had managed to travel without landing in the thick of it. Then I noticed the fire alarm was going off.

"We should go," Charis said. "Divine Suggestion won't keep these people away if they feel their heritage is threatened."

I couldn't argue with that. I peeked out from beyond the large crates placed on either side of the rift, looking down a long aisle filled with crates, boxes, and shelves. It was amazing to think of how much stuff they didn't have on display. There was shouting now, coming from the right. At least know we knew where the exit was.

"Adam, can you get us some bearings?" I figured if we had an angel with us, we might as well take advantage.

Adam responded by reaching up and pulling off his polo shirt, revealing the perfectly chiseled form underneath. He handed me the shirt stepped past, finding a spot where he could extend his wings. I dared a glance over at Sarah, unsurprised at her red face and o-shaped mouth.

He flew up near the ceiling, his wings flapping slowly and gracefully. I had never seen an angel in regular flight before. They were usually diving down at me, or in the midst of landing. It was an awe-inspiring sight, and I was impressed with the lift he got with so little effort. Of course, he wasn't really flying in the sense of air and thermals and lift. He had a little help with his ratios.

"The exit is that way," he called down, pointing. "There are about a dozen

167

mortals a few rows away, and they're running towards you. They must know where the alarm was triggered."

There was no time to get around them, and no time to hide and wait for them to investigate why the rift's packaging had melted. I was hesitant to ask Sarah to handle them, because she'd been using that particular skill quite a bit, and I had a fear that every time she did it moved her closer to the madness. We needed another way out.

"I'll lead them away," I said. "I'll meet you at the exit."

I didn't wait for them to argue. I started running down the aisle, glamouring myself into my vision of a ninja. I figured that would look espionage enough to get their attention.

It did. They turned the corner as a group, a clutch of Egyptians with fire extinguishers in hand. These weren't soldiers, these were scientists. When they saw me, they skidded to a stop. Then one of the guys in front shot his fire extinguisher at me.

I danced out of the path of the white foam, and then turned ran past them, trying to lead them down a different aisle, hoping they would all follow, and wondering if Divine Suggestion, as Charis had named it, could be used to attract them, especially since they saw me as the threat.

Apparently, it could, because when I turned my head to look back, I had twelve angry egyptians right behind me. I could only imagine Adam's perspective. He would probably fall to the ground from laughing too hard.

I didn't focus on speeding myself up, though I could have outpaced the men easily. That wasn't the idea, and so I ran slow, staying just out of reach of the fire extinguishers, and letting them feel like they could catch me. I looked up at Adam, and he was indeed laughing, but he had enough wherewithal to give me a thumbs up.

Broken

I'd only just turned down the second aisle when I saw Adam put both his thumbs up, and then wave for me to join them at the exit. I returned his gesture, and reached for my power so I could outrun them at last. He swooped down to join the others.

"Landon."

One of the men had just said my name. It broke my focus, and I stopped running.

CHAPTER EIGHTEEN

I didn't turn around right away. I stood there, taking in the sounds and the smells. There was one that was overpowering. Death.

"How did you find us?" I asked.

I turned slowly, knowing what I was going to find, even if I didn't know how it had happened. When I finished the half-circle, I saw that there was only one Egyptian left standing, a younger man with a thick mustache and an athletic build. The others were on the ground behind him.

"How many times do I have to explain this? I'm a god, Landon. I don't need to 'find' you. I always know where you are."

Was that how he had found us on the train? Then why hadn't he attacked us in New York? I had an idea that maybe being inside a church had something to do with that.

"You didn't have to kill them," I said.

He cackled with laugher. "Didn't have to kill them? That's what I do, you moron." He took a few steps back, and kicked one of the bodies. "So fragile, humans. So easy to break."

His anger was enough to change the pressure in the air. I could feel it coming off his host like a static charge.

"Not feeling as confident, are you?" I asked. "Not after we've slipped past you and yours, what? Three times now? It's happened so often, I'm losing count. Some god."

This only enraged him more, but I wasn't that concerned. Sarah Commanding his host had shown he was limited when he was possessing another's consciousness. I probably shouldn't have been goading him, but I had my own share of anger.

"What are you doing here anyway?" I asked.

"I was curious."

"Curious?"

He took a few steps forward. "What would you be doing in Egypt? Something brought you here."

"You think I'm just going to tell you?"

He chuckled. "I know you aren't going to tell me," he said. "That's why I had to come and see for myself. I just couldn't resist revealing myself to you. I wanted you to know that I'm here. That I'm always here. And I can be anyone. Oh, and I'm not limited to only being here. Right now, I'm also in the body of a fiend in Mumbai."

"Mumbai?" I asked.

"I'll tell you what I'm doing in Mumbai, if you tell me what you're doing here," he said.

"I have an idea of what you're doing in Mumbai," I said. He was the Beast, after all. "You can't say the same about me."

"True enough, kid. I guess I'll have to settle for a different kind of satisfaction. I'll admit, you're pretty good at this game, for a rookie. You've managed pretty well, and I applaud you for that." He started clapping. "Like I told

171

you before, my power is growing faster than even I expected. So, I'm moving up the time table on phase two. If you think it's been fun so far, you ain't seen nothing yet."

His face changed, growing into that freaking smile. That damnable grin that I despised.

"Are you ready?" he asked.

I focused, preparing myself for whatever he intended. "Bring it on."

He raised up his right hand, and I watched in horror as the bone of the forearm pushed out through the skin, growing and changing shape until it resembled a blade of bone, leaving the man's hand hanging limply attached below it. His other arm went through the same transformation

"This is just a preview, kid." He said. Then he charged.

There was no time to shift, but at least I had Josette's fighting prowess to rely on. I focused, pouring power into my body, sidestepping the first attack and countering with a solid right hook. The Beast brought a forearm up to block it, and I heard the bones crumble beneath the force.

"Ouch," he said, without emotion. He brought the right bone-blade around, slashing at my face. I caught his arm and held it.

"Do you really think you can take me like this?" I asked.

"Don't be stupid, kid," he replied. "That's not what it's about."

I shoved him backwards, sending him twenty feet in the air to crash down on the rest of the dead. He pushed himself to his knees, facing me.

"Watch this," he said. He stabbed one of the bodies with the bone-blade. A second later, it began to climb to its feet. "Are you starting to get it?"

I felt my heart start to pound, my mind starting to catch up to the Beast's display. He could re-animate the dead. How many at one time? I didn't know, but Malize had said the angels sent entire armies up against him, armies that fell to

172

their once fallen brethren. He could also possess the living. It was a vicious combo that brought all of the hope I'd started to gain from his prior defeats to a screeching halt. How could anyone stand up to that?

"Ah," he said. "I see you are. I-"

His head fell forward, detached from his body. Adam stood behind him. "Okay," he said. "I believe you."

Was it a surprise the statement didn't bring me any comfort? I motioned to the man he had animated. "What about him?"

In response, a grenade of hellfire hit the corpse, setting it on fire. Adam backed away from it, and in a few moments it was consumed. Izak stood there, a grim look on his face. He might not have been happy, but watching the body burn gave me back a little bit of my lost hope. At least we could burn the dead, to keep them from coming back.

The three of us ran through the warehouse, meeting up with Sarah and Charis near the exit.

"We need to move fast. The Beast-"

Another Egyptian man rounded the corner and leaped at Sarah. Before I could react, Izak got in front of her and grabbed his head in his good hand. It burned away beneath his touch, the body flopping to the floor.

"He's possessing people and sending them at us," I finished.

"Come on," Charis said. "The Pyramids are ten miles away."

That wasn't that close. Not when we had to get through a city of hundreds of thousands of people, and any one or more of them could be the Beast.

We ran as fast as we could, up a flight of stairs and out the back door of the museum through an emergency exit. We had to keep going, to keep moving faster than the Beast could get people after us. Even if we killed them with fire like Izak had, he was still destroying people. People with families, and homes, and

173

lives of their own.

"We need a car," Sarah said.

We had come out the back. There was a fence, and a roadway on the other side. I focused, tearing open the fence with a thought and running for the road.

As we approached, a car skidded off the pavement, headed straight for me, the driver laughing. I crouched and focused, ducking to the side and lifting the front corner of the car with a tug, sending it corkscrewing away to land upside down with a crash. A second later, two more cars veered towards me.

"Stay close to Sarah," I shouted. Not to protect her, but because she could protect us, at least from the cars. He wasn't going to risk killing his prize. They skidded to a stop, and the drivers got out.

They didn't get far. Izak hit them with hellfire, sending them falling away, but more cars were pulling over, and then I felt the sudden heat of a demon in my Sight.

"Get in the car," I yelled, pointing at one of the abandoned vehicles.

"I'll meet you there," Adam said. He spread his wings and shot into the air, circling above us.

The rest of us made a beeline for the car, some run-down rust bucket of a thing. Charis slid in behind the wheel, and I took shotgun. She peeled out as best she could in the clunker.

"Which way?" she asked me. I dug into my pocket and pulled out my cell. I never thought I'd be Googling directions to the Great Pyramids like this.

"Left," I said, looking at the map that had come up. I was still waiting for the GPS to locate us, so I hoped that it was right.

"I can't go left from here," she shouted. "It's one-way."

I looked at her. "Are you kidding me?"

She smiled and turned the wheel, forcing the tires to whine while she pulled the car left, up a curb, and over into oncoming traffic. They split around us, avoiding an unseen obstacle. That didn't save them from the Beast, who was moving those he possessed behind us. We could hear the crashes in the background.

"Son of a bitch," I yelled.

We passed more cars, and I heard the screaming tires as the Beast took the drivers and turned the cars around, angling them into other oncoming traffic. Within seconds, the cars ahead of us saw what was happening behind us, and they came to a stop.

"Not good," Sarah said.

Charis hit the brakes. "Now what?"

I tried to think. This had gone bad faster than I could have imagined. I had thought the Beast would adapt his strategy, and he had in a big way.

"We'll have to fight our way through." I opened the door and got out of the car. They followed my lead.

"Do you give up?" Three of the drivers were walking towards us. The words came from all of their mouths at once.

"Not a chance," I said. As much as I hated that people were dying, if he won, *everything* would die. "You're going to have to do better."

Three faces smiling in unison. "Oh, I plan to. This is just the warmup."

"Izak?"

The demon walked towards the drivers.

"Nice hand," they said. "That looks like it hurts."

He held out his palm, the hellfire flaring in it. He bathed them in it.

"Good for you." Two more people approached from the other side, another man and a woman. "You can keep me from bringing them back, but you can't stop me from taking them, and there are quite a few people here in Cairo."

"Landon," Charis said. "This isn't going to work."

175

"We don't have a choice." I took Sarah's hand. "Be careful with your puppets," I said. "You don't want anything to happen to Sarah."

"Don't worry. I'll be careful."

I let go of Sarah's hand and ducked as a vampire crashed to the ground in front of me. I had Seen him coming. He rolled to his feet.

"It isn't just humans, you know," the vampire said.

Maybe not, but vampires could still burn.

Or lose their heads. When he leaped at me again, Charis intervened.

"Turn right onto Nile Corniche in two hundred meters," came the automaton voice from my phone. It had finally gotten the directions.

"Come on," I said. "We have to run for it. Now!"

I reached out for Sarah's hand, and then paused, feeling a coolness enter my Sight, and hearing a buzzing in the distance. It seemed ridiculous, but what about the rest of the situation was any more sane?

"Sarah, when I say the word, grab onto me as tight as you can."

"Okay, but why?"

"You'll see. Also, tell Izak to get back over here."

She nodded, and I could feel her power reaching out to the demon.

"Getting defensive?" the Beast asked. He was moving his pawns in closer. Ten more doors opened, and ten more drivers got out. "I can do this all day," all twelve of him said.

The buzzing was getting louder. We just needed to hold them off for another minute. "Charis, the glass."

She looked at me, and then focused. There was shattered glass from the crashed cars all over the road. She brought it to us, and started spinning it around.

"That isn't going to work," the Beast said. A dozen voices laughed in unison.

He sent them forward, into the maelstrom. Some of the bodies were torn up, but one would block the onslaught from another, and half of them made it through. The buzzing was much louder now.

Izak turned on those that had gotten through the barrier, burning them with hellfire and putting his palm to their heads. They didn't last long, but already a dozen more people were headed towards us.

"Landon?" Charis asked.

I turned my head and looked up.

"Charis, grab Izak," I shouted. "Sarah, hang on."

Charis reached out and took the demon by the arm. Sarah jumped on my back and wrapped her arms around my neck. The buzzing was clear now, easy to identify as an airplane propeller. I watched the plane swooping in, coming down towards us, ready to snatch us up like one of Tolkien's giant eagles.

The only difference was, we'd have to grab on ourselves.

I focused, flexing my legs and preparing to jump, hoping both Charis and I would get the timing right. I could see Adam now, inside the cockpit, his brow arched in concentration. Who knew an angel could fly a plane?

"Hey Ross," I said looking at the incoming puppets. Their eyes fixed on me, and I gave them the finger. Then I jumped.

"*Hah. Now this is what I call awesome,*" Ulnyx cried, his excitement rattling my soul.

Sarah screamed, and her arms gripped tighter around my neck, threatening to choke me. The plane rocked from side to side as I wrapped my arms around the left landing gear, swinging wildly back and forth while my body absorbed the shock, praying Sarah would hold on. I looked over and saw that Charis had made it, having wrapped one arm around the right gear, and helping Izak find purchase with the other. Satisfied, and greatly impressed with Adam, I peered back towards the roadway. At least one hundred pairs of possessed eyes followed the plane as it zipped away.

CHAPTER NINETEEN

We hung there, the four of us, from the landing gear of the small airplane
that Adam had commandeered from I don't know where. It was less than ten miles to
the Pyramids from the air, and the distance fell away fast. We had climbed up over
the wheels by the time Adam circled the plane and brought it down in the sand next
to the Great Pyramid.

There was no time to waste though. No time to congratulate the angel on his
daring rescue, or even to just be thankful we had made it.

The Beast was here too.

Even worse, the Pyramids were patrolled by armed guards.

They started firing on the plane the moment it stopped moving, the bullets
pinging off the aluminum, peppering it with holes. The only one they could kill
with the rounds was Sarah, but they could still be effective at inflicting pain and
slowing us down. I was surprised he was taking the risk of hitting her, but he
seemed to be a pretty good shot.

I took two bullets in the arm and another in the leg, wincing each time I
felt the stinging pain blossom through my body. I knew by the grunt and groans and

curses that the others were hit too. We made a run for the Pyramid, trying to keep the plane between the bullets and us, and casting aside any of the possessed tourists that tried to block our path.

"This look familiar, kid?" one of them asked, flipping me the bird right before I tossed him to the ground. Maybe I shouldn't have saluted him like that.

"Do you have any idea where we're going?" Adam asked. His arm was bleeding from a bullet wound.

"I don't even know if this is the right pyramid." I really, really, hoped Obi had been right about the whole secret room thing. It sounded like something that could have been left by Malize.

"How do we find out?" His hand shot out and blocked a punch from an old woman in a purple skirt. He grabbed her and pushed her to the ground, as soft as he dared. She fell to the ground laughing.

"Unless hurting them will make you fall, you don't need to be gentle," I said. "They die when he lets them go."

Adam's angry look reflected what I was feeling.

"There has to be an entrance somewhere. A glamoured wall, or maybe a hieroglyphic that looks like Malize's signature. It could be anywhere, or nowhere."

We kept running, from one side of the Pyramid around to another. At least the corners gave us respite from the gunfire. It didn't stop the puppets though, and I could swear they were multiplying.

"We should have come in the middle of the night," Charis shouted.

"Just look for the symbol."

We were around to the south side, opposite where we had landed, when we found it. I had focused to enhance my eyesight and see the lines in the stone more clearly, and even then I attributed at least half the discovery to luck. Someone had defaced the Pyramid more recently by scratching their initials into the rock.

The change in texture had drawn a closer inspection, and I had found Malize's sigil behind it.

"Izak, Adam, you're on defense. We need some time."

"How do we open it?" Sarah asked.

I put my hand to the symbol, feeling around it. The stone was solid. I focused, reaching past it, trying to feel the density of the structure beyond. It was solid too.

"I wish I knew."

"The Great Pyramid?" The Beast asked, from the voice of a small girl. "Interesting."

I ignored him, and kept searching. Charis knelt down next to me, wiping away the sand under the symbol, to see if there was another clue that had been buried by time.

"I don't know what you think you're going to find in there," he said. Both Izak and Adam were occupied with the larger puppets, so they allowed him to walk right up to us and lean over our shoulder. "Maybe you need to piss on it?"

"Sod off," Charis said, without looking at him.

The Beast laughed, a child's chipmunk laugh. "Am I bother-" He stopped mid-sentence, shoving me to the side so he could look at the pyramid wall. His head snapped towards me, long hair whipping around behind it.

Every voice joined in chorus at the same time. "Malize?"

So, he remembered the name. "You know him?"

He didn't get to answer. Sarah reached down and grabbed the girl by the shoulders. "Go to sleep, child," she said in a gentle voice. "It's a nightmare, that's all. Just a nightmare."

"Your nightmare," the Beast said, his fear and surprise masked by the normal smugness. "It's just start-"

181

The child's eyes fluttered back, and she fell to the sand.

"She's alive," Sarah said.

The realization face-palmed me. "He's spread too thin to resist your power." It wouldn't stop the assault against us, but it would certainly limit it. "How many can you Calm?"

Sarah turned to where Izak and Adam were doing their best to knock the Beast's prisoners back. I could feel her power building. "Rest, all of you," she said. It was a Calm Command, an ability unique to her. "You're all having a bad dream, and you must rest."

The power spread out from her, a charge in the air that I could feel throughout my soul. The Beast began to growl in frustration, but he wasn't strong enough to hold on. The mass of people rolled their eyes, and fell.

"Landon, look," Charis said.

I turned back towards the pyramid, and saw that Malize's symbol was glowing.

"What do you think it-"

The pyramid was gone. The sand was gone. The collapsed mortals were gone. Adam and Izak were both gone. Charis, Sarah, and I were standing in the middle of a large limestone room, filled with dry air and lit by the sigils etched into the walls. Templar script, tightly drawn. It began to glow brighter.

"This is unbelievable," Sarah said, turning around to look at the glowing writing.

"Look." I pointed at the wall, where a small door was pressed into the stone, so well measured that there was no seam. I only knew it was there because of a small gold handle. "I guess Obi was right."

The symbols grew brighter, and brighter still, until the entire room was bathed in white light. It reflected off the polished sandstone, and off the gold handle. It reflected until there was nothing but light, in a whiteness that

182

reminded me of the wall between what Ross had once told be was the 'staging area' and Purgatory.

He appeared as though stepping through the light, or maybe stepping out of it. Malize. The archangel looked different from when we had seen him only two days ago, older and more wise. His hair was streaked with white, and he was a wearing a white cloak that flowed to his feet and covered most of his form.

"Diuscrucis," he said, bowing to all of us. "I'm glad that you made it."

"Malize," Charis said, returning his bow. "What's going on?"

"You were too late to prevent the Beast from being freed," he said, looking directly at Sarah. Her face turned red and she looked down. "Do not be ashamed, child. I had feared that such a thing would come to pass. So many thin threads, so many lost hopes. I knew one day the Pure One would come, and the Beast's prison may be shattered. You should be proud for escaping his grasp."

She looked up at him and smiled. "You're beautiful," she said. "So many colors."

He held up his hand, and as before we were transported back in time. To the building of the Great Pyramid. While thousands of workers lifted stone around him, Malize stood at the limestone panels that would line this room and carved his symbols. "From the first moments after Lucifer and I had imprisoned it, I surmised that the balance would require a way for it to escape, and that the likelihood that it would succeed was not minimal. To that end, I began to prepare. This room is one such preparation, a means by which I could intercede if needed, and offer guidance based on the experience and wisdom I have gained. More millennia than you can count have passed in the Cave of Christ since I first begged of my Lord Jesus to assist me in removing myself from your universe. I have spent much of that time in meditation and contemplation, waiting for this day that I prayed would come."

Of course. The Beast hadn't known Malize was still around, because he had never heard a peep from anyone about it. That was because nobody could remember who or what he was.

"And the clue to get us here?" I asked. 'That was another of your preparations?"

He smiled. "Yes. That was another. It was much harder to execute, as it required finding the right soul. One who would spend time in Purgatory, who could leave the clue. That; however, is in the past. What is more important is what I can tell you today. You have Avriel's Box?"

Charis reached into her pocket and removed it, holding it in her palm. "How did you know about it?"

"I would not be very prepared, if I had no way to observe," he replied. "I have seen your efforts. You've done well, although losing the Redeemer may be a challenging misstep."

"The Redeemer?" I asked.

He nodded. "The Canaan Blade. I had hoped it would provide useful to you. It was difficult to obtain."

"I saved Landon with it," Charis said. "So it did come in handy, even if we lost it."

"It only works on demons anyway," I said.

He smiled. "That is not the whole truth of it, but it is enough."

"What else does it do?"

"It is of no importance, now. It may be that losing it will cost us. It may be that it won't. I have made arrangements to help us adjust for its dispossession."

The location around us faded and changed. Now we were inside the Beast's prison. "This is the prison, the day it was completed," Malize said. It didn't look much different than I remembered it. "Hold up the Box, and compare."

Charis held it up, and we each looked at it, and then back at the prison. Both had sigils etched everywhere, though the Box's were in seraph runes, not Templar script. Other than that, I didn't see any similarities. I wasn't looking close enough.

"The symbols," Sarah said. "There." She pointed at the prison. "There." She pointed at the Box. "They are almost the same. Those also." She pointed at another section. "And those."

Malize nodded. "Yes. Almost the same. So many of the symbols are similar, yet different. Avriel's design is a wonder, a work of art. He had no knowledge of what we had done to capture the Beast, and yet he was so close to creating the perfect prison."

"Perfect? He ended up trapped in it himself."

"Not because the design is flawed," Malize said. "It was his understanding of the power needed to keep a creature like Abaddon contained that failed him. That is why I am glad you came, and why I am especially glad you have the Box."

"So, we can trap the Beast in it?" I asked.

He nodded again. "In time, yes."

Huh? "What do you mean in time? He's getting stronger, not weaker."

"Yes, I know. The trouble is that while the design of the Box is incredible, these symbols were made to catch a demon. You need to catch something else entirely."

I glanced over to Charis when I saw her smile. She must have been thinking the same thing I was thinking. We're gonna need a bigger boat. "So we need to make some modifications?"

"Not you," he said. "Avriel. He's the only one who can work out the calculations. He needs to convert these seraphim runes to Templar script."

I didn't like the sound of that. "Malize, I hate to sound ungrateful," I

185

said. "But first, the Beast has Avriel. Second, I don't think he knows Templar script."

The room changed around us again. We were on a mountaintop, at what looked like an old monastery. I could swear I had seen the place before in a kung-fu movie.

"Avriel is here. Mortals call it Mt. Popa, in Burma."

"And..." I said, knowing it couldn't be that simple.

"The Beast convinced Abaddon to join him. This was how. He promised him that he would place Avriel somewhere that the demon could always return to torture him, even after the destruction of the rest of the world. After you slipped past him, the Beast had him return to wait for you. He knows the Box can hold him, but he also knows the Box can hold anything, if enough power is fed into it. He needs Avriel for his endgame."

It was the way he said it that made my spine tingle. "You mean he hopes to trap God?" That was a tough idea to wrap my head around.

"Yes. If the calculations are correct, with the full power of the Beast... I believe it can be done. You need to rescue the archangel from Abaddon."

I felt an uncomfortable rocking in the pit of my stomach. "How are we supposed to do that? Even Izak is afraid of him, and I got lucky with the sucker punch."

Malize smiled. "The Redeemer would have suited you well for this purpose, but as I've said, I've made preparations. It may indeed work out for the best, for the Deliverer is a much more potent weapon against a creature like Abaddon."

"The Deliverer?"

"Another of the Canaan Blades," he replied. "There is a Templar waiting for you in Kyoto, at The Golden Pavilion. He will assist you in acquiring it."

"You mean you don't already have it?" I asked. I didn't like the sound of that.

"Unfortunately, we do not. The Canaan Blades were stolen almost one thousand years ago. It took extraordinary effort and the deaths of many Templars to even recover the one."

"Wait," Charis said. "Malize, why was I never told about this?" She sounded upset.

"I'm truly sorry," he said. "The less you knew about the Blades, the better. We could not afford for you to attract the attention of the Inquisitors."

She still didn't look happy. It seemed like the perfect time to interject. "Okay, so I go to Japan and acquire the Deliverer. We use it against Abaddon. We rescue Avriel. Great. He still doesn't know Templar script."

"No, but Charis does. She can guide his hand. Based on the advanced nature of his original design, I have no doubt he'll master the language in no time."

I laughed. "Which is about how much we have."

"Do not fear," Malize said. "Remember, as long as the Pure One lives, the Beast cannot claim his full strength. As long as you live, you have the ability to stop it." He reached under his cloak, and pulled out a pair of silver bracelets. They were covered in Templar scripture, and the white light refracted strangely off the etched surface. He tossed one to me, and one to Charis.

"I don't know how, but the Beast is using the power of your Source, of Purgatory, to track your movements. These bracelets will subdue that power, and prevent it from being visible to him. Be cautious, as this also means you will not be able to affect change to anything outside of yourselves for as long as you are wearing them."

I knew how. The power in Purgatory was the Beast's power. It made sense that he could track us with it. I put the bracelet over over my wrist and squeezed it closed. "Thank you."

"Yes, thank you, Malize," Charis said. "For everything."

"I have done what I can. If you need to speak to me again, the Templar can help you find the other portal I've left in the mortal realm." He walked over to Sarah, and knelt down in front of her, putting himself below her. He took her hands in his and looked up at her face. "I know of the war that rages in you, child. Do not be afraid to open your heart, for it is that common thread that binds all of His children that will lead you to your destiny."

Sarah didn't respond. She just kept her head down at him. Were there words being exchanged in the silence? I'd never know.

Malize rose back to his feet, and bowed to Charis and I. "Godspeed to you both," he said. He took another step back, and was collected by the light.

I turned to Charis and Sarah. "At least we know what to do," I said. I didn't get a chance to say more, because the light began to intensify, reaching for us in blinding fury. Before I could even move, we were back out on the sand.

"Well?" Adam asked. "Is anything happening?" He was still facing the people Sarah had put to sleep, watching them for any signs of movement. In the twenty minutes we had spent with Malize, not even a second had passed here.

"We're done," I said. "We need to get to Japan."

We made our way back around the Great Pyramid, keeping an eye out for any more mortals possessed by the Beast. Between Sarah shutting down his vessels, and learning that Malize was involved, he seemed to have retreated.

"Who did you speak to again?" Adam asked.

I had explained everything to Izak and the seraph as we ran, in a condensed version. The details weren't that important anyway. Even so, he had already forgotten the archangel's name.

"The important part is that we get to Kyoto as soon as possible," I said. "Today is your lucky day. You might get two of your swords back by the time this is over."

"I still can't believe it," he said. "We've been searching for the Deliverer for over a thousand years. To think we have a lead on someone who knows where it is."

"Yeah, crazy," I agreed. "You said the Canaan Blades have special properties? What does this one do?"

"It makes the wielder immune to demons. Hellfire, cursed weapons, claws, Command, everything. It will deliver the carrier through any battle."

I could see how that would come in handy against Abaddon.

We pulled up next to the small airplane. It was riddled with bullet holes. Charis stepped up into it. "Let's see if this thing can still go," she said, hitting switches and starting the propeller. I knew from her memories she knew how to pilot pretty much anything that flew. She even knew how to drive a train, if needed. We rarely needed to sleep, after all.

I felt a tug on my shirt, and turned to look at Izak. He had a pissed off, dour expression on his face.

"What's up?" I asked him. ,

He knelt down and drew a circle in the sand, and a few runes. A rift. Then he drew a rectangle with a circle in it. He wiped both of them out with his foot.

"No rifts in Japan? Are you kidding?"

He shook his head, holding out his palm and quickly squeezing it closed. Destroyed.

"When?"

He shrugged, and then motioned with his finger. Not too long. Did someone know we were coming? Or had they destroyed them to stop something else?

"Next closest option?" I asked.

"South Korea," Charis said for him. "Across the Sea of Japan. It'll take us days to get there."

"Crap," I said, looking at the ground. I didn't like the chances of humanity surviving the Beast for hours, never mind days.

"I can take one of you," Adam said.

"Take?" I asked. I had an outside understanding of what he was suggesting, but I didn't think it was possible. "Won't you fall, if you help us like that?"

He smiled. "Before, yes, but I'm the Ninth now. As you know, we have certain... freedoms, that the others do not. Since helping you will allow me to retrieve one of the Canaan Blades, I believe the cause is just."

Angels and their games. I returned his smile, and then leaned into the airplane. "Can you get Sarah and Izak back to the rift?"

"Of course," she replied. "Meet at the church?"

"Yeah." I reached into my pocket, pulled out my phone, and tossed it to her. "Try to get in touch with Obi, if you can. Tell him what's going on and to stay as close to the church as possible." I looked back at Adam. "I'm hoping Mr. Ninth back there can convince Kassie to give up the hunt and help us out with the Beast."

"Things are going to get messy, Landon," she said.

"They aren't already?" I replied. "We need to get the rest of the Divine involved, or we'll never have a chance of getting close enough to the real Beast to put him in the Box. Adam believes, so it's a start."

I helped Sarah into the plane. Izak hopped up on his own. "Take care of them," I said to him on his way by. He nodded.

"I'll see you soon," I said to Charis. I wanted to say more, but the words wouldn't come.

"You're damn right you will," she said. I saw her pull the bracelet off her wrist, and then she leaned over and pulled the door closed, and the plane began to roll forward. It would have been tough going in sand, but I could see it flattening

190

and compressing in front of the wheels as she made herself a runway.

"Are you ready, diuscrucis?" Adam asked.

I walked back to him. "Watch where you put your hands," I said.

CHAPTER TWENTY

He laughed as he put his arms up under my shoulders. "This is going to feel strange, since you've never done it before." He crouched slightly, and then pushed off, his wings spreading and flapping a few times. I felt my heart drop beyond my stomach, passing down to my groin as we rocketed into the sky. It took me a few beats to get my breath back, and when I did I let out a scream of fear and joy. I felt like a kid on his first roller coaster.

"This is awesome," I shouted. I had flown myself in Purgatory, but it wasn't the same. This was real.

"*I have missed this,*" Josette said, her voice rising up for the first time in a while. I could feel her excitement beneath my own, adding to it.

"It almost makes you wish you had been a little less evil, doesn't it?" Adam asked.

In other circumstances, I might have called him an asshole for making a statement like that. Right then, I was having too much fun to care.

"*Enjoy it while it lasts,*" Josette said. "*There is little enough to be had in times like these.*"

We were above the clouds in no time. Adam wrapped his legs around mine as he turned horizontal, holding me below him like a tandem skydiver. His wings swept back, and I felt our velocity increase beyond anything possible with mechanical flight.

The ride only lasted for a minute or two at most. Then we were falling, dropping towards the ground thousands of miles from where we started. I saw the Earth approaching once we cleared the clouds, and felt the blood rising to my head. Below us, I could see the grey of the city of Kyoto, and the green of the ground around it.

"That's the Golden Pavilion over there," Adam said, motioning with his foot. "I'll bring us down over on that brown area, where it's more quiet."

As we neared the ground, he flared his wings out again, turning the ends so they caught the air like a parachute, and slowing us down to a still jarring speed. The impact would have crushed human bones.

"Thanks for the lift," I said when he let go of my arms. "I take it you've been here before?"

"This is one of my favorite places," he said. "Heaven is amazing, but there is a lot to contemplate within the beauty of this world that He created."

We walked through the surrounding brush and down to a quiet path. There were only a few tourists and a small collection of locals still walking the gardens. The sun was hidden by a thin layer of high clouds, but even through them I could tell it would be setting soon.

"Who are we meeting?" Adam asked.

"I don't know," I replied. I hadn't told him about the Templars. It was too big of a secret to just go spilling to an angel, even if they had proven themselves at least somewhat reliable. Instead, I had just said there was someone waiting for us. "Either I'll know when I see them, or they'll know when they see me." In fact, as long as I was wearing Malize's bracelet I couldn't use my Sight beyond its natural range, which was visual. I'd rather be surprised by a seraph or a demon than the Beast and his puppet armies.

We turned right at the sign that pointed to the Pavilion, an impressive, gold-painted pagoda sitting on the edge of a small pond. It was a perfect Japanese botanical landscape, and despite everything I couldn't help but admire the composition. There were only a few people standing around, looking out at the water.

I recognized our contact right away. I should have known. I tapped Adam on the shoulder and pointed him out.

"Max," I said, shouldering up to him and leaning over the railing. Adam stopped on the opposite side.

He didn't move his head, only his eyes, from my side to Adam's and back. "Diuscrucis," he said, a little too excited. "You brought a playmate?" He looked back at Adam. "Not the companion I would have expected. Was it wise to leave our little peanut on her own?"

"Sarah's hardly on her own," I replied. "Charis and Izak are with her. Besides, it would have taken forever to get them here. Did you know someone's been destroying the rifts?"

He rubbed his chin. "Hmmm... yes, well I suppose it makes sense. The Beast freed Abaddon. He doesn't care about how you're aligned, only if you make a tasty treat. I'm sure the demons want to keep him away as much as anyone else does. I expect more of the rifts will fall in a hurry." He shrugged it off, and his eyes brightened. "You did say Izak? Oh yes, I've been hearing rumors about that one. Is there any truth to them?"

"If you mean that he's a badass? Yes. That's why I know Sarah's in good hands."

His grin spread from ear to ear, and he turned to Adam, holding out his hand. "A pleasure to make your acquaintance, mister..."

Adam looked at the fiend's hand, and then at me. Max pulled it back.

"Too much of a stretch, I suppose," he said. "No matter, my good man. One you've been through the torture of Hell, a little surliness is a walk in the park. No pun intended. Ha-ha."

"Max, you know why we're here," I said.

He reached up and put his arm around my shoulders. "I do, old chap. I'm prepared to lead you on this little adventure. First, I need you to do one thing."

"What's that?"

"Just say the words you know I want to hear." He put his face in mine, his huge grin too comical for me to be annoyed.

"Fine. You were right about the trap. I trust you."

He let me go and slapped me on the back. "Bully!" he cried. "Jolly good. Well then, off we go." He turned and started walking back up the path.

"Max," I said, trailing behind him. "Where are we going?"

He stopped again. "I should tell you that, shouldn't I? Very well, have you ever heard of the Nicht Creidim?"

I had no idea what he was talking about. "Nick Creedem? No, is he a demon, or an angel?"

"Ho-ho. Not Nick Creedem. *The* Nicht Creidim. I'll assume that since you can't pronounce it you don't know who I'm referring to. They're mortals. Awake mortals. A 'family' as it were. They're collectors of Divine artifacts. Anything that has Divine power, they want."

I had definitely never heard of them.

"*Josette?*"

I felt her presence illuminate my soul. "*I have heard the word before, but I*

195

*have never met them. Some think they are a myth. Others believe they exist, but
they don't meddle much in the affairs of the Divine."*

"*They're vultures,*" Ulnyx said. "*They hide in dark corners, and pick at the
remains on the battlefields. They'll collect anything Divine - weapons, clothing,
blood. Anything they can get before it wastes away.*"

"They're vultures," I said to Max. "My question is, why?"

"Why, what?" he replied.

"Why do they take Divine stuff? For what purpose?"

"Divine 'stuff' as you say, is very powerful stuff, especially for a mortal.
They take it because they feel it can help them maintain the power and influence of
the 'family', and perhaps one day even grow it. I wouldn't call them vultures. It
was Nicht Creidim assassins who murdered the seraphs given the Canaan Blades. It
took hundreds of years to find out where they were keeping the Redeemer, and now
the Deliverer. It took the deaths of many to get the Redeemer back."

"What about the other blade, then?" I asked. "What about the Swords of
Gehenna?"

He cast his eyes at Adam, hesitant about how much to say. "It is likely they
have them as well, though we don't know where."

"You're a fiend. Can't you just Command them to tell you?"

He shook his head. "Ah, no, my good man. You see, the Nicht Creidim are an
interesting lot. They tend towards inbreeding, with just enough breakage in the
direct lineage to prevent the genetic deficiencies normally associated with such
activity. The reason they do it is because it has allowed them to develop
certain... resistances to the Divine. Most likely stemming from an initial contact
with an artifact that gave the original progenitor some amount of immunization."

"Like someone who drank from the Holy Grail?" I asked. Wouldn't that be a
pisser, if one of the original Templars had gone off and created his own cult?

"Precisely," he said. "They're a secretive lot, as you can imagine. They don't tend to fight the Divine unless threatened, so for the most part they stay under their radar."

"Not if they have the Canaan Blades," Adam said. "When First hears about this, she's going to be on them like a bee on a flower."

Max stopped walking and rounded on the seraph. "Landon, you naughty boy, you didn't tell me he was an Inquisitor." He got right up in Adam's face, his expression turning dark. "One, that was the least manly simile I could imagine. Two, you'll say nothing to Kassie about the Nicht Creidim and the Blades. You have no idea what trouble you would be causing by bringing your little S.W.A.T team down on them."

Adam backed up a step and raised his hands. "Whoa, no offense, little man," he said. "I'm just trying to do my job. You know, the Lord's work."

"The Lord's work does not include mass murder," he said.

"We won't kill them," Adam replied. "Not unless it is absolutely necessary."

Max started laughing. "Ha-ha! Now that is what I love about the seraphim. I'm talking about the mass murder of angels," he said. "Don't underestimate them because they're mortal. There is a reason they've held the Blades for over a thousand years."

Adam backed down, but he didn't look convinced.

"Guys," I said. "It doesn't matter right now. Nobody is going to be getting anything if the Beast has his way."

"Right you are," Max agreed.

"So, let's try this again. Where are we going?"

"Port of Osaka," Max said. "The Nicht Creidim own a shipping company. It makes it easier to move the artifacts around. I'll bring you as close as I can, but you have to go in alone."

"Go in alone?" I hadn't been expecting that.

"They're mortal, but they have a kind of Sight. They'll know if there are Divine headed their way, and they'll prepare a pretty nasty defense. So, old chap, you'll have to disguise yourself and try to talk your way in. Show them that fancy bracelet, and tell them you're looking to sell it. See if you can get them to show you around. I have it on good authority the Deliverer is in there. I just don't know where."

I looked at Malize's bracelet. I wasn't too keen on taking it off. "Where are you going to be?"

He clapped his hands. "Waiting nearby, of course."

"Fine," I said, taking a deep breath. "How do I recognize the sword?"

"Have you ever heard of Excalibur?" he asked.

King Arthur, the Knights of the Round Table. Who hadn't? "Of course."

"That's its stage name, so whatever you think Excalibur looks like, there you go. Just be sure not to use it until you're ready, or you're going to bring a lot of attention to yourself."

I did a double-take. "Wait. You're telling me the Deliverer is Excalibur? That Excalibur is real?"

He rolled his eyes and spread his hands. "Well, duh. Arthur was one of ours. So were his knights."

Unbelievable.

Max had a car, and we piled into it. It wasn't a long drive from Kyoto to the port, especially with the traffic subconsciously moving out of our way. Within thirty minutes we were pulling to a stop in a dirty, industrial part of town. Darkness was beginning to settle here, and there was a distinct quiet that had me on edge. I rubbed my hand absently on Malize's bracelet, hoping that it was doing what he had claimed it would. There was no sign of the Beast, but I was still getting a creepy feeling.

Max pointed ahead through the windshield. "Three buildings down, turn left. Walk until you hit the water, then turn right. Keep going until you see a long, low stone building with a blue roll-up door. That's it. Knock out S.O.S in Morse code, and they'll open up to check you out. Do you know Mr. Morse?"

I didn't, but Josette did. I nodded. "One question. Will they be able to see my eyes?" They would be a dead giveaway that I was more than human.

Max opened the glovebox and reached in, then handed me a pair of mirrored aviator sunglasses. "Just don't take them off," he advised.

It didn't seem like the best plan, but what else could we do? I pushed open the door and climbed out, making sure to focus, adjusting my signature to true neutral and vanishing from the Sight of anyone who had it. "You two lovebirds say out of trouble," I said. Neither looked pleased at being left with the other. I gently closed the door and started walking.

There wasn't much to it. I turned left where Max had instructed, until I got to the edge of the bay. I stopped when I reached the water, looking out at the ships in the harbor, and then at the glow of the rising moon, diffused by the light clouds. It took some doing to imagine all of it going away, under the Beast's destructive thumb. I wasn't going to let that happen.

"*I've always loved the moon,*" Ulnyx said with a chuckle. "*Do you know why weres are so often associated with howling at full moons? It's when the bitches get the most horny.*"

"*Shut up,*" I said, ignoring his amusement.

The sound of my tapping Morse code on the blue door echoed in the emptiness of the late evening. No sooner had I finished the last rap than I heard a click, and the door moved, sliding up and out of view and revealing a face behind it.

"Who are you?" the girl asked. She was maybe eighteen or nineteen, with long

199

black hair and a pale complexion. Her eyes were almond-shaped, and she had a pert little nose on a small face. She looked like a mix of Japanese with something more European.

I didn't give her a name, I just held up my arm and tapped on the bracelet. "I heard I could find someone who might be interested in a piece like this here."

Her expression didn't change, but she leaned in and looked at it. When she backed away, she was smiling. "You heard correct, Mr..."

"Smith," I said with a smile.

She gave me a small bow. "Of course. Follow me."

She led me into the open area of the warehouse. It was filled with shipping containers, crates, and boxes. Forklifts sat half-loaded, as though they had been abandoned as soon as it had hit closing time, and only the auxiliary lights were on. I scanned the area visually, but I didn't see anyone else in there.

"That's an interesting piece," she said as we walked. "How did you come by it?"

"I stole it," I said. "I'd heard there were buyers for stuff with this kind of etching on it. What is it, Japanese?"

She laughed, a cute little choppy chuckle. "Oh no, Mr. Smith. Not Japanese. Something much older." We reached the end of the warehouse, and she put her palm up to an electronic lock. It beeped, and she bent down to lift another door. Behind it was an elevator.

"Pretty cool kit," I said.

"We can never be too careful," she replied. "We deal in priceless antiquities that are highly desired by a number of parties. Not all of whom are willing to be above the table in working with us."

"I can imagine. You don't have a problem with the means by which I obtained this, do you?"

She turned and looked at it again. "Oh no. One man's loss, is another's gain. If they didn't want a professional such as yourself to take it, they should have been more careful."

I couldn't help but smile at that. "My sentiments exactly," I said.

The elevator descended fifty or sixty feet, and then opened up into an empty cement corridor that was about twenty feet long. The whole thing reminded me of how the Templars had positioned the Cave of Christ in order to keep it safe. I guess it was a common tactic.

She used her palm to open a huge iron door at the end of the hall, and we had to wait upwards of a minute for the machinery behind it to get it open. She stared at me the whole time.

"Can I help you with something else, Miss...?" I realized I hadn't gotten her name.

"Smith," she replied, with a wink and a smile. "To be honest, I was just admiring your physique."

I didn't know what to say. I wasn't glamoured, because they' d probably have seen right through it anyway. That meant it was just me, which in my opinion wasn't really that impressive. Thin build, a little bit of muscle, but a Hollywood idol I was not.

"Did I embarrass you?" she asked. "I promise I can make it up to you later, once your business with father is concluded."

The door finished its slide up into the ceiling, and she led me ahead, into a red carpeted hallway. Hanging from the walls on either side were display cases of thick, bulletproof glass. Inside of them were a whole mess of things. Arrowheads, daggers, chalices, clothes. It seemed they'd put the demonic stuff on one side, and the angelic stuff on the other.

"You don't look like you need any more of this stuff," I said, trying to get off the last topic. I have to admit, her giggle was really cute.

"We can never have enough, until we have it all," she replied. We reached the end of this corridor, stopping at a pair of heavily runed wooden doors. She used her palm one more time, and the doors swung inward.

It was like an underground palace. Glossy marble floors, a high ceiling with a fake skylight at top, and two decks of hallway connected by twin staircases. It reminded me of Rebecca's father's penthouse, except much, much grander. In the center of the room, glinting in the fake sunlight that was focused on it, was the hilt and last six inches of the blade of a sword. The rest of it was jammed into a large, smooth stone. I couldn't help but stare.

"Do you like it?" She asked me.

"It's incredible," I replied. "It reminds me of King Arthur's sword. Excalibur?"

She giggled again. "I have to go get father. Please wait here." She headed off to a door on the east side of the room.

"*Just take it,*" Ulnyx said. "*You can get out of here before she gets back.*"

"*Don't be foolish, Were,*" Josette replied. "*There is nothing natural about the light that's shining down on it. It's probably an alarm.*"

"I was thinking the same thing," I said. Still, I wasn't sure I would have much choice. I wasn't about the let the bracelet go, even on the off chance they would be willing to trade for it.

"Oh, what would that be?"

I hadn't meant to say it out loud. I turned east to where Ms. Smith was standing with an older man. He was a military type, with a white flat-top, a grizzled face, and a tough expression. He also looked like he could whip me six ways to Sunday.

"I've never seen anything like it." I walked over to him and held out my hand. He ignored it, his eyes going right to the bracelet.

"I've never seen anything like that," he said. His voice had a weird, constant hoarseness to it. Like he spent ninety percent of his time yelling. "Where'd you come across something like that?"

I didn't answer right away. I was still considering my options, and realizing I didn't have any. I took a deep breath, reached up, and took off the sunglasses. "An archangel gave it to me," I said, dropping my disguise and letting them See me if they could.

"Divver," Ms. Smith cried. Before I could blink, she had a dagger in her hand, and was crouching down, ready for a fight. Her father hadn't moved.

Divver? That was a new one.

"Interesting," he said, looking me over. "I've heard about you. I didn't think you'd be making an appearance though. It's Landon, right?"

I wasn't that surprised he knew who I was. You couldn't collect so many Divine artifacts without being pretty up on our day to day. "That's right," I said. "And you are?"

"Joe," he replied. "Father Joe to my family." His daughter was still crouched, ready to fight. He looked over at her. "I'll tell you what, Landon. You beat my girl in hand to hand, I won't call in the rest of the troops and I'll listen to whatever it is you came to say. I figure if you were here to fight, you would've gotten to it already."

It was more reasonable than I'd expected, based on what Max had told me. "F-"

Before I could finish speaking, she had launched herself at me with a speed that should have been impossible for a mortal. I got my hands up in time, crossing them over to block her downward strike with my forearms, then pushed back against her to break us up.

"Not bad," she said with a smile. She turned the knife over in her hand, putting it against her arm, and came again.

I had enough time to focus now, and I slipped away from her attacks without too much difficulty, twisting and turning away from one slash after another, then a kick and a leg sweep. They wanted to test me, so I decided to test her.

"More than not bad," she said, her breathing a little heavier. "Do you do other things as well as you fight?"

I could only imagine what she meant. I felt a little rush of blood headed upwards. "You'll never know," I replied.

"Don't count me out so quickly." She came at me again, faster than before. I don't know how she did it, but even pulling on my power it was tough to keep ahead. It was time to stop fooling around. I went on a short offensive, returning her strikes with some of my own. I got one through to her chest, and with my enhanced strength and speed I thought it would be over, but she didn't even bat an eyelash.

I hesitated for just a second, trying to figure out why she hadn't gone flying away. Something on her had to be shutting me down. She took advantage of my confusion, bringing the dagger up and across my face, digging it deep into my cheek. I grunted and took a few steps back, ready to defend against her next blow.

It didn't come. She stood there, shocked that she had cut me? I glanced over at Joe. He had a curious expression. Then I realized they were waiting for me to die. The blade was enchanted after all. I hadn't gotten a good look at whether it was Cursed or Blessed. Either way, the wound healed.

"So it's true," Joe said. "Divine weapons can't hurt you."

"No, they can hurt me," I said. "They just can't kill me. Not unless you take my head off."

I shouldn't have said that. She crouched down and charged towards me again, somehow dialing her speed up another notch.

I moved away, looking for something to use as a weapon. My back smacked into the stone in the center of the room. Why not?

The light burned my hand as I reached in and grabbed the sword's hilt, pulling it out of the rock in one smooth motion. I shifted it to my other hand just in time to start deflecting dagger strikes, the burning causing more pain than I thought it should have. I could only imagine how Izak felt.

Ms. Smith sped up, I sped up. We both moved faster and faster, the two blades smacking against each other in an impossibly quick rhythm. Block, parry, dodge, strike. On and on it went, twirling around the room like some kind of sharp waltz. It was a work of art, I knew. A composition even Mozart would have been proud of.

Then it was over. I caught the dagger between the blade and the guard and twisted, pulling it from her hands and sending it tumbling away. She tried to go after it, but I managed to put the edge against her neck and stop her cold.

"I win," I said.

She looked at me and smiled. She had a hunger in her eyes. A hunger I'd seen before, in someone else. It made me uncomfortable.

Joe's clapping got my attention.

"Bravo," he said. "My dear, I'm amazed by how much you've improved." He looked at me. "And you. You're a virtuoso."

It wasn't really me. It was Josette's connection that guided me in the fight, but he didn't need to know about that.

"So. What can I do for you, Landon?"

CHAPTER TWENTY-ONE

The blue door rolled open, exposing me once more to the outside air. It was much later than when I had gone in; too much later for my taste, but the fact that I was going out with the Deliverer in hand had made it worthwhile.

It had taken a long chat with Joe to convince him of my need to borrow the weapon. In the end, he had been wise in recognizing that the Beast was a threat to all of our ideals, not just those of the Divine. It didn't hurt that the Nicht Creidim had a credo that fell pretty close to my own goals. They believed the end of the world was unavoidable, and they wanted to be sure to have the best chance of defending the remainder of humanity from the coming Divine hordes.

I wish that could have meant they would agree to more of an alliance than a loan, but their goal was to survive the Apocalypse and get rid of the Divine once and for all, not prevent it and keep living in the current state of stalemate. From my position I could see where they were coming from, even if it meant that in the end, if I were the last 'Divver' left standing, they would be out for my blood too.

"Good luck, Landon," Elyse said, putting her arms around me and leaning up. I tried to turn my head to let her kiss my cheek, but her other hand came up and held it. Her lips found mine, sending me off with soft, warm passion. "I hope to see you again."

I didn't kiss her back, but she didn't seem to notice, or care. "You will," I said, holding up the sword. "I promised I would give this back to you."

That was the one hitch in my successful retrieval of the weapon. I'd sworn to Joe I would return it once the Beast was defeated. I swore on an ancient copy of the Bible, and I'd felt the inner chains that made the promise binding. I didn't know what would happen to me if I reneged, but I had a feeling it wouldn't be pleasant. Somehow, I had to convince Adam, Kassie, and the rest of their crew that it had been necessary, and they'd have to pay Joe a visit on their own if they wanted the Canaan Blade back. The good news was it only mattered if we succeeded.

I gave Elyse one last wave, and the door rolled closed. I stood out on the empty street for a minute and took a deep breath, and then headed back to the car.

"*You should've taken her up on her offer,*" Ulnyx said. "*A body like that.*"

Her body had been the work of a higher power. I was surprised they had shown none of the physical signs I associated with the inbreeding Max had claimed.

"*Shut up,*" I replied.

"*There* was *something about her,*" Josette added. "*Not her looks, Were, before you comment. It was the way she fought. If she were a Divine and appeared that young, I could understand, but she was all of twenty years old?*"

"*I thought the same thing,*" I said, remembering her speed and skill. "*I just assumed it was her Divver kit.*"

"*It may be,*" she replied.

It also may not.

"Sure took you long enough," Adam said when I reached the car. "I've been stuck here with this one for hours. It's one thing that he's a demon. It's another that he never stops talking."

Max turned around. "You should appreciate my good humor, instead of sitting there pouting."

"I wasn't pouting, I was thinking."

"Guys," I said. I held up the sword. "Mission accomplished. Adam, it's time to fly."

The angel got out of the car, his eyes fixed to the sword. "May I?" he asked, reaching for it. I pulled it back.

"Sorry, Adam, but I'm not letting this thing out of my hands until Abaddon is disintegrating in front of me. I've been screwed too many times."

Adam nodded, but he didn't look happy.

"There he goes pouting again," Max said. "Chin up, my good man. You'll be caressing that lovely soon enough. How many did you have to kill? Were they tough? So many questions, so little time."

I turned the blade over so I could hold it against my body, and lifted my arms for Adam to get a grip. "I didn't have to kill any of them, but yeah, they were really tough. See you around, Max. Thanks."

Adam hooked his arms under mine and bent slightly. Max put his fingers to his forehead and gave me a mock salute. "Give 'em Hell. Or Heaven. Or whatever kills 'em the best," he said. Then we were going up.

I didn't get quite as much enjoyment out of the second flight as I had the first. It probably had something to do with the fact that I was headed for a direct confrontation with the most powerful demon on Earth; a demon that even Izak ran away from. I could still remember the cold feelings of hopelessness just being near him had given me. It wasn't something I was looking forward to. I gripped the Deliverer tighter.

"You won't be able to get too close," I said to Adam once he started descending. There was a thick layer of clouds here that left us blinded to the

208

world around us. "You'll have to drop me."

I wasn't looking forward to that either. With the bracelet on, I couldn't

slow my descent. All I could do was accept the broken bones and pain, and wait for

it all to heal. It would be an excruciating and vulnerable couple of minutes,

during which I was dependent on getting lucky that Abaddon wouldn't notice, or

couldn't reach me in time.

"Are you sure?" he asked. I could tell by his voice he thought I was crazy.

It was crazy, but also necessary. I wasn't sure what would happen to the

seraph if he got too close. "Positive."

The clouds gave way about a thousand feet over the monastery. Immediately I

could see why they had chosen it. It sat on a level mountaintop, at least five

hundred feet over the surrounding landscape, making it a difficult proposition for

someone like me to approach unseen. Except, they hadn't been planning on me taking

the Angel Express.

The second thing that registered was the desolation and destruction of

everything around it. From up here, I could see the surrounding land, and the green

of verdant field and forest. Until it got within a half-mile of the monastery.

There, everything was brown and dead. Everything.

I knew there would be no other Divine, save for Abaddon and Avriel. I knew

there would be no people either, that they would have been killed or have fled.

Would they even know what had done it? To mortals, Abaddon was plague and

pestilence, not a demon with a shrouded but very real face. Just more casualties in

the hidden wars raging around them.

I could tell when Adam began feeling Abaddon's effects. His descent lost

control for just a hair in time, his body seizing up and his grip on my arms

tightening. He didn't let me go then, he kept trying to go further. We were still

seven or eight hundred feet above the ground.

"It's time for me to drop," I said.

"I'll get you closer," he replied.

"Adam, let me go." I tilted my head so I could see his face. He was getting pale, and his forehead was beginning to sweat.

"I can get you down."

"Dammit, he's going to know I'm coming, you idiot," I shouted. I shoved my elbow back into his stomach, and he let go with a grunt. Trying to ignore my velocity, and block out the fear of the pain I knew was coming, I focused on making myself Sight neutral. I could only hope the demon hadn't caught me already.

To say it hurt would be understating the pain of hitting the ground from a five hundred foot free-fall. I did get lucky to land in a somewhat soft spot, my drop broken by a few branches of a tree before I smacked into the soft ground. I had held the Deliverer point down, knowing it would sink into the earth, which was better than having it go flying off to wherever.

I felt the bones break. Ribs, arms, legs, spine. The shock ran up my entire body, and I think it may have even caused some brain damage, because my eyesight dimmed and everything felt off for a minute. I bounced once, high enough that when I let go of the sword I could see it buried in the ground to the hilt, and then laid there.

I did my best to keep my focus, to hide myself from Sight and beg myself to heal. In the moment I had dropped contact with the blade, I could feel the dark helplessness of Abaddon's power circling around me, trying to catch me in its emptiness.

"*That rocked it pretty hard,*" Ulnyx said with a laugh.

"*You don't feel the pain,*" I replied. "*So, shut up.*"

I laid there for three or four minutes, looking out for the demon. In this case, his power was a benefit, because I would see the dark tendrils arriving long before the actual creature did. It was a tense few minutes, but my body mended itself, and Abaddon didn't appear.

I pushed myself up, pulling the Deliverer from the ground as I did. I was only a dozen feet or so away from the monastery walls. I could see the gold towers rising above them. Was Avriel somewhere in one of those?

The place was larger than I had expected. How long would it take me to find the angel, even if I did defeat Avriel? Time was still an issue. Even though the Beast couldn't find me now, I knew he was doing something in Mumbai, and I didn't need to know what to know it wasn't good.

I skirted the wall until I came to a tower with a porch and an open doorway. I stowed Excalibur and shifted, pulling on Ulnyx's power and giving myself the size and strength I needed to leap the distance. Huge claws dug in on the floor, and I climbed up, shifting back once I reached the doorway.

The inside was as stunning as I expected, filled with a mix of ancient oriental architecture and modern renovations. It was also deserted, dark, and cold. Dead monkeys lay huddled together on the floor, along with a pair of dead people. They were frozen on the ground, their mouths open, as though they had died of sheer terror.

I kept walking, letting go of the alterations on my Divine signature. Now that I was whole and inside, I wanted Abaddon to find me. It would make everything much easier.

It didn't take the demon long. I had only just reached the main courtyard when the pitch black tendrils of his power began snaking along the sides of the buildings and covering the sky in unnatural darkness.

"Diuscrucis," it said, the word reverberating through the tendrils. "Did you come to die?"

I couldn't see him, not yet, but his power was wrapping around me, trying to trap me. I held the Deliverer a little tighter, feeling it warm in my palm. The runes along the surface of the blade began to glow in a soft white light, pushing back against the demon's power.

"You know why I came," I said. "Give me Avriel, and I'll leave without a fight."

His laughter shook the entire building, spreading a film of dust and mortar. "You won't be leaving. There is no need for me to fight."

The tendrils moved closer bunching in, surrounding me, placing me in a cocoon of total darkness. I couldn't see anything around me. I couldn't see anything except the sword, glowing in my hand, preventing me from losing myself to the despair and disease Abaddon wielded like a sword.

"The Beast will destroy you too, once he has the power. You aren't immune because you're strong." It was probably pointless, but I didn't think it could hurt to try.

"Perhaps," Abaddon said. "But ask yourself this, diuscrucis. Where do you see yourself in ten thousand years?"

I was ready for a fight. Now I paused. I'd never thought about such a distant future. I'd only been here for five years. Heck, I wasn't even through a mortal lifetime yet. Was Abaddon that old? Older? What was the future like? What would it be, when the whole world had changed? If I had tired of the fighting and the killing in five years, where would I be in one hundred? Where would I be in ten thousand?

"No smart answer?" he asked. "No idealistic retort? Maybe now you begin to understand what the Beast has to offer? Torturing the angel has its enjoyment, but even that will grow old in a millennia or two."

He showed himself then, stepping out into the open, his body barely visible to me through the shroud of panic he threw out around him.

212

"This isn't about me," I said. "This is about the billions of people who live here."

"Think, child. One hundred years is a millisecond to those who cannot die. One hundred years and nearly every single person you are protecting today will be dust. All any of them lose is one hundred years. What do you gain?"

Rebecca had tried to recruit me. Rachel had tried to recruit me. Even Sarah had in her own way. None had made a case quite like Abaddon, but how could they? He was a destroyer, like the Beast. In fact, he had been made in that mold. He understood life and time in a way that they couldn't. What did I gain, fighting against them and surviving? More war? More killing? More death?

"*Landon*," Ulnyx said, trying to get my attention.

Ten thousand years. Could I picture doing anything for ten thousand years?

"*Landon*," Josette said.

"You're hesitation proves what you know to be true," Abaddon said. "Mortals think in such short terms, because it is all they have. You are a Divine. There is a bigger picture for you to look at."

I was looking at it, and I didn't like what I saw. Emptiness, hopelessness, sameness. Death, destruction, loss.

"*Landon*," Ulnyx and Josette shouted, together.

It was like an electric shock. I looked at the Deliverer, hot in my hands, the once glowing scripture turning black. Somehow, he was overpowering it.

I closed my eyes and focused, pushing my own power to my hands, trying to bypass the bracelet and feed it directly through into the sword. It must have worked, because the darkness began to retreat again. Abaddon shrieked, and attacked.

How do you fight a creature shrouded in blackness, when you could never be sure of where his actual form was? He had dug his claws deep into my shoulder and

213

thrown me to the ground before I had a chance to find out.

The Deliverer wasn't enough to keep him from hurting me, I realized. Not when I had my hands full holding off the life sap that came from his innate design. I rolled to my feet in time to hop back away from the darkest part of him, and then struck out at it with the sword. It sliced only through air.

"Your weapon is impressive," Abaddon said, shifting himself so I could see his fanged mouth, his dark skin and sharp red eyes. "I have not seen its like before."

"That's because you were trapped in the Box, like a chump," I said, focusing and leaping towards one of the walls, avoiding a black blade that had shot from somewhere within his shroud. I bunched my feet against it and shot towards him, stabbing downwards where his head had been.

Except it wasn't there anymore. A leg came up at me, but I blocked it with the flat of the blade and spun myself over, landing on my feet. I jumped at him again, the Deliverer raised to strike from directly overhead.

He flowed out of the way like water, and a claw came out and caught me in the chest, holding me impaled. I coughed on blood filling my lungs, but turned the blade and lashed out at him anyway. He let me go, sidestepping the weapon.

"It has been so long since anyone has challenged me like this," he said. "It's an honor."

I wasn't expecting that. I brought the blade up and deflected two more strikes, and then went back on the offensive. I could never seem to get close, his dark, shrouded form slipping away as if it were carried by the wind.

"Just freaking die," I shouted, launching another flurry of thrusts and slashes, searching for him within the darkness.

He only laughed, and then clawed my face, sending me tumbling backwards.

"One last true challenge before the end," he said, suddenly sounding tired.

"Thank you, diuscrucis."

I couldn't see him, because he'd ripped out my eyes. I couldn't See him, because of the bracelet. I held the Deliverer in my hand, but I knew it was over, because he would kill me before I healed. We both knew it.

The bracelet. It wasn't doing anything to help me right now, but I couldn't pull it off without dropping the sword. Could I survive his power on my own for that long? I had no idea, but I needed to find out.

I let the hilt fall from my fingers, and reached over to the bracelet, ripping it from my wrist and dropping it. I focused, fighting against the despair and desperation, sure that he was right on top of me. I could feel the pressure against my soul, needling in to tear it apart.

I reached for the Deliverer again, but a clawed hand caught mine and held it. "I will enjoy the taste of your essence," Abaddon said. I could feel his breath against my face, and my eyes began to regain themselves.

Ten thousand years. At least I wouldn't have to worry about it anymore. I got a blurry view of the demon's face right on top of mine, opening to literally eat my soul.

A gust of wind, a loud crunch, and Abaddon was gone.

I grabbed the sword and got up. Adam was laying against a wall, covered in blood. Abaddon was near him, getting back to his feet. I didn't waste any time.

"Sorry to be less than honorable," I said, grabbing his neck with my free hand. "But... you know." I brought the Deliverer forward, into empty air. "What the...?"

There was a dark spot on the ground, like a pool of spilled oil. The black tendrils of his power were retreating into it, condensing into a shrinking point of evil.

"He's retreating," Adam said. "Back to Hell."

The angel was still against the wall, and he looked completely dazed. He stared back at me with one eye open, the other with a gash over it, hissing from the demon's poison.

I ran over to him. "I guess it's your lucky day," I said, handing him the sword. As soon as he took it in his hand, the wound stopped sizzling, and began to heal.

He looked at the Deliverer, his eyes wide. "Amazing," he said, with reverence.

"Not that amazing," I replied. "It wasn't enough to stop Abaddon from kicking my ass."

"It wasn't designed to stop Abaddon," Adam said. "He had already been dealt with when the Blades were created. Lucifer poured so much power into him, we knew he wouldn't gift another like that."

I wanted to pick him up by the neck and punch him. "You couldn't have told me that before I challenged him to a duel?"

He chuckled. "That would have been entirely detrimental to your confidence."

I still wanted to punch him, but he had a point. Instead, I held out my hand and helped him to his feet. "You saved my life, again."

"You know what you can give me in return." He held the sword out to me. "Just not yet."

Except, there was one promise I wouldn't be able to deliver on. The only question was who was I lying to? I was glad I didn't have to decide that yet.

I went back to where Abaddon had knocked me down, picked up the bracelet, and returned it to my wrist.

"We need to find Avriel, and be quick about it. The Beast knows we're here. If he knows Abaddon isn't anymore, he won't be a happy camper."

CHAPTER TWENTY-TWO

We found him in the largest of the golden temples, naked and bound to the ground by chains. Runes ran up the length of them until they reached the manacles themselves, which were ordinary metal. He was filthy, covered in his own blood, which had been splattered around the room so often that it was nearly a dark red coat of paint on top of the floor. Spread out on either side of him, beyond his reach, were his wings, somehow shorn off without killing him.

I had my own anxiety about facing him, even before we had entered the temple. Seeing what the Beast and Abaddon had put him through, it took an extra helping of courage to continue forward.

"You."

That was all he said when he saw me. Despite what he had been through, he was defiant.

"Avriel," Adam said, going down to one knee. "We've come to save you, brother."

The archangel looked at him. "You've come to save me? Save yourself, brother. Get away from this one before he breaks whatever promises he's made to you."

Adam turned to me, a questioning look in his eyes. I ignored it.

"Avriel," I said. "I'm sorry."

That was all I said. No excuses, no trying to weasel out of it. I had spent hours trying to think of a way to explain, but in the moment I knew there wasn't one. I got down on my knee and bowed my head, ready to take whatever he dished out.

There was silence for at least ten seconds. Finally, he let out a huff of air. "I felt the demon retreat. You came back for me, and you apologized with sincerity. The Lord would not approve if I could not find it in my soul to forgive you. Rise, diuscrucis, and help me get away from this place."

"*Well done, Landon,*" Josette said.

I got to my feet and walked over to the chains. A single stroke from the Deliverer not only snapped them, but made them disintegrate entirely. I pulled the manacles off with my bare hands.

"What manner of weapon is that?" Avriel asked. He rubbed his wrists as they began to heal. The wings stayed mangled on the floor.

"A weapon of the Lord," Adam said. "Created after your disappearance." He rose to his feet and approached the archangel, wrapping him in a hug. "I am honored."

"Thank you," Avriel said. He looked at his blood-soaked wings. "My days of flight are behind me it seems."

"Take the sword," I said, holding it out to him. "It will heal you."

He surprised me by shaking his head. "Let it be a reminder to us all. The value is in survival, not in lamenting our wounds."

"I can't get you out of here any other way," I said. "Adam can only carry one of us."

Avriel laughed. "Fear not for me, diuscrucis. The wings are for more local travel. Besides, we won't be alone for much longer."

Before I could ask him what he meant, sixteen seraph charged into the temple, organizing in a circle around us. I didn't need to ask who all of them were; I already knew. The Inquisitors, and their backup.

"Adam." A woman stepped forward, with long wavy blonde hair and an equally long face. She was a little bit pudgy, a little bit butch, and she exuded power.

"Kassie," Adam said, dropping to his knee once more.

She turned to the archangel. "Avriel. It is an-" That was when she noticed his wings, and all the blood. "What has been happening here?"

"Kassie," I said, stepping towards her. "It's-"

Her sword was out and headed towards me before I could finish my greeting. I brought the Deliverer up in plenty of time to block it, but I didn't appreciate her attitude. When the swords met, hers cracked and crumbled to dust.

Her eyes grew wide. "Is that?"

"The Deliverer," Adam said. "But why did it just shatter your blade?"

Kassie didn't say anything. She looked at the other assembled angels. Then her face changed.

"Darn," the Beast said. "You got me." A small demonic dagger appeared in his hand, and he lunged at Avriel.

The archangel didn't flinch. He put his hand out and caught the Beast's wrist, twisting and breaking it with ease.

"Ouch," the Beast said, his other hand coming around in a fist and slamming into Avriel's face. The archangel fell backwards.

I rushed to help him, but everything erupted in chaos, with the Beast's servants turning on the loyal angels. "Adam," I shouted, getting the angel's attention. I threw him the Deliverer, and shifted.

He caught the blade and turned, just in time to block one of the angel's attacks. As had happened with Kassie, the sword shattered when it came into contact

219

with the Canaan Blade. The seraph tried to back away, but Adam caught him with the tip of the Deliverer, and it tore through him, the wound opening with a blinding white light. The seraph didn't turn to ash. He vanished.

I heard an angel try to sneak up behind me, and I leaned on my hands and kicked back with Ulnyx's powerful hinds, feeling claws ripping through flesh and sending the angel flying. Then I brought the legs back in and used them to spring towards another of the now fallen Inquisitors, grabbing his neck in my jaws as his blade smacked into my side. I didn't even notice such a puny wound, and I took a sick pleasure in feeling the crunch of his spine in my teeth.

"*Not bad*," Ulnyx said. "*You're getting better at being me every time you shift.*"

The statement made me catch myself. It was too easy to be corrupted by the Great Were's power if I didn't keep myself grounded. I turned and looked for Avriel, finding him still going hand to hand with the Beast. He was more than holding his own, and had managed to knock the dagger form his hand.

"Getting sick of losing yet?" I asked the Beast, coming up from behind and grabbing him. Avriel might have been able to kick the crap out of the host all day, but without a weapon all the damage would just heal.

"Who says I'm losing?" He twisted in my grip, trying to turn around. I focused and tightened it, keeping him straight.

"You're down one Abaddon. I've got the Box and Avriel. I've got Sarah. I've got a bracelet that hides my location from you, and I've even got a pretty sweet sword. Where exactly are you coming out ahead?" I brought my forearm around his neck. He grabbed it and fought against the motion, knowing that I was getting in position to break it.

Somehow, he managed to slip the move, ducking his head under my arm, turning and elbowing me in the stomach. He followed up with a punch that launched me across the room.

"You don't have Avriel yet," he said. He held out his hand, and the knife flew into it. Avriel was coming at him, ready for another round. He turned in one smooth motion, and the dagger launched from his hand and pierced the archangel's heart. "I just wanted you to think you were winning, so it would hurt more when I did this." He motioned with his hand, and Avriel's entire torso collapsed inward on the dagger. His expression was one of surprise, and then he fell to ash.

"The Divine aren't the only ones who know how to channel power with symbols," he said, laughing. "Let's see how well Avriel's Box works for you without Avriel."

I didn't say anything. I just stared at the pile of dust that used to be Avriel the Just. I could hear Josette crying in the back of my soul, and I could even feel the shock of the Were at the sudden turn of events. I felt sick to my stomach, the hope and despair pouring in as though Abaddon were still standing right outside the door. All the while, the Beast laughed.

"Keep underestimating me, kid," he said. "I'll find out where you've got Sarah stashed sooner or later. I know it's somewhere in New York, thanks to the hours this sack of feathers I'm wearing spent chasing around after your sidekick. I'm just glad she came in useful after all, she was almost as much of a loser as you."

He smiled his stupid smile, and left her body.

I walked over to Avriel and knelt down over the ashes, my eyes threatening to fill with tears, my heart ready to burst. I heard footsteps, and looked back. Adam was approaching, along with five other seraph.

"Using the sword told the angels where I was," I said. "It's all the Beast needed." I turned back to the ashes. "He was our only hope."

Adam put a hand on my shoulder. "We'll figure something out. The Inquisitors are with you. What's left of us, anyway."

It didn't bring me any comfort. "We need to go back to the church, and meet up with the others. We need to tell them what happened. I don't know if we can recover from this one. Even Malize thought Avriel was the only one who could make the Box strong enough to keep the Beast contained. Without him? I just don't know."

I stood up and faced the other angels. There were two men and three women, of varying ages and features. They all looked upset at the loss of the archangel.

"Do you believe in the Beast now?" I asked them.

"We do, Landon," Adam said.

"This fight isn't about Heaven and Hell. It's about survival. For all of us. Can you abide by that? Because I can tell you right now, you *will* have to fight side by side with demons if we're going to take him out."

The angels weren't happy about that, but they didn't argue.

"We'll do what we must," one of the women said. She was dark-skinned, and spoke with a thick Haitian accent.

"Which of you is the First?"

The same woman stepped forward. "I am. I speak for the Inquisitors. We will help you however we can."

"Can you get us some more angels?" I asked.

She smiled. "We can try."

I held out my hand, motioning for Adam to give me the Deliverer. Joe was going to do his best to kill me for this, but Adam handed the sword to me, and I handed it to the woman.

"What's your name?" I asked her.

"Fredeline." She gazed at the Deliverer, holding it with reverence.

"Fredeline, it appears the Deliverer will tell you who is true, and who is a servant. Use it to root out the faithful, the ones that are willing to join you."

She brought the blade to her lips and kissed it. "I will," she said.

222

"Starting with my own." She brought the sword to each of the remaining angels. Each of them put their lips to the sword, including Adam.

"This is a temporary truce, diuscrucis," she said. "Once the Beast is taken care of, it will be business as usual."

Somehow, I doubted anything would be usual once this was done, but I nodded.

"Then we will take our leave of you," Fredeline said. "Adam, stay with Landon. He needs someone to keep him out of trouble."

Adam bowed to her, and the angels left the temple.

"Why didn't they turn to ash?" I asked him, seeing that Avriel's wings were still lying on the floor.

"He rejected them," Avriel said. "The wings don't make us what we are. Our faith does."

I knew there was a deeper meaning somewhere in there, but I wasn't in the mood to look for it. The Beast had won this round, and negated every other victory we had scored along with it. It was a challenge to keep my head up and keep fighting, but I knew the stakes.

"To the bat-cave, then," I said, the humor feeling flat, and falling flat.

We walked out of the temple, and Adam tucked his arms under my shoulders.

I didn't even notice the flight.

CHAPTER TWENTY-THREE

"What are we going to do?" Sarah asked.

We were all gathered in the nave of the church, after having forced a reluctant Father Tom to close it off to worshippers. I hated to ask him to do it, but the church was the only place we had that felt somewhat safe. Rebecca's place under the Statue of Liberty may have been a viable alternative, but it was too hard to get into and out of. Still, he had submit without complaint, after I gave him the short version about what had happened to Avriel. He had been crushed to hear about the death of an archangel, and had retreated to his office and locked the door.

"I feel like the 2006 Yankees," Obi said. "Up three games to none, looking like a lock for the Series, and then pow! Sox kick our ass."

"Maybe we're the Red Sox?" Adam suggested. "Down, but not out."

"We need to find someone who can understand Avriel's work," I said. "His design. Malize said there's a lot of math involved, so maybe we just need Stephen Hawking or something."

Obi huffed. "Man, it takes him an hour to say one sentence. How long would it take him to tell us how to alter the Box?"

"I'm open to suggestions," I replied. "Come on guys, we've got negative time to find a solution."

"Landon, do you remember when we met at the tower in Thailand?" Charis asked. "I told you I might know someone who knew about the Box?"

I did remember. I tried to think of who she was referring to, but she knew too many people to cherry pick one of them from her memories. "Yeah, but if your source is reliable, why didn't you push him on us earlier?"

She shrugged. "I didn't say he was reliable. I just said he might know about the Box. He's more of a last resort."

"Which is where we're at," Obi said.

"Sad, but true," I agreed. "Who is he?"

"He's a demon. I think Dante knows him. His name is Alichino."

"It doesn't ring a bell," I said.

"His name means harlequin. He used to serve in Hell, but he got kicked out and sent back to Earth for allowing someone to escape their torture."

"That doesn't sound like much of a punishment," Obi said.

"For a demon who was created in Hell, and wants to stay in Hell, Earth is the worst punishment there is."

Obi huffed again.

"Okay," I said. "So, where do we find him, and why do you think he can help us with the Box?"

"Brazil. I'm not sure he can help us with the Box, but I know he was obsessed with it. He always wanted to be the one to find it and free Abaddon. He was hoping that Lucifer would be so grateful, he would let him go back to Hell."

"Is he good at math?" I asked.

Charis nodded. "He claims that he can prove the Euler-Mascheroni constant is irrational."

"Whatever that means," Obi and I both said in unison.

"We've got to go find this Alichino. Melody?"

The angel had been quiet during the conversation. She had taken the news about Kassie in stride, but she looked pissed that she hadn't guessed at her true allegiance. "Yes, Landon?"

"Can you go find Fredeline, and stick with her? She'll need someone to lead her to us when we're ready for them to join the fun."

She got to her feet and nodded, walking over to Obi and kissing him on the cheek. "See you around, mate," she said with a smile.

"Don't be long," Obi replied.

She winked at him, and headed out of the church.

"O-"

"Don't even tell me I'm not coming," Obi said.

There was a rift in Brazil. "Fine, you're in. Charis, you too. We need Vilya to get us there."

"I want to come," Sarah said.

"No," I said. "I'm sorry. I wish you could, but you're safer here. The Beast is stepping up his game, and we need to stay focused on the task, not on protecting you."

She frowned, but stayed quiet.

"Besides," Charis said. "We need to stay inconspicuous. We can't do that trailing a big entourage."

"Which is why you want Thomas and I to stay here?" Adam asked.

I nodded. "Hold down the fort. With any luck we won't be gone more than an hour or two."

"The First asked me to keep an eye on you," Adam reminded me.

226

"If she stops by, tell her I'm in the bathroom. Izak, can you come unlock the door for us?"

The demon stood up and followed us as we descended the stairs into the church basement. He knelt down in front of the rift and used his good hand to scratch out the runes to connect this one to the one in Brazil. He did it fast, almost impatiently, and started walking away as soon as it flared to life.

"Thanks, Izak," I said.

He waved his hand at me and left.

"He's in a good mood," Obi said.

"You wouldn't be too happy if you lost your hand," I said.

"True."

"Are you boys ready?" Charis asked.

Obi shrugged and walked in. We followed behind him.

"Where are we?" I asked. We had stepped out into a small room encased in stone, with a metal door at the north end. "No, wait. Let me guess." I knew a little bit about Brazil. "Christ the Redeemer, in Rio?"

"You're getting good at this," Charis said.

"Whoa, hold on." Obi pointed up at the ceiling. "There's a demon rift under a huge statue of Jesus Christ?"

"It's under the chapel too," Charis replied. "Look, I didn't put it here. Alichino might have. He has an irreverent sense of humor."

"He's a demon. Doesn't that just come with the territory?" Obi asked.

"You asked," Charis said.

"Touche," Obi replied.

"So, how to we find Alichino?"

The door swung open. A small demon stood there. He was three feet tall, with a long snout and leather skin, the left half of which was black, the other half white. He was wearing a pair of tight lycra bicycle shorts and Pumas, and holding a thick book under a spindly arm.

"You don't find Alichino, diuscrucis. Alichino finds you."

I laughed. Could it actually be this easy? "You knew-"

"No," he said, before I could finish. "Well, yes. But, no. Dante looked me up and asked me if I could help you. Me and him go way back. You have the Box?"

Charis took it from a purse at her hip. When the demon saw it, his eyes lit up.

"Wow. You really do have it?" He scampered over, reaching for the artifact.

Charis pulled it away. "Hold on. You don't get to touch it until you agree to help us. In blood."

He snorted. "My word isn't good enough for you? Even if Dante vouches for me?"

"You have a reputation," she said.

His laugh sounded like a chainsaw. "Okay, fine." He reached down and produced a small knife from his sneakers. "I promise to help you with whatever you need me to do with the Box. In exchange, you'll get me back to Hell." He cut his finger and held it up.

Charis looked at me, and then took the knife. She cut her finger, and put it to his. "I promise we'll do our best to get you back to Hell, in exchange for helping us with the Box."

I hadn't made the agreement, so I didn't feel the pressure of the binding, but I knew Charis would. Alichino laughed again and reached for the Box once more. Charis handed it to him.

"Amazing," he said, turning it over and over in his three-fingered hand. "Do you see these lines?" He traced some of the angel scripture in a fine pattern. "The calculations to reach this kind of simple complexity are beyond insane."

"So, you understand it?" I asked.

He flicked his head towards me. "I've been studying everything I could about Avriel's Box since the day that bastard Bonturo tricked me. I know you guys don't like Abaddon much, but he could have sent me back just by touching me and willing it. Anyway, yeah I understand it. I learned to read the seraphim scripture so I could reverse engineer the calculus. The best mortal nerds would have an orgasm if they could read the source code."

"Wow, nice choice of words," Obi said.

Alichino laughed again. "Yeah, I knew Avriel got trapped in there, even if nobody else did. Well, until they let him out I guess." He held up his book. "I can show you the math if you want."

"How about summarizing?" I said.

He looked disappointed. "Fine. He missed an exponent in the containment algorithm."

"How about summarizing in English?" Obi asked.

Alichino rolled his eyes. "Look, you want to keep something behind an electrified fence, you need to make sure you have enough juice to power the whole fence, right? You don't cover the whole fence, it's all useless. Are you following me?"

"He didn't have enough charge for the fence?" Obi said.

"Exactly. He fed his power into the Box, but not enough. He had two choices then. One, give up and let Abaddon keep eating everything. Two, give it more power. The only way he could satisfy the equation was to feed himself to the Box with Abaddon. Bada-bing, bada-boom, he's stuck inside."

"Fine," I said. "We already know most of this. The question is, how do we feed it enough power to trap the Beast inside, and hold him?"

The demon stopped laughing, and looked at me. "Are you serious?"

229

"I'm afraid so."

"Look, there's some fuzzy math to calculate the power of a demon, or an angel. Leave enough wiggle room over the top, and you're good to go. There's no way to quantitate the power of that thing."

"We have it on good authority that it can be done," Charis said. "We can up the innate 'charge' by converting the seraphim scripture to the Templar language."

"Templar?" he asked.

"The original writing of the first children of God," she replied. "If the Divine symbols were solar panels, Templar script is the most efficient at conversion."

"Ooh," Alichino said. "That sounds exciting."

"I'll teach it to you. Then you need to figure out how to use it to maximize the charge."

The demon squealed with delight. "What are we waiting for?" he asked.

As soon as we were back in the church basement, Charis shooed us away so she could share what she knew with the demon. Is wasn't that we couldn't have stuck around if we wanted to; but who wanted to?

I found Sarah in the vestibule, kneeling in front of a statue of the Virgin Mary. She had her hands clasped in prayer, her head down. I stood behind her and waited. There was nothing else to do. I knew she would know I was there.

After a few minutes, she lifted her head and stood up. "Hello, brother," she said, turning to face me.

"Hey, kiddo," I said. "I was just checking in with you. Making sure you're okay."

She smiled. "I'm good. Better than ever, believe it or not."

"Not afraid of the end of the world?" I was.

"I have to make choices," she said. "I can choose to believe that what I've

230

seen is all that can be, or I can choose to believe we can change it."

"What do you see?"

"It wouldn't help you to know, any more than it helps me."

Fair enough. "Do you still kill me?"

Just the slightest change in her face, and I knew that was still the future she saw. "Yes. I'm not going to let that happen."

"I know you won't," I said. I wasn't sure how much I believed it. If it came down to it, I would have to make sure she didn't.

"How is mother?" she asked.

I smiled. "She's fine," I said, tapping on my head.

"When this is over, do you think I'll be able to spend more time with her?"

"If I'm here, she'll be here. You know how to get into my head, so I don't see why not."

She returned my smile, and then walked over to be and gave me a hug. "I love you, brother."

I rubbed her back, my eyes fixed on the Mary statue behind her. "I love you, too."

"Landon!"

I let Sarah go and turned my head. Thomas was running towards me.

"What's going on?" I asked.

He stopped and motioned for us to follow. "You've got to see this."

We followed him out of the vestibule and around to the left, into the hallway that led to Father Tom's office. The door was finally open again, and most of the crew had crowded around. I pushed my way in.

"What's the panic?" I asked.

Father Tom was sitting in his chair, his face completely pale, a look of absolute fear written across it. There was a simple wooden box sitting on his desk now, an old AM radio.

"We're getting reports of a civil war breaking out in the Indian city of Mumbai," the voice on the radio was saying. "People on the scene say it is complete chaos in the streets, with civilians attacking one another across the city. According to our sources, the rioters are even going into apartments and attacking people in their homes. The exact cause of the unrest is unknown, but it has been reported that it started at a downtown restaurant, when two of the patrons got into an argument, and quickly escalated from there."

I took a deep breath and looked around the room, at Father Tom, Sarah, Adam, Thomas, Izak, and Obi. "This is not good." I felt a small twinge in my gut. The balance, beginning to slide. We were running out of time. Was the Beast going for the end zone, or trying to lure us out of hiding? "This is really not good."

"What should we do?" Thomas asked.

I looked around the room at them. "We can't do anything right now. We have to wait for Alichino."

"Landon, there are people dying out there," Obi said.

"I know," I said. "There's nothing we can do. The Beast is possessing them, making them attack one another. If we kill one, he'll just take another, and another. Whether we take the lives or he does, the end result is the same."

"We have to stop him," Adam said.

"How?" I asked. "Right now, we can't. Believe me, I know you want to do something. You aren't the ones who can feel the balance starting to-"

A pounding on the door of the church interrupted me. It wasn't a knock. It sounded like somebody was trying to break it down.

"Think they found us?" Obi asked.

"How?"

"They've been fighting out there for hours," Thomas said. "They've stayed mindful of the balance. I think they're done with that approach."

The pounding intensified.

"Izak, go cover the front door. Adam, take the east entrance. Thomas and Obi, you're on the west. I'm going to go check things out from the roof. We need to give Charis and Alichino time."

"What do you want me to do?" Sarah asked.

"Stay here. Izak, if you can't hold the front you need to get Sarah out through the rift." I tried to think of where. "Take her to Brazil, and stay there."

Izak nodded, and headed for the front of the Church. Thomas, Adam, and Obi headed off to take up their own positions, while Father Tom bowed his head in prayer.

I made my way down the hall. Opposite the stairs to the basement were the stairs to the belfry. I could hear Charis speaking to Alichino down the steps. She had to know the balance was shifting, but she was speaking with a sense of patience and calm. The demon was cooing at her explanations.

"*We're screwed,*" Ulnyx said as I scampered up the steps.

"*Whose side are you on?*" I asked him.

"*It looks like the wrong side.*"

The belfry was a small room, with the bell a dozen feet up in a small tower. I focused and jumped, reaching the tower and anchoring myself with my feet against both sides. I peeked out, and then ducked back in just in time to keep my head from being cut off by an angel. I heard the sound of Obi's Desert Eagle down below.

The seraph crouched down to find me inside the tower, and I wrapped my hand around his throat. I shifted my other hand to a claw, drove it through chest, and then tossed him away. Before I could begin looking for the next target, I felt the heat of flames headed towards me. I let myself drop, falling to the floor and dropping to my stomach as a gout of hellfire roared through the tower, and it exploded in a mess of mortar and dust. I rolled out of the way just in time to keep the white-hot and melting bell from landing on me.

"Freaking fire demons," I said, getting to my feet. The whole building shook, and I knew it had landed on the roof.

I shifted, bunching my hinds and leaping to the gaping hole in the ceiling. I landed on the roof in front of the demon. It had a huge blade raised over its head, ready to bring it down into the church. A pair of angels stayed airborne behind it, letting it lead the assault.

I closed my eyes and focused, willing myself to be stronger, pushing the focus so hard I thought my head would explode.

The sword came down.

I caught it.

It was blazing with hellfire, but I had made the skin of my claws so tough that it couldn't penetrate, and I didn't feel it. Neither did I feel the bite of the edge. It started to sink into the flesh, but I had forced the huge hands to be as hard and dense as adamantium. I heaved against the force, muscles flexing and threatening to pop, feet scratching along the roof to stay rooted. I focused even harder still, and pulled the huge blade from the demon's hands. It was way too big for me to wield it, but I had another option.

I pulled off the bracelet.

It was useless right now. Even if he didn't know where I was, he would soon enough. As soon as it had fallen down the hole into the church, I focused on the tremendous sword, pulling it around in a wide arc. The fire demon saw it coming, and it raised its arms to defend itself.

It needn't have bothered.

The blade went right through the demon's arms, and right through its neck, severing its head. It fell backwards in the middle of a huge screech, one of its wings slamming into a waiting angel, the sharpness of it leaving a huge gash. The angel hadn't attacked yet, so he hadn't fallen. The demon's poison killed him before the demon had even hit the ground.

The bracelet gone, I focused on my Sight. I wished I hadn't.

If the church was an island, the enemy outside was the Pacific Ocean.

I jumped back into the hole, grabbed the bracelet, and ran downstairs. I scrambled out into the main part of the church. I could see Obi with a knife in hand at the west entrance. The door had been blasted in, and a group of devils was trying to get past him. I found Thomas on the floor. He wasn't moving.

I turned around. Adam had drawn some kind of runes on the east door, and it seemed to be holding for now. He was on his knees in prayer.

"Adam!" I shouted. Obi needed help. He didn't respond. "Adam!"

He was ignoring me. I ran over to him. I was reaching for his shoulder when he stood and turned. "Sorry, Landon," he said. "I was just calling for backup."

"Backup?"

I felt a rush of air, and then Fredeline, the Inquisitors, and Melody came down the stairs from the hole in the roof. The First was carrying the Deliverer.

"It looks like you needed us sooner than you expected," she said on her way by.

She raised the blade and started yelling and running for the devils attacking Obi. It attracted their attention and his, and he watched dumbfounded while she tore into them with the sword. The devils in front crumbled to dust as the weapon dug into them, and those in the back started screaming and trying to run. She and the Inquisitors followed them out, while Melody stopped next to Obi.

"Are you hurt?" she asked.

He shook his head. "Nah. It'll take more than those a-holes to put me down." He looked over to where Thomas was laying. His voice dropped to little more than a whisper. "We weren't all so lucky."

"Thanks," I said to Adam, before going over and kneeling down next to Thomas. He was dead.

"I'm sorry," I said to his corpse, reaching out and pushing his eyes closed with my hand. He hadn't turned to dust, and I wasn't sure why. I guess Purgatorians didn't get such a clean end.

"*He died well*," Josette said.

"*For once you said something I agree with*," Ulnyx remarked.

It didn't make it any easier to take. I closed my eyes and grimaced, feeling the twisting of my gut from the balance continuing its slide. I closed my eyes and focused, using my Sight to check on our situation. I could sense the line of Inquisitors outside, digging into the mass of enemies around us, led by Fredeline and the Canaan Blade.

"What now?" Obi asked.

When I opened my eyes, he was kneeling on the other side of Thomas, looking down on him with his fist to the fallen angel's heart.

"We need to hold out until Charis and the harlequin are done. I just hope that happens before the balance tips." I got to my feet. "I'm going to go check on Izak. Watch the stairs, they'll be coming through there next."

Obi gave me the thumbs up, and he and Melody joined Adam by the stairs up to the demolished belfry.

I moved through the nave and out the back doors to where Izak was sitting, cross-legged on the floor. He had scratched a bunch of demonic runes in front of the doors, and it looked like so far none of the other demons had tried to pass it.

"Having a nice rest?" I asked him.

He turned his head, and shrugged.

"Keep doing what you're doing," I said, starting to turn to go ask Charis for a time estimate. I felt a wave of heat blast towards me, and for a split-second I thought it was my Sight, but then the doors of the church exploded inward behind a blast of hellfire.

I dropped flat onto my stomach as the splintered wood and flames roared overhead, threatening to melt the skin right off my back. I could see Izak stretched out on the floor too, and he didn't look very happy. As the flames subsided, a new demon joined the party.

She was without a doubt the most attractive creature I had ever seen, with long, shining black hair, olive skin, and crystal eyes. She was wearing only slightly more than nothing, a sheer dress that only barely covered the important parts, that shimmered and changed colors as she moved, and gold bracelets that ran up perfectly shaped arms and legs.

She walked into the church, stepping onto Izak's runes. They exploded in another round of light and heat, the blast so strong I had to look away. When I turned my head back, the stone walls of the church had started reducing to slag, but the woman was still standing there, unharmed.

"Mephistopheles," she said. "It's been a long time. Still as predictable as ever, I see."

He rose to his feet and stared at her. He wasn't impressed by her beauty. In fact, he looked like he wanted to rip her face off with his bare hands.

"And you are?" I asked. I could see a swarm of demons beyond her, and the glow of the Deliverer at its center. She didn't seem to care about the angels at her back.

"Ardat Lili," she said. Her voice was as sultry and appealing as her body. I could feel myself reacting, despite any of my best intentions.

"*Keep it calm, meat,*" Ulnyx said. "*It's a bunch of crap. She's a succubus. Actually, she's the succubus. The original that all the other designs are based on.*"

He must have brought her out of Hell. She is something else, though."

Even with his warning, I could tell he was succumbing to her power too.

Izak wasn't. He charged towards her and threw a heavy punch. She slipped to the side, grabbed his arm, and planted her knee in his gut. Then she threw him backwards, sending him sliding along the floor.

"Where is she?" she asked.

She had to mean Sarah. I swallowed, feeling my body building up to some kind of freakish ecstasy, and my tongue moving almost of its own volition, ready to tell her what she wanted to know.

"*Landon,*" Josette shouted.

It snapped me out of it. I reached for Ulnyx' power, to shift and go on the offensive. I found myself cut off.

"*Ulnyx?*"

"*So beautiful,*" the Were replied. "*I don't want to hurt her.*"

She started walking towards me, her hips rocking from side to side, every action causing an equal and opposite reaction. I swallowed again, fighting against the waves of attraction and passion that were pouring out of her.

"Where is she?" she asked again. "I'll make it very worth your while to tell me."

I felt my mouth moving again. Then another shot of hellfire slammed into her, knocking her away. It didn't burn her though. It just made her more sexy, the shadows of the flames enhancing every perfect curve.

"*Landon,*" Josette shouted again.

I shook my head to clear it. The succubus was on her back, smoke pouring off her. She started to get up. Izak walked towards her, his hand out, ready to launch another round of fire.

"Stop," she said to him, a Command so strong it almost made my ears pop. Izak

238

stopped moving.

"*This is bad*," I said to Josette.

"*He'd have to send a demon that could stand up to Izak,*" Josette replied.

"Mephistopheles, help me up."

He reached out with his good hand. She took it, and he pulled her up. She turned and looked at me, and I felt her power reaching out.

"*How do I stop her?*" I asked. I could feel my body reacting again, and my mind returning to its sexy woman mush state.

"*Let me in*," she said.

She'd never asked to drive before, because unlike Ulnyx, she respected that my consciousness was mine. I gave it up to her easily, feeling the soul of her rising up and taking control.

The demon seemed to know it, as soon as it happened. "I can make it worth your while too, my innocent darling," she said. I could still feel her power. If Josette did too, she didn't show it. "No? Izak, kill them."

Izak took a step towards us.

"*How was this a good plan?*" I asked.

"Izak," Josette said. My lips moved, but the voice that came out was hers. "Izak, don't." The fiend paused.

Ardat Lili grabbed his shoulder, turned him and looked into his eyes.

"What?" she said. "You fell in love with an angel? You?"

"Izak," Josette said. "She wants to hurt me. She wants to take Sarah. You can't let that happen."

"No," the succubus said. "Mephistopheles, we have a past. You know what I can offer you. Kill her, kill the diuscrucis, and help me take the girl. I can give you everything you need, in his new universe."

Izak turned his head, looking back at us.

"Izak," Josette said. "You-"

Before she'd even finished speaking, the fiend's hand came up and wrapped around Ardat Lili's throat. He lifted her off the ground, while her eyes filled with fear.

"Izak, no," she said, her voice little more than a croak. "Think of the pleasure."

He smiled and nodded. He squeezed tighter, the palm of his hand igniting in hellfire as it sunk into her neck. She screamed in pain and anger, her body frantic to fight him off. He held on tight, pressing harder and harder, until she stopped moving.

He never let her go, and she turned to ash in his grip.

CHAPTER TWENTY-FOUR

We spent the next two hours trying to keep the Beast's forces from getting into the church and claiming Sarah. All the while, I could feel the balance twisting and rocking, like a glacier moving towards an inevitable end. It seemed as though the Beast had convinced half of Hell to join his cause, by the number of creatures that kept pouring into the area through an unseen rift, joining with a much smaller cadre of fallen angels. If it hadn't been for the Inquisitors and the Deliverer, I don't know that we would have lasted ten minutes.

We were still spread out at the different entrances, with Izak and I manning the gaping hole in the front of the church while Adam, Melody, and Obi took the rear. The angels roamed the streets, cutting a swath of destruction through the hordes, but it was all they could do to keep a small enough number from coming at the church that the rest of us could hold them back. I kept waiting for reinforcements from Heaven, or for the archangels to get themselves involved and the true meltdown to occur. It seemed they were willing to wait it out, as long as the balance didn't go too far.

"Landon!" Charis and Alichino came running through the doors behind us. The demon had the Box in his hand. I knew from a glance it didn't look any different.

"Good news?" I asked. I was tired, dead tired, having spent more of my time in Ulynx's skin than I would ever have wanted to. It was an unfortunate side effect that using his power made me overly arrogant and lustful. I had to fight against the bad thoughts that seeing her put into my head.

"I haven't figured out the conversions yet, no," Alichino said. "But I have done some calculations on the energy output. There's a way we can pump enough strength into the Box to make it the most power dense prison ever constructed."

I liked the news. I didn't like the way he gave it.

"But?"

"You have to inject it with the Beast's own energy."

I put my arm up to block the sword of an incoming devil, then brought my claws around and severed its head. I would have thought after killing a couple hundred of them, that they would have tried a different tactic. It was no wonder Hell hadn't won this war yet, despite vast numbers.

"So we have to trick him into powering the box?"

"Not exactly," Charis said.

There was only one other source of the Beast's energy I knew of.

"We have to power it?"

"Yes," Alichino said. "Both of you. You need to mix his pure energy with that of the true diuscrucis. It has to be a balance of all of the forms. Based on my calculations, that should get you a ten thousand percent improvement over Avriel's original design."

I kicked a devil out of the way, and turned to him. "Did you say ten thousand?"

The demon hopped up and down, excited. "Yes. Impressive, no? It's a combination of the power source and the Templar script. I can show you the math

242

downstairs if you'd like?"

"Just make it work," I said, looking at the Box. "You haven't changed anything."

"Landon," Charis said. "There's a catch."

Of course there was. There was always a catch. "What?"

"The Beast's power has to be pure. We need to find a way to empty our souls."

I shifted back to my human shape. "Izak, I need a few," I said. He looked over at us and nodded as he put his hand to a hell hound's forehead and crumbled it with a thought. I took Charis' hand and pulled her back to the nave.

"When you say pure, you're talking about-"

"Extraction," she said. "We have to get our absorbed souls out."

"Extraction isn't possible."

"*Lylyx said there was a djinn in Moscow,*" Ulnyx said. "*If you can get me back into my own meat, I'd kiss you.*"

I didn't know what to think, or how to react. I'd been carrying both the Were and Josette around with me for more than five years. I didn't know if I would have lived any of those without the power they had brought. I couldn't imagine what Charis was feeling. She'd had Vilya's soul for longer than that.

"It has to be," Alichino said. "There's no other way. I can show you the math?"

I shook my head. "Lylyx said she had heard there was a djinn in Moscow who could do it. I don't know where she heard it from, or how reliable the intel is, but that's all I've got."

"Then we go to Moscow," Charis said. "The slimmest thread is the strongest we've got right now, and let's face it - we can't stay here."

I had stuck Malize's bracelet in my pocket. I pulled it out now, and put it back on. Charis followed my lead.

243

"Go set up the rift," I said. "I need to round up the troops. It's time to retreat."

Charis and Alichino headed off to the basement. I ran back out to the front and got Izak's attention. "When I come back, head for the basement. We're getting out of here."

He responded with a short nod. I looked through the hole in the front, finding the glow of the Deliverer in the distance. Then I ran to Father Tom's office.

The priest was still at his desk, his head in his arms, a wet spot spreading from the arm of his vestment. He hadn't stopped praying and crying since the fighting had started. Sarah was there too, her head straight forward, her body stiff. I imagined she was watching as much of the battle as she could through Izak's eyes.

"Sarah," I said. A slight tremor in her form, and then she turned her head. "Get down to the basement. Charis and Alichino are there. We're leaving."

She got up and ran out the door.

I walked over to Father Tom, knelt down, and took his arm.

"Father, it's time to go. The demons are going to take the church."

He lifted his head and looked at me. His eyes were bloodshot and puffy.

"I could have been Touched," he said. "There was an angel once, she was such a beautiful lass. She offered to give me the power, because of my piety and faith. I turned her down. I said I couldn't continue to touch humanity with His word if I wasn't fully human myself. If I had been Touched, I think I could have saved this place."

I put my other hand on his back, and started lifting him from the chair. "You saved something a lot more important, Father," I said.

His eyes caught on mine. "Only if you win. Otherwise, we'll all be nothing more than a blip in time. A quickly forgotten blip in time."

The games of gods. It was a game I was determined to win. "Come with me," I said. Plain, old mortals couldn't go through the rifts, so I would need Adam to get him out of here.

I led him out into the nave, where Adam, Obi, and Melody were doing their best to hold off the hordes of demons pouring in from all sides. The altar of the church had been desecrated in the fighting, crucifix shredded by angry Hell spawn. I heard Father Tom gasp beside me, and I had to grab his arm to keep him standing.

"Time to go," I shouted from the back of the nave. Obi turned to acknowledge they had heard me. I couldn't help but wince when I saw the deep cut across his face. I couldn't be sure if his left eye was still functional or not beneath the torn flesh. "Adam, I need you."

The angel shoved his blade into a demon and hopped backwards, his body launching the full length of the nave. He spun as he landed in front of me.

"What do you need?" he asked.

I pulled Father Tom forward. "You need to get him to safety. Then, find Fredeline and tell her to bail. This isn't the fight we need to worry about right now. If you can get to Mumbai and scout the place out, great. Otherwise, meet us in Moscow. Oh, and see if you can get me a sword." If we managed to find a way to extract Ulnyx, I was going to need one.

He nodded, and took hold of Father Tom's shoulder. "Come with me, Father," he said, his voice gentle as he Calmed the priest. Father Tom followed without complaint, out to the stairs and up towards the hole in the church's roof. He had to fight through a few demons to get there, but he dispatched them without trouble.

I ran back out of the nave to the front of the church. Izak had retreated closer to the doors. "Come on," I said. He backed out with me, and we met up with Obi and Melody near the stairs.

245

The demons were still pouring into the building, overrunning the spaces we abandoned. I'd never imagined how much force they could actually bring to bear, if they had enough of a motivation to work together to do it. That none of the archfiends could manage the singular sense of purpose that the Beast had told me a lot.

"I can heal that, when we have a minute," I said to Obi when we reached the bottom of the stairs. Izak took up the rear, and held the flood of Hell from reaching us.

He wiped some blood away with his hand. "Just the eye would be good enough. A scar might be sexy."

"You don't need a scar to be sexy, mate," Melody said.

I looked to the back of the room. The rift was awash with hellfire. "Go. Now," I said.

Alichino went first, followed by Charis and Sarah, and then Obi and Melody. I tapped Izak on the shoulder, and motioned at the rift. We both made a run for it, and went through one behind the other.

A few demons managed to get through the rift before Charis could disconnect it. They didn't last long.

"First stop, Moscow," Alichino said, giggling.

"You think this is funny?" Obi asked, headed for the demon.

I put my hand up in front of him. "Let it go, Obi," I said.

He growled under his breath, and then lowered his guard. "So, what are we doing here?" he asked.

"We need to look for a djinn," Charis said. "That's all we know."

"Seriously?" Sarah said. "Do the words needle and haystack mean anything to you?"

"Whoa, whoa, whoa," I said, stepping into the middle of the gang. "Everybody take a deep breath and chill out." I felt the balance in my soul, resting on a

cliff and inching towards the ten-million-mile drop with every passing second.

"We're all on the same side. Let's get our crap together and come up with a plan."

"Okay," Obi said, sucking in a mass of air with his nose, and blowing it out

through mauled lips. "That hurts."

I put my hand to his face and closed my eyes, focusing on my palm, and his

skin beneath it. I felt for the damage, and willed it to repair, demanding it to

put itself back together. The act left me short of breath, but within a minute his

face was as good as new.

"Thanks, man," he said, reaching up and rubbing the new, pink, skin. "You

forgot to leave the scar."

"Shut up," I replied.

I needed some recharge time. Looking around, we all needed some recharge

time. None of us were going to get it.

"So, how do we find a djinn?" I asked. Between everyone present, we had to

have nearly three thousand years of experience to go on.

"Djinn are shape-shifters," Charis said. "They can be anyone, anywhere."

"Are they good or bad?" I asked.

"*Nobody knows*," Ulnyx said. "*Neither side wants to claim them.*"

"What do you mean nobody wants to claim them?" I said it out loud, so the

others would know I was talking to myself.

"*Nobody likes to talk about the djinn*," Josette said. "*They live like

mortals, though with a much longer lifespan, but they have Divine power. Some have

said that God created the djinn to keep an eye on humanity, because the angels were

too busy with the demons. Others have said that Lucifer created the djinn to cause

trouble for God's creation.*"

"What do you think?"

247

"I think it doesn't matter. We just need to find the one that supposedly lives here."

"If somebody heard the the djinn could do extractions, then somebody must know how to find him," Melody said. "Who in Moscow would be that somebody?"

I knew the answer. So did Charis. There was an archfiend in Moscow, a ruthless, cold, violent, and powerful woman who went by the name of Darya. She wasn't the most gifted with demonic runes, hellfire, or even personal combat, but in some ways that made her more of a challenge to deal with. She had risen to power through fear, intimidation, and manipulation, and held a tight grip over one of the most powerful vampire clans on Earth, as well as a pretty nasty pack of weres. The good news was that I knew where to find her.

"Darya," I said. "She should have a lead on any Divine stalking around the city, and probably anywhere in the former Soviet Republic."

"Great," Obi said. "Where do we find her?"

"We don't find her anywhere," I said. "I don't know about the rest of you, but my tank is getting low, and I'd rather avoid another confrontation right now. Charis and I will go talk to her, and see what we can find out. The rest of you should go to Mickey D's or something."

Obi sighed. "Yeah, I guess the whole lot of us headed for her HQ wouldn't make the right impression." He reached into his pocket and pulled out his cell. "Who wants Starbucks?"

CHAPTER TWENTY-FIVE

Charis and I split with the rest of the gang a few blocks before we reached the Stolnik building, leaving them to follow Obi to a nearby Starbucks. It was a shorter, older building that had been renovated recently to put a penthouse on the roof, a massive apartment that spanned the entire length and width of the building, complete with a pool, a yard, and, oddly enough, palm trees. The apartment had been paid for by a local architecture company, a front for the Stolyev family, a massive and far-ranging cadre of vampires who had been subjugated by the archfiend.

"How are you feeling?" I asked her, as we treaded the block up to the building. I couldn't throw my Sight out to check on the number of demons hanging out around us, so I was a little more tense than normal.

"Tired," she replied. "And a little apprehensive. Vilya and I have been together for some time. She gave herself up in Hell to be with me. Let's say we find the djinn, and he can do the extraction. What's going to happen to her?"

"We find her a body to take over," I said. "That's how the whole thing usually works." Ulnyx had tried to absorb my soul, and take my body after I destroyed his. He hadn't known what I was, and had been caught off-guard, allowing me to turn the tables on him.

Charis stopped walking and looked at me. "I know we can but... she defied
Lucifer by helping me escape. Can you imagine what will happen if we stop the
Beast, and the demons find out she's vulnerable?"

"You can still protect her."

"It's not the same, and you know it."

"I'm sorry," I said, putting my hand on her shoulder. "We don't have a
choice."

She nodded. "I know. You asked me how I was feeling. That's it. Neither one
of us likes it, but we'll do what we have to. Even if the outcome is scary, the
Beast winning this thing is much worse."

We kept walking until we reached the entrance to the Stolnik building. There
was a doorman standing outside, and a second man in a black suit standing behind
him. I didn't need my Sight to know he was a vampire.

"Good afternoon," the doorman said as we approached.

"Good afternoon," I replied. I looked over at the vampire and motioned for
him to join us as we entered the lobby.

He was short, but well-muscled, with cropped black hair and a thick face.
"Diuscrucis," he said. "I hadn't heard the Mistress was expecting you. Either of
you."

"She isn't," I replied. "We need to talk to her. To ask a favor, actually."

He smiled. "You need a favor? One moment." He leaned away, reaching into the
top of his shirt for the small microphone that would allow him to communicate with
the security upstairs. "The Mistress will see you, on the condition that you make
the deal in blood that you will come and go without a fight. She doesn't want to
waste so many of us stopping you."

Of course, she would never tell her subjects she was afraid of what the two of us together could do to her and her goons. She also didn't know we'd lost a bit

of our mojo since then, and that our worn state had reduced the juice further. I

don't know if we could have taken her if we needed to. I didn't want to find out. I

shifted my right index finger into a thick claw, and used it to slice open my left

thumb, and then Charis' left thumb. The vampire cut himself on a tooth, and we

pressed our thumbs together.

"Deal," Charis and I both said. I felt the weight of the binding. It wasn't

that strong, but it was an act of good faith that would put the archfiend at ease.

The vampire led us over to an elevator, separate from the rest. "It will take

you straight up," he said when the doors opened. We stepped in, and went up.

We ascended to the penthouse, and the elevator doors parted to reveal a huge,

open living space. It had lots of white leather furniture, some rare artwork,

ancient Chinese vases, and some strange apparatus hanging from the ceiling.

Attached to the chains and leather were two female vampires, both in skimpy leather

something or others, their backs raw and bleeding.

Darya stepped out from in front of them to greet us. She was an ugly one,

with features too large for her head, straw-like black hair, and a gaunt frame that

made everything on her face look even bigger. She was wearing a simple white frock,

and red stiletto heels.

"Charis, I thought you were on our side?" she reached up and unclasped the

two vampires. "Go get cleaned up," she Commanded. They rushed off to another part

of the apartment.

"I'm on my own side," she replied. "And Landon's."

Darya's smile was crooked. "So the Demon Queen is who now, I wonder?"

The question made me wonder too. It had been Charis, but that had been while

her allegiance had trended evil. Then it was Rebecca, but she was dead. I imagine

Ardat Lili could have made a claim, but she hadn't survived either. "Maybe it's you?" I said. "Although, I don't know if you want the title. Demon Queens don't seem to have much of a future lately."

She laughed. "Too true. Especially with the Beast making a mess of things."

"You know about the Beast?" Charis asked.

"I've heard the news reports, and I've been in touch with some lesser demons from New York who told me about a massive battle over a church. A church that you were supposed to be holed up in."

"We had to abandon ship," I said. "Anyway, the million dollar question is, where do you stand with the Beast?"

"Do you mean am I a servant?" She scowled. "I serve none but myself, and the Beast is threatening to ruin my lifestyle. Why do you think I let you up?"

"What do you know about a djinn who's been rumored to be hanging out in the city?" I asked.

"More than a little," she replied. "What is it worth to you?"

It was my turn to smile. "I think a better question is, what is it worth to you? That djinn may be our only chance of stopping the Beast from ruining your lifestyle."

She pursed her lips. "That is an enticing offer," she said. "I'll tell you what. You make a deal with me, in blood, that you'll leave me to control Moscow and its surrounds, unimpeded, for a hundred years, and I'll tell you everything I know."

"I'll give you one hundred years, if you promise not to reach outside of your area for more power. Plus, I want fifty of your best fighters."

"You're bargaining for my vampires?"

"And your weres. The djinn is useless if we can't get close to the Beast. If you've heard the news, you know he'll have a possessed army in the thousands by the time we go after him."

"Fifty won't be near enough to help you with that," she said.

"It will keep them busy. The possessed are mortal after all. Still, you're probably right. Let's make it a hundred years, for a hundred vampires and weres, plus everything you know about the djinn."

She looked down at her feet, and ground her stiletto into the floor while she thought. "Fine," she said at last. "I'll have them meet you at the rift in one hour."

She reached out with a finger and used her nail to slice open her arm. I cut my thumb again, and pressed it to her. "Deal," I said. The weight of it was heavier this time.

"His name is Kafrit. He's been in Moscow since Stalin was running the place, though he doesn't like to talk about those days. Before that, he spent a thousand years in Iran. You can usually find him in Solntsevo, running with the Brotherhood. He likes the high stakes games they play, and the men they can provide him. When he's laying low, he usually takes the form of a big black dog."

"Do you know about the rumors?"

"You mean soul extraction? I've heard he can do it, but I've never seen it done. Angels don't take souls, and demons never want to give up the power they've gained willingly. You'd want to part with the power of the Great Were?"

I didn't really, at least not while we still had the Beast to stand up against, but I had no choice. "It's complicated," I said. "Lots of math."

She laughed. "Tell the Brotherhood that Darya sent you. It will make things easier."

"On us, or on them?" Charis asked.

She didn't answer. "Unless you'd like to stay and take a turn in the machine with me, I believe our business is done." She motioned to the chains hanging from the ceiling.

"I think we're done," I said. "Remember the deal. One hour."

"You remember the deal, diuscrucis. One hundred years. Not a second less... But maybe a little more." She laughed, and walked away, headed in the same direction the vampires had gone.

"So, Solntsevo it is," I said. "Let's go get Obi so he can Google it for us."

Charis nodded. I could see the apprehensiveness return to her expression. I put my hand on her face.

"It'll be okay," I said, trying to sound more confident than I felt.

She put her hand over mine and gave me a forced smile. "Thanks for trying," she said.

We made our way back to the elevator, and out onto the street. Obi had given me directions to the Starbucks from our current location, and I traced them in my mind as we walked, hoping I got them right. I was pleased when the little green mermaid-circle came into view.

They were all sitting around a table, paper cups spread among them. Alichino was in the corner, looking impatient.

"It's about time," he said when he saw us. He hopped over the table. "I don't know how you stand this stuff. It tastes like somebody took one of my craps and let it soak in hot water for a while."

"Awww, man," Obi said. "That's disgusting."

The demon turned and picked up Obi's extra-syrup, extra-espresso latte. "This is disgusting."

"Nectar of the gods, man," he said, taking it from Alichino and downing the last swallow.

"I doubt that."

"Did you find him?" Sarah asked.

"We have a lead," I said. "We need to get to Solntsevo. Obi, can you look it

254

up?"

He took out his phone and started putting it in. "Twenty four kilos," he said. "We're gonna need a van or something."

I turned and headed outside. There was a UPS truck stopped across the street. I ducked my head back in. "I found a ride."

We piled in, with Obi taking the wheel. The driver came out of the office across the street just in time to watch us pull way. I felt kind of bad for the guy. Sarah thought it was hilarious.

"Did you see his face?" she asked.

I let her have her laugh. The opportunities were few and far between as it was.

It was about an hour to the small city, a city that I had expected to look a little more slummy, based on Darya's description of its inhabitants. I was surprised to find it reminded me of pretty much anywhere in the developed world. Sure, it had its older apartment buildings, its warehouses, and its seedy looking characters, but so did New York.

"An hour drive, great," Obi said. "We need to make this quick, man. How many people do you think the Beast can have kill each other in an hour?"

I had felt the balance sliding. Mumbai was big, but it was still only a fraction of the world population. It would take more than one city to trip the wire. At the same time, India as a whole had a lot of people, and the Beast's power was like a virus, spreading from soul to soul until it had covered the earth. It's speed would increase with each passing minute.

"That's an interesting question," Alichino said. "If you-"

"Spare us," Obi said.

"There's only one way to do this," I said. "Stop the truck."

They all looked at me curiously, but Obi pulled the truck to a stop. I hopped down and took a deep breath, focusing on strengthening my lungs.

"Kafriiiiitttttt," I shouted, as loud as I could. It was loud enough that the mortals who couldn't register my existence in their minds all stopped, dead silent, and looked around for it's source. I waited, and then shouted again.

Within a few minutes, a few muscle-bound guys in black cargos and grey vests turned up. Fiends.

"Hey guys," I said.

The looked at me, confused. There were still a few demons out there who didn't know about me, I guess.

"Do you know Kafrit? I need to talk to him."

"What do you want with Kafrit?" the biggest one asked. He was almost big enough to put Ulnyx's Were form to shame.

"Extraction," I said.

He looked at his two buddies, and charged me.

I only had two seconds to react, so I focused and leaped, up and over the raging bull, coming down on the other side, between his friends. They reached out for me, and I planted an enhanced fist in each of their faces, sending them sprawling. The big one turned and came back at me, throwing a heavy fist towards my gut. I caught it, and tossed him to the ground too.

"Kafrit?" I asked again. They all regained their feet, while the rest of the gang rushed over. When the three fiends noticed them, they put up their hands.

"He doesn't want to see anyone," the big one said.

"Does he want to continue walking the Earth? Gambling, whoring, all of that good stuff? Because it's all going to end, if he doesn't see us."

He tightened his jaw and narrowed his eyes. "One second," he said, turning around. He whispered something to his boys, and turned back. "He'll see you."

I was expecting the big guy to be Kafrit. I had been since they had shown up.

It wasn't, though. Kafrit was goon number two. He stepped forward and shifted into a small, thin man with olive skin and a slight goatee.

"A pleasure to make your acquaintance," he said, with a deep bow. "And you are?"

"Landon," I said, holding out my hand. He smiled and took it.

"Not *the* Landon?"

I hadn't realized I'd earned a 'the'. "The same."

"Well, what is the world coming to that has brought a boy like yourself to my doorstep, and I've shown such poor manners." He motioned towards a building across the street. "Come," he said. He turned to the rest of my entourage. "Come. Delight in the hospitality of Kafrit Al Niraj, Efreeti Especiale." He started walking towards the building, his men close behind.

"I like this guy," I heard Alichino say as we followed.

He walked right into a stark apartment building that had seen better days, leading us to the stairs down, where there was a casino in full swing. He brought us through, past the mortals that couldn't see anyone but him, to a private room with a poker table and a bar.

"A drink?" he asked, wiggling his fingers. It must have been a signal, because the big guy went up to the bar and started mixing a drink. He motioned for us to sit around the table.

"Do you have blue curaçao?" Alichino asked. "I love that stuff."

I glared at the demon, who shrank to the back of the line. "I appreciate your hospitality, Kafrit," I said. "We have about four hours to stop the end of the world."

"So, right down to business, eh? You hurt a humble djinn's feelings." He pouted, until the big guy handed him his drink. It was some kind of martini, and he sipped it gingerly.

257

"I'd rather stay and play," I lied, "but the end of the world won't wait."

He sighed loudly. "No, I suppose it won't. You want to know if I can extract the souls you have inside of you, right?"

I nodded. "Can you?"

"I can," he said. "Only a djinn can, because it requires a very light touch, and an almost neutral power. I've done it twice before. You should know, there is a chance you'll die."

"We're as good as dead if we don't. Two from me, one from Charis."

He looked over at Charis, focusing on her red eyes. "If you want the souls to survive, they'll need another body. Did you bring any prisoners in that truck of yours?"

I paused. It wasn't that I hadn't considered it, but we'd been in such a rush I hadn't thought to bargain for replacement flesh from Darya. "No."

He laughed. "I can help you there, for a price," he said. "And I can do the extraction, for a price."

Desperation was leading to a lot of bad debt. What was a little more? "Name it," I said.

He shook his head. "I need more time," he said. "An opportunity like this only comes once in a lifetime."

"Kafrit."

He waved his hand. "I will do the extraction, but you owe me one boon. A price you will pay at the time I ask for it."

It wasn't like I had a whole lot of choice. "Two conditions. One, no sexual favors. Two, nothing that will tip the balance."

He laughed. "You just ruined one of my ideas, but as you wish." He held out his hand. As I reached for it, he drew it back. "Remember, diuscrucis. I am not an angel, or a demon. A deal with a djinn cannot be unbound. If you try to renege, you will be twisted in agony for the rest of eternity."

It sucked, I admit. I had to do it. "I know."

He put his hand back, and we shook. His smile was wide and white, and just a hint devilish.

"Now, I need to find a few shells for you," he said. "I assume they prefer to occupy the same sex?"

"*You're damn right*," Ulnyx said. I could feel his excitement at the prospect of being free.

"Yes," Charis said for Vilya.

Josette was silent.

"*Josette?*" I asked.

It took her a few seconds to respond.

"*I won't take someone else's soul*," she said. "*I'm sorry, Landon.*"

CHAPTER TWENTY-SIX

I wish I could have said I was surprised. I wish I could have said that her decision wasn't something I should have expected. It was just that I had never considered that she would be so adamant about it.

I had retired to a private room Kafrit had provided, to be alone, and yet not alone. He needed time to find some willing, or less than willing participants for Vilya and Ulnyx to overpower, and I needed time to try to convince Josette that she couldn't just let me let her die.

"Landon, I'm sorry, but I will not do it," she said to me, for the hundredth time.

I had put myself down in a bare corner of the room and pulled myself back to my Source, where we could talk face to face. Ulnyx had tried to pop in, but I had banished him with a thought. I couldn't imagine anything he had to say being helpful at the moment.

"Josette, what about Sarah? She needs you. I need you to be there for her. She's been holding up pretty well, but you can imagine what losing the mother that she just found is going to do to her."

260

She glared at me, an angry look in her eyes. "Don't you think I know that, Landon? This isn't an easy decision to make, or an easy thing to do, but I don't have a choice. I have lived seven hundred years believing in the true sanctity of life. All life. I never harmed a mortal soul. I never even considered not having my brother's child. You can't take me out of your body without letting me die, or giving me someone else's form, and I am not willing to do that, under any circumstances."

"Even if it means the fate of everything?"

She nodded. "Isn't that the truest test of one's beliefs? When everything is on the line? I still believe in Him, Landon, and in you. I believe you will triumph, with or without me."

I took a deep breath and tried to stay somewhat reasonable. "What if we find someone with terminal cancer, or is brain dead, or something? Someone who is as good as dead anyway?"

"No."

"Josette, please. I understand your faith, but-"

"If you understood my faith, you wouldn't say 'but'. I've enjoyed our friendship, and I've enjoyed the time we've had to spend together, both before and since you took my soul. The fact is, I was supposed to die five years ago. What I've had since then has been a blessing, and the work of the Lord, for me to help guide you and bring you to this place. For me to meet my little girl. I want her to survive, Landon. It's what I've always wanted. You know how to make that happen. You have to do it."

It sucked. It completely, and totally sucked. I loved Josette like the sister I never had, and a best friend at the same time. Even for all the years we couldn't communicate, she was there, and I was living her life and sharing in her joys and pains. Learning how to speak to her had been one the best things that had happened

261

since I'd become a Divine, and now she was going to be gone. Not just out of touch, but gone, gone.

"I can't," I said, the tears rolling from my eyes.

"You have to," she replied, her own face just as moist. "It is His will."

"I don't believe that."

"I do."

That was the crux of it. She believed in the Goodness of God, and that even the nastiest demon shared some kind of lineage with Him, and as such was one of His creations. She wouldn't destroy what He had created except when she had to. Even the first night we had met, when we had fought the vampires in the alley, she hadn't killed them. She had tried to scare them off, but she had a sword, and she didn't use it. She was pro-life, and nothing in the universe, not even it's end, would change that. I hated her choice, but I respected it.

"You know I love you, right?" I asked her.

She smiled. "I love you too."

"I'd miss the hell out of you, but I don't think you have any in you. Nothing's going to be the same once you're gone."

"You'll defeat the Beast. Everything will be better."

I stepped forward and wrapped my arms around her. I don't think I could have held her any tighter. "Maybe for everyone else." I held her close for a minute, and then gave her a chaste kiss on the lips. "What's going to happen to you, anyway? I mean, what happens when a Divine dies?"

"Nobody knows," she said. "I'm curious to find out."

"Well then, maybe we'll meet again."

"Perhaps we will."

"I'm not saying goodbye yet. Not until the last second."

She kissed my cheek. "You have an exceptional soul."

The words were awesome, but they didn't help at all.

"I'd like to say goodbye to Sarah," she said. "And Izak. He deserves that."

I couldn't disagree. He had saved my ass more times than I could count. "Wake me up?" I asked. I always had trouble getting myself out of these weird dream states.

She reached up, and slapped my face.

A new face had been added to the group by the time I returned to Kafrit and the others. A female vampire. A young, and pretty one, with shoulder length hair that she had dyed a dark red, and strong but delicate features. She looked confused, and uncomfortable. In fact, the big guy was holding her arms behind her back.

"*Do you not see, Landon?*" Josette asked.

I did see, but I didn't care. Maybe I should have thought it was wrong. Maybe I should have been at least a little bit unsure, but it didn't change that I believed Josette was more important then one more gutter vampire.

Izak and Sarah both looked at me, their nerves obvious.

"Can I talk to both of you, in private?" I asked.

"My friend," Kafrit said. "It would be best to get this done soon."

"I know," I said. "Just a few more minutes." I walked out of the room, with Sarah and Izak behind me.

"*Are you ready for this?*" I asked Josette, surrendering control to her one last time. I felt her spirit flood into me, her soul rising up to take hold of my body. She walked us into the room, and closed the door behind Sarah and Izak.

"Sarah, I-"

Sarah didn't let her speak. She wrapped her arms around us, and buried her head in our shoulder.

"Don't do this, mom. Please don't do this. I never got to know you, I barely

263

got to spend any time with you."

I could feel the tears through my shirt.

"Sarah," Josette said. She pulled her back gently. "You know I have to do this. Everything I sacrificed was to keep you safe. How could I refuse now, when you need me the most?"

"I need you here," Sarah said. "I need my mother. Everything has been so much better since we talked. I feel so much better. Why can't you just take another body? Vampires are scum."

"All life is sacred, and all life deserves respect. I had my time. It should have ended long ago, but the Lord saw fit to give me a gift in a beautiful child. I could not have asked for anything better, or a life more complete."

Sarah bowed her head. "It isn't fair. If I hadn't set the Beast free, you wouldn't have to die. It's all my fault."

We reached out, putting our hand to Sarah's face and cupping it tenderly. "No, my love. This is His will. Think of all of the many things that had to happen to bring us to this day. Think of how many ways we might never have met, or you might never have been. Yet here you are, and here I am, and we have this chance to say goodbye. Only God can make such blessings so."

Sarah was crying harder, and she took us in her arms again. "I love you," she said.

"I love you too."

She backed away, and Izak stepped in front of us. For as tough as the demon was, even he couldn't keep his eyes from running. He looked miserable.

"Izak, of all of the beings I have ever had the honor of knowing, you have been the greatest." We stepped forward, and she kissed him. Not a small peck, but a solid, loving, intimate kiss. The demon was surprised at first, but he didn't resist. He wasn't seeing me in that moment, he was seeing Josette, his forbidden love. This was his last chance, and he didn't waste it.

We backed away, and smiled at him. "You have made me so proud. Thank you."

He smiled, and put his hand to his heart. We did the same.

"*I'm ready*," she said to me then, letting go of her control, and allowing me to reassert myself.

"*Believe it or not*," Ulnyx said. "*I'm going to miss you too, princess.*"

"*And I, you, wolf,*" she replied.

I looked at Izak and Sarah, both red-eyed and stricken. I felt the same way they looked, and it was taking a lot of effort to keep myself together. "Come on guys," I said, my own voice sullen. "It's the way it has to be."

They both looked at me, but didn't say anything.

When I returned to Kafrit, Charis was unconscious in her chair, and the red-headed vampire was leaned over her, stroking her face.

"Vilya?" I asked.

She turned and looked at me. Her eyes were as red as her hair. "Landon," she said. "I wish we could be meeting under different circumstances." She held out her hand.

I took it. "Me too."

"Well my friend," Kafrit said. "Now you see the proof, I can do the extraction. She'll be okay, but it is taxing on the body and soul. I expect you'll have the same reaction, possibly worse because you have two in there."

"What does he do?" I asked Obi.

He shrugged. "He just put his hand on her forehead, whispered some gibberish, and a black cloud came pouring out of her mouth and went to the vampire. She moaned a bit, but it didn't sound too painful."

"Please, have a seat," Kafrit said, pointing at the empty chair.

I walked over to it and sat. The djinn stood over me, looking into my eyes.

As he did, he brought his hand up to my forehead. I could swear I saw an eye appear on his palm, right before it touched my skin. He started mumbling under his breath, words I didn't understand and could never repeat.

I felt Ulnyx shifting within me. I focused, and saw the threads of him that bound us together, coming unraveled, spinning apart, and gathering into a single dense ball of *him*. It was an odd feeling, and it tickled and hurt at the same time. I also felt his power leaving me, and in the first seconds after it washed away I felt weaker and more naked than I could ever remember. Ulnyx had been my personal monster, my warrior armor, my key to winning so many fights. I felt his soul separate from mine.

"*See ya on the other side,*" he said, his voice echoing in my mind. Then I felt like I was choking, and I let my head fall back. The black cloud that had shoved itself into me all of those years ago came pouring out of my mouth, pooling in front of me until it was completely external. I watched as it flowed towards the big guy, whose eyes grew wide with shock. Kafrit hadn't told him he was the host. Ulnyx poured in, and a few moments later he smiled.

"I never thought I would get the chance to do this," he said. It suddenly occurred to me that maybe we weren't on as good of terms as I had thought.

Ulnyx walked towards me, his eyes menacing. I grabbed Kafrit's hand, to pull him away, because he was still chanting and he hadn't noticed the Were. Ulnyx reached me, a long, sharp smile extending across his face.

"Boo," he said, then he started laughing.

"Shut up," I whispered, finding my voice hoarse.

I felt the process starting again, Josette's soul being unwrapped from my own once more.

"*Goodbye, Josette,*" I said. "*I love you.*"

"*Goodbye, brother. I love you too. Good luck.*"

Broken

    Her spirit was torn away from me, gathering into one mass of white light that slipped more easily from my body. She floated for a second above the table and then shot towards Sarah, circling around her, enveloping her in one final hug, bringing more tears and a smile to her daughter's face. Then she spun around Izak.

    In an instant of blinding white light, she was gone.

CHAPTER TWENTY-SEVEN

I woke up an hour later, my head resting on the poker table, surrounded by my friends and family. Well, most of them. I had lost two today, and one that hurt more than all of the others combined. I tried not to think too much about it, because there was nothing good to come of it. She had made her choice, and we all had to live with it.

I picked up my head.

"Welcome back, meat," Ulnyx said. His voice was strange to me, outside of my body and in the form of the large Russian.

"You're still here," I said. I hadn't been sure he would stick around once he was free.

"I'm not missing this action," he said.

"Landon." Charis' voice. I looked at her, almost doing a double-take at the violet eyes that looked back at me. I wasn't expecting that.

"Your eyes," I said. "They're amazing."

She smiled. "Yours too."

I turned my head, looking for Sarah. She wasn't there.

"She's out in the truck with Izak and Alichino," Obi said. "She couldn't stand being in here, once Josie was gone."

"Why is Alichino in the truck?" I asked.

"He's working on the Box," Charis replied. "He's making the modifications."

"How long?"

"Not long."

"So, my friend, you are awake!" Kafrit stepped into the room, a huge grin on his face. "I told you I could do it, didn't I?"

"You did. I guess I owe you one."

"Yes. You will do well to remember."

"I'm sure you won't let me forget." I pushed myself to my feet, ignoring my body's complaints. It felt weaker than I remembered, without the Were to help augment my strength. Other things felt more dull too; my hearing, my sense of smell. It was going to take some readjustment. I could still remember some of Josette's fighting style at least. I had learned something by practicing it for five years.

"Ulnyx," I said.

"What's up, meat?"

"I'm glad you're willing to help me out. What about the rest of your pack?"

"What about them?"

I looked at him. "Think you can get them to Mumbai?"

He scowled, and then nodded. "Better for them to die in a blaze of glory. I'll have to go round them up myself. It's going to take a few hours, and I need some help with the rifts."

We had two demons who could manage them. I needed Izak. I turned to Vilya. "I don't know you that well yet, but-"

"You know me better than most," she said, interrupting. I had Charis' memories, so in a way that was true. "Consider it done.We're all on the same side, right now."

"I'll stay on your side," Ulnyx said, his face a little too much of a leer.

"Watch yourself, Were," Charis said. "You're dealing with a daughter of Baal."

He laughed. "Even sexier," he said. "Just warn me if I'm going too far, and you're tempted to hellfire my balls off."

"This should be interesting," Obi said.

Vilya scowled at the Were.

"Kafrit, can you spare an extra car?"

He sighed. "You take advantage of my friendship, diuscrucis. There's a Maybach in the garage out back. Pietr will drive you."

His remaining stooge pulled a set of keys from his pocket and started walking. Ulnyx and Vilya trailed behind.

"Sorry," I said to Charis once Vilya was gone. "I know you're worried about her, but she's in good, if not overly hormone-driven hands."

Charis nodded. "I understand the need. Besides, she can take care of herself. I forget that sometimes."

"Now what?" Melody asked. She was sitting next to Obi, her hand on his shoulder.

"Back to the rift. As soon as Alichino finishes with the Box, we head to Mumbai."

"So, we have the pure energy, and we'll have the Box soon enough," Charis said, "but the Beast is still trapped, isn't he? Which means we need to get back to his original prison to try to catch him again."

"The prison we don't know how to find," I said. "We need to talk to Dante. He got us out of there, he must know how to get back."

270

"Sounds like a great plan," Obi said. He stood and headed for the door. "Let's do it from the truck. I'll drive, you meditate; or whatever it is you do."

I couldn't argue with that. "Kafrit, do you have a cell?"

He reached into a pocket and pulled out a gold-plated smartphone. "What kind of respectable businessman would I be if I didn't?"

I took it from him, and put in my own phone number. "I can't guarantee how long this number will work for, but I have a feeling you'll be able to find me, when you're ready."

He laughed, and wrapped me in a hug. "Good luck, my friend," he said. "Don't think dying will get you out of our bargain."

Most times, I would have thought it could. With Kafrit, I wasn't too sure. I left the room without another word.

We piled into the UPS truck. Alichino was tucked into the back corner, hunched so far over the Box I couldn't see what he was doing to it. Sarah was sitting at the opposite corner with Izak, her head resting in his lap while she slept. The demon looked pained, and he didn't acknowledge us when we joined him in the rear.

Obi and Melody rode up front, while Charis and I took one of the free corners. We sat down with our shoulders pressed together. Obi started the engine, and got us on the move.

"Hang in there, Landon," Charis said, nothing but warmth in her eyes.

"You too," I replied, taking her hand in my own. "Let's go find Dante."

I closed my eyes, focusing on the trickle of power coming through from Purgatory and following it back once more. The power looked and felt strange to me, no longer hued with the energy of the Were and the angel, and I felt a pang of sadness at the thought. Time seemed to stop, and I stepped forward out of my body, into a world so much like our own, but so much different. Charis was standing next to me.

She reached out and took my hand. A thought, and we were at Dante's 'house', but I knew right away he wasn't there.

"The library," I said. We were there in a blink.

Marble columns and lots of books and scrolls. That was the only way to describe the library. It was sixty feet high from floor to roof, with a tremendous dome in the center that made it look even more massive. There were a number of souls inside, some working returning items to the shelves, others reading, and a few just standing amidst the books, as if they didn't know how they should be spending their eternity.

We found Dante amidst his own pile of tomes, having amassed enough of them that he was using a larger stack as a stool to sit on. He was already looking at us when we approached. He didn't look happy.

"Millions of books," he said. "Millions, and I have found nothing but a single scrap of paper. I did go to see an acquaintance of mine, to see if he could assist you with Avriel's Box."

"Alichino," Charis said. "He thinks we can trap the Beast. He's altering the design right now."

His mood turned on a dime. "Excellente," he shouted, drawing stares from the souls around him. "So, you will be able to stop the Beast?"

"We're going to try," I said. "There's one little problem."

"We don't know how to find him," Charis said.

Dante hopped off his book-stool and held up a finger. Then he closed his eyes. "I have a connection to his prison, because it was leaking into this realm." He was still for a minute, during which he began to shake his head. "This is very, very bad," he said.

I was used to it. "What?"

272

"He isn't there."

"What do you mean, he isn't there?" I asked. "I thought he was trapped."

"Much of his power is still there, signore. Power that he cannot unlock without the rest of the true diuscrucis' blood. He has gathered the rest faster than I would have thought possible, and has taken form to walk the Earth."

"And lure us in," I said, the objective becoming clear. "He tried to stop us a few times, but it didn't work out. Now he's betting that he'll be able to get Sarah, before we can get him. He wants us to go to Mumbai. He wants us to bring the Box. He has an army in the millions, not even counting the demons and angels on his side, and it only grows with each passing minute. We have to go to him, or he'll destroy everything, and break the balance."

"He can't know we've altered the Box," Charis said.

I smiled. "No, he doesn't. He killed Avriel, believing that was enough to stop us. But he'd know we'd make a run for him anyway. We don't have any other choice."

Dante rubbed his chin. "So you must walk right into a trap," he said. "How will you get through these millions to reach him? How will you even know where he is?"

I thought about it. They were tough questions, that I had to answer, but had no good answer to.

"Do not be concerned, signore. I can help you with the second part. As I've said, I can feel his power and use it to find him, even as I can use it to find you. I will locate the Beast, and I will make his location known to you. There will be... consequences."

"What do you mean consequences?" I asked.

"Every time I use my power in your world. Every time you use your power, or the Beast uses his power, it changes the very fabric of the reality that God shaped

273

within the universe. Like any fabric, it can take a certain amount of pulling and twisting and still go back into form. Pull too hard, twist too tightly, and the fabric tears, or stretches, and never goes back the way it was."

I had always understood the principle. "But what is the consequence?"

He shook his head. "I don't know, signore. What I can tell you is that I have already stretched the fabric to deliver you from the Beast's prison, and the Beast is stretching it even now. For me to use the strength of Purgatory, the true strength of Purgatory, in the mortal realm might be the proverbial straw that throws reality into chaos."

Charis laughed. We both looked at her, confusion on our faces.

"There are a million plus human beings being possessed at one time by a single entity bent on destroying all of God's creation, and every other mortal he kills becoming the walking dead. Haven't we already thrown reality into chaos?"

Dante smirked. "What about getting past these millions, to reach my signal?" he asked.

"We'll get by with a little help from our friends," I replied.

CHAPTER TWENTY-EIGHT

Adam was waiting for us when we returned to Ivan the Great's Bell Tower. So were Darya's promised troops, in the form of fifty vampires and fifty weres. They were an interesting assortment of male and female, though most had athletic builds and the calm toughness that came from being a trained badass. They didn't look too happy to be waiting outside anywhere near the angel, who had taken a perch above them.

He dropped down when he saw us pile out of the truck. "Fredeline sent one of the Inquisitors to Mumbai to try to get a feel for the situation. They never came back."

I wasn't surprised. I could feel the balance in my gut, and with it a coldness that I had never felt before. The demons had been winning when I had come onto the scene five years ago, but the scales were tipped even further on their side now. Except, it wasn't their side. It was that the universe didn't know it.

"We've got it as good as it's going to get," I said. Alichino had complained about the bumpy ride in the back of the truck, but he had finished his changes and hopped out of the corner beaming and proud of himself for what he had accomplished.

275

He had shown Charis the Box, and tried to describe the math before she diverted him to teaching Sarah how to activate it.

It would take all of our power to ensnare the Beast, and to hold him. All three of us would have to have a hand on the Box, with Charis and I focusing our energy into it, powering it up. Sarah's role was to use the gathered juice to Command the Beast into the prison. Since the energy was partly his own, according to Alichino he would be unable to resist, and would find himself trapped.

"You even scrounged up a little morsel for them," Adam said. "A distraction?"

"With any luck."

"Fredeline is waiting. Once we've gone through the rift, I'll put up a beacon for her to follow. She talked a few dozen seraph into following her, and outed a bunch more as servants. We locked them away until this is over. We can worry about their penitence if we win. Oh, I have something for you." He held out his hand, and a sword materialized in it. It was a standard issue blessed seraphim blade, which was good enough. I took it from him.

"Thanks."

I waded into the gathered demons, looking for whoever Darya had put in charge. I found an older vampire named Vincent. He had white hair and a bushy white mustache resting on top of a heavy frame, and he peered at me with cautious eyes when I approached.

"Diuscrucis," he said. "Darya Commanded me to come here with my best, to assist you with a small problem. I don't know why she agreed to help you, but here we are."

I wasn't friendly or gentle with him. He didn't seem the type to warm to that approach. "We're going to be attacked as soon as we step through the rift," I said. "Your job is to make sure we don't get killed before we can get our bearings, and then just to kill as many of them as you can, without getting killed yourself."

He smiled a fanged smile. "It's been a while since I got into a real brawl. I'm looking forward to it."

It was because he didn't understand what he was getting into. Otherwise, he wouldn't be so eager. "Get your charges to the rift. Izak over there is going to activate it for you. As soon as me and mine get into the room, start going through. Be ready to get hit immediately."

It was the worst part of our otherwise desperate plan. A single transport rift that led to the High Court building, on the southern end of the city. It sucked because we couldn't see what we were walking into, and it was a ridiculously easy place to stage an ambush, or even to pack a million possessed or dead mortals to rip all of us except for Sarah apart. Then, there was Gervais. I hadn't forgotten he was out there, one of the Beast's dead servants, a puppet on a string who could push Sarah to a bad place without much effort. I knew Izak would do his best to neutralize him whenever he made his appearance, but down a hand, I wasn't sure the fiend could handle him.

I made my way from the demons back to my group. They were all spread out around the area, Sarah and Izak in one spot, Alichino with Charis in another. Obi, Melody, and Adam made up their own group. I didn't like the fracture.

"How about a little togetherness," I said, putting some force behind my voice. It was enough to rally the troops, and bring them all together.

"Sorry, man," Obi said. "Just trying to set up a date for after we stop the end of the world."

Melody punched him in the shoulder, and he laughed. It was nervous energy, because none of us really thought we were going to get out of this alive. I looked over at Sarah, whose slumped posture worried me.

"Talk amongst yourselves," I said to them. I took Sarah aside and tapped my head. We needed to talk in private.

I felt the pressure of her knocking, and I opened her up to me. "*Sarah. I'm worried about you.*"

"*This is it, brother,*" she said. "*I've seen this part, this gathering.*"

"*When you kill me?*" I asked.

"*Yes. We make it to the Beast. Gervais is there. He tells me things, and I believe them. He promises me gifts, and I want them. All he asks is that I clear the way for him, and everything I want will be mine. I do it for him. I kill you and Charis. Without you, nothing can stop him. I do it because he says he can bring Mother and I together again in the world that he will create. I do it because he says I can have Gervais, to do whatever I please.*"

It was a chilling sequence of events, but not a believable one. "*Sarah, the Beast can't create, only destroy. That alone means your vision isn't true.*"

Her voice was hopeful, but guarded. "*How do we know that? I mean, can we be sure everything Malize says is right, or true? The Beast says he is a god. Maybe's he has only destroyed because that is what war is? Maybe the creation comes after?*"

I had no way to know if Malize was right or not. I had no way to know which Sarah I was even talking to. She had calmed so much after being reunited with Josette, but now she had lost her again, at the very moment she needed the most strength. Sarah was a total unknown to me, a wildcard. I loved her, but I had no idea whose side she was on right now, or whose side she'd be on ten minutes from now.

"*Bringing her back would mean killing everything else,*" I said. "*Is there any part of you that believes that your mother would have wanted that, when she wouldn't even accept the sacrifice of a single demon?*"

She was silent for only a moment. "*No. You're right. I'm being stupid.*"

"*You're not stupid, but be careful reading too much into what you see. For all we know, the Beast or Gervais are planting those visions in your head somehow.*"

278

I didn't really believe that. Father Tom had said all true crossbreeds were destined to go insane. I had been inside Sarah's head. I understood why.

She broke the connection, and then walked over to me and put her arms around me. "I love you," she said.

"I love you too," I replied. "I know you won't let anything happen to us, and I know you'll make your mother proud."

We returned to the group. There still wasn't too much communication between them, but what did I expect? For the most part, they weren't friends. They were allies, rallying around me for their own sake as much as everyone else's.

I took center stage, and coughed to get their attention. "If you've seen one of those cheesy speeches from the end of one of those movies where the fate of the world is on the line... yeah, that." I smiled and put my hand into the center of our jagged circle. Obi was next, followed by Charis, Melody, Sarah, Adam, and Izak.

"I'm not a fighter," Alichino said. "I'll stay here and wait for you to come back for me."

"You're coming," I said to him, looking at our group. We had two mortals, two Divine diuscrucis and two angels. We needed a second demon. It was a better balance. "Even if Sarah has to make you do it."

Alichino frowned, and hopped forward to put his hand in.

"One... two... three..."

We shouted as one, all of our different histories, different goals, different motivations, and different allegiances for a moment forgotten.

"Break!"

CHAPTER TWENTY-NINE

It could have been Hell on Earth, but I didn't think even Hell was that bad. We came out of the other side of the rift into a war zone unlike anything that could be described, or make any kind of sense. There was no logic to it, only destruction.

The rift had once been below the High Court of Bombay, a judicial house that saw many of the legal cases in the city. The High Court had been decimated around it, the rift left intact in order to give us passage through. The hundred demons I had borrowed were nearly all gone in the four seconds it took to enter the maelstrom, ripped apart by a pair of wraiths that were circling the rift, a crowd of thousands behind them.

It was early evening. The sky was dark, with heavy clouds blocking out the sunlight, although no rain was falling. The ground held a sheen of sweat from earlier precipitation, and the heat of the fires burning throughout the city was enough to add a few degrees to the ambient temperature. There were possessed and undead as far as I could see, and plenty more people who were no longer moving under any circumstances. They hung from windows, dangled from cars, and lay broken in the streets. There was smoke everywhere, the sound of alarms, screaming, crying, pain, and suffering.

It nearly took my breath away. It nearly broke me before I could act, ripping the bracelet from my arm and pulling in the power I needed with a ferocity I couldn't remember having felt before. I leveled the blessed sword in front of me, and rocketed towards one of the wraiths. Black tentacles reached for me, contorting and shifting to pointed edges and heavy balls that aimed to crush my body. The ground below me cracked and tore into dozens of cement shields, rising up to block the creatures efforts, and I brought the blade down with a cold satisfaction.

I turned towards the second wraith, and was blinded by the beam of light that shot up into the sky, courtesy of a small etched disc Adam had placed on the ground. Before the wraith could move in on any of us, Fredeline fell from the sky, tearing into it with the Deliverer. Fifty angels fell into the surrounds, crashing up against the evil creatures the Beast had made the mortals into.

"It's about time you arrived," they said, a hundred thousand voices all rising at once in his voice. It was a wave of sound that crashed over us, threatening our sanity and will. "You seem to be a little outnumbered." He laughed, and they laughed. "Did you bring the Box?"

I stepped right up to one of the possessed. "Why don't you tell me where you are, so we can make this quick?" I asked.

Thousands of heads shook at once. "What would be the fun in that. I told you I would win." A hand grabbed for me. I brought the sword up and around.

"Landon, where do we go?" Sarah was standing in the center of our group, and we circled up around her and began wading into the masses. They tried to push past, to grab, to strike. Izak brought up a wall of hellfire around us, incinerating the slow and knocking the rest back. As soon as the flames subsided, they charged in again.

"Dante is going to send us a signal," I said. I knew it couldn't be too far from where we came in. He would want to grab her, and take her back to his prison before we could even think about stopping him.

I heard wings then, and a mass of devils and fallen angels dropped over the throng, landing right in front of Sarah and reaching for her.

"No," she shouted. Her Command went out like a shockwave, and the ambushers froze in their steps. "Kill them." She pointed past us. Most of the demons complied. The ones that fought off the order fell before they could recover their momentum.

I swung the sword, focusing my strength on my body, enhancing my sword arm to make clean cuts, and my other hand to throw solid punches. I tried to ignore the faces of the people I was killing, their human eyes and heads and clothes. I tried to see them only as they were, shells for use by an angry being. I tried to keep us from being swallowed in it.

Was it even possible? With each passing second, it felt less and less so. There were almost seventy of us now, between the angels and the controlled demons and our initial group, yet it was barely enough to keep the circle intact, and to keep them from reaching Sarah. Nobody was tired yet. Nobody had fallen.

Then came the signal, Dante's signal. I had no idea what it was going to be, but he didn't disappoint. All I had to do was look up, and see the change in the formation of the clouds above us. With one look, it was dark and threatening. With another, I could see the reddish orange of the setting sun against much higher clouds, and all of the dark nimbuses had pulled together, creating a series of arrows that all pointed to a ring shaped formation that from my vantage looked to be a mile or so away.

I felt something else when it happened, something I couldn't describe. As if I could sense that the universe had just been stretched beyond repair. Whether it

282

was a minor pucker, or a complete tear, I couldn't know.

"There," I shouted, my sword reaching through another neck, my foot lashing out and throwing back a dozen undead from my left. I had lost Josette, but a lot of her skill had stayed, learned subconsciously through repetition.

"That's not close," Obi said. He had his knife in hand, and he was doing good business with it, but I could see he was getting bruised and bloodied by the sheer number of flying arms and legs.

I heard a scream, and shifted my attention backward. One of the angels had been lost beneath a sea of humanity. A second later, and another vanished.

"This thing has no power against them," Fredeline shouted, the Deliverer nothing more than a sharp piece of metal when demons weren't involved. She was a good fighter, but she didn't have the power to overcome them. She could Calm them, but they would be replaced faster than she could talk.

"Dante?" the Beast asked. "You sent Dante? You thought he could stop me?"

They started laughing again. All of them. An insane thunderclap of mirth that would have drove the courage from anyone. We were losing. We were going to lose.

A great howl pierced the din, rising above the laughter of thousands. It was followed by a dozen more, than even more. The laughter stopped. I looked back, and I could see the bodies flying away from a dark mass, thrown aside like matchsticks. A gout of flame rose up in front of us, searing the bodies in our path before subsiding. It was hellfire, but it was nearly blue from the intensity.

"Cavalry's here," Alichino said. He was hunched behind Charis, doing his best to stay alive, bringing his claws down on the foot of an enemy when he could so it safely.

The Great Were's massive shape landed next to me, a single slash sending a dozen bodies away from us. Ulnyx turned his sharp maw towards me and grinned. "I thought I was going to miss the good part," he said.

"How many did you bring?" I asked.

"All of them that were fit to die. Three hundred."

Another blast of hellfire removed another ten feet of flesh from our path. We moved forward to fill it as fast as we could. Another angel died, and two of Sarah's controlled demons. The reinforcements had helped us double our distance in a matter of seconds, but I still wasn't sure it was enough.

"Great Were," the Beast said through his multitude of mouthpieces. "I can offer you anything. Don't waste your time on the wrong side of this fight. Grab the girl and bring her to me."

Ulnyx looked at me, and then back at Sarah.

"Can you bring back the dead when their bodies and souls are lost?" he asked.

"I can," he replied. A lie.

The Were was unimpressed. "I'll think about it. Killing you is too much fun right now." He smashed another pile aside.

We moved forward another two blocks before the Beast upped the ante. Sitting in the road in front of us was a huge stack of crushed cars, melted together with a blast of hellfire. The wall ran across from one building to the next, completely choking our ingress. We cut a channel through the undead and possessed, and then came face to face with the barrier.

"Now what?" Obi asked. He was out of breath, and his arms and hands were covered in bleeding cuts. Pieces of flesh were torn from him, and his clothes were tattered. Melody didn't look much better standing next to him, covered in blood, though her body was healing underneath.

I focused, reaching out the the metal, forcing it to corrode. It started to happen, but there was just so much, and a new distraction made itself known.

"Sarah." The voice echoed through the streets. A familiar voice. I looked up to the top of the wall, where Gervais was standing, staring directly at his offspring.

It was as if everything else paused while the parent and child had their moment. They locked eyes, and I stared at Sarah, waiting to see how she would react to him once more.

"Kill him," she Commanded the two fallen angels that remained of those she had taken. They flew up at the demon, but all it took was a touch from him to make them fall to ash and ruin.

"Now that is no way to treat your father," he said. He gathered himself and jumped, falling towards us. He never made it.

Izak's own leap brought him slamming into Gervais, and the two of them knocked back against the wall of cars. Gervais tried to put his hand to the demon's head, but he held it off with his good hand, while the broken remains of the other lit up with hellfire, pressed against the archfiend's chest. He might not bleed, but fire could still incinerate him. He shoved Izak away, and jumped back up the wall.

"We need to go around," I said, finding the door to the building on the right. It was a hotel or something, with a revolving glass door that had been shattered to pieces, and a formerly glitzy inner that was shredded and mangled. We changed direction, still moving the mass of humans aside.

"Don't you think I wanted you to go in the building, kid?" the Beast taunted. "Why don't you just give her over now, and save us all the trouble. It will hurt less for you."

I didn't answer. I used my fists, feet, and sword to punch through the mob.

"Melody!" Obi's shout broke that focus, and I glanced over to see the angel on the ground, a vampire hunched over her, a cursed blade in her gut. He kicked the vampire off. "Holy water!"

"There isn't any," Adam said. "We used it all."

285

He broke free of the fight and knelt next to her. More demons began appearing amidst the mortals, sneaking along with them and launching themselves at us. Obi had a pair of fangs in his neck before he brought the knife up and into his assailant, and he cursed and yelled. Melody lay at his feet.

"Damn you all," he roared. He threw the corpse of the vampire into the crowd, knocking a few more back. I smelled a sour odor, like bad citrus, and then the vampire was up at and him again. When Obi stabbed him, there was no blood.

"Ulnyx, help him," I said. The Were broke from my side and hopped over, grabbing the vampire and ripping him in half, throwing the pieces away. I covered his spot, focusing harder to keep them at bay.

"Melody," Obi said. He joined Adam kneeling with her.

"We have to move," I told them.

"Landon, she's dying," he said.

"We have to move, or we're all going to die."

He knelt and lifted her, throwing her over his shoulder. As he did, Izak crashed into the ground in front of Sarah, his back breaking under the force. Gervais landed on top of him.

"Hello, my love," he said to her. She punched him in the face.

It didn't do any damage. He started to laugh, but then a streak of heat blasted into his side and threw him away. Vilya.

"Get inside," I shouted. "Get inside."

Izak healed, and regained his feet. We started moving again. Two more angels fell, and then a few of the weres. From what I could see, the nearly four hundred plus we had started with had been reduced to less than fifty. We were only a quarter of the way there.

"It still isn't enough," I said to nobody.

"No, it isn't," the Beast replied in a thousand voices. "It never was. Just

give it up, and let me take her. I'll tell you what. You hand her over now, and
I'll kill you quickly. Maybe."

I saw Gervais just in time.

He was headed for Sarah again, at a full run, trying to grab her and get away
like a thief. I was out of physical range, but there was more than enough detritus
lying around. I focused, pulling up a heavy block of concrete and smashing it into
his head. He tumbled away, his head partially caved in, but he didn't stay down. He
grabbed Fredeline, and destroyed her., turning her to ash with a touch.

"No," Adam shouted. He threw himself at the archfiend, almost getting his
sword down before Gervais knocked him to the ground. He would have killed him too,
but Izak got back into the fight, scalding him with a well-placed ball of hellfire.
The angel picked up the fallen Deliverer, taking up her place in the circle.

I smelled the bad citrus again, and looked to where Fredeline's outline of
ash lay on the street. A moment later, Obi screamed.

It was Melody. She had died while he carried her, and the Beast had taken her
body. She had planted her sword into his back, and it stuck out the front of him.
He hefted her up in his strong arms and threw her away, then dropped to his knees.

"Get it out," he shouted. Sarah came up behind him and took the sword,
pulling it from his body while he cried out in pain. Blood poured from the wound,
but he got back to his feet, fueled by his anger.

We reached the doorway, and stumbled inside. Izak had vanished, lost in the
scrum with Gervais, and we had only a small collection of weres and seraph
remaining. The hotel had already been used up, and so it stood empty. As soon as we
were all inside, I focused, bringing up every bit of junk that I could find to seal
the windows and the doors, to keep the crowd outside from getting in.

"Ulnyx, Adam, make sure the entrances are covered. We need to regroup."

The Great Were growled orders to his pack, and Adam directed the remaining

287

angels. I rushed over to Obi, who fell to the ground on his side, gasping for air.

"I'm sorry, man," he said to me. "I wanted to do this."

"Shut up," I said. "You aren't dead yet." I put my hand on his wound. He pushed it away.

"No way. You're too weak."

"I'm not going to let you die," I said.

"I'm not going to let you save me," he replied.

I could feel the tears rising to my eyes.

"Don't cry for me, man. I'm going to be in Purgatory, waiting for your sorry ass."

No. He was going to be taken by the Beast. Unless we burned him. I looked for Vilya, who was sitting on the ground, exhausted. Where was Charis?

"You aren't dying yet, Obi," she said, coming up to us from the other side. She looked like crap, but she was still alive. She knelt down, and took my hand, putting it back on his wound with hers. "It will be easier if we both do it."

I smiled at her, and then focused. I felt her energy joining mine, and our hands grew warm together. Obi coughed, but the color started returning to his face.

"I lost Mel," he said, once he had healed. There were tears in his eyes.

I didn't know what to say. I just nodded.

"Come out, come out, wherever you are." An avalanche of sound blasted the hotel, shaking its foundation. My barrier vibrated from the pounding of thousands of fists.

I looked around the room. Adam, Ulnyx, Vilya, Charis, Alichino, Sarah, and I; plus a few dozen other weres and seraph, against one million or more.

We had lost.

Broken

CHAPTER THIRTY

I closed my eyes, and tried to figure out how we had gotten to this place, this moment. I had only been dead for five years. I had been a champion for man for a blip in time, such a tiny fraction compared to Josette, or Charis. I had failed, and miserably. It sucked.

I kept my hold on Charis' hand, leading her to where the others sat, trying to regain some strength. I could hear fighting in the background, the back door, the loading dock, wherever there was another way in. It was a tight fit though, and the bodies would pile up and make it harder for more than one or two at a time to get through. A Divine could handle two at a time with ease.

There was no way out. No way to win. We had the Box, but we wouldn't be able to get it to the Beast before one of us died, or Sarah was taken. There was only one reasonable thing to do, that would save some of what remained.

I had to kill Sarah.

If she were gone, the Beast would take this world, but he wouldn't be able to gain a foothold on the others. He wouldn't be able to rise to the power that had allowed him to fight such a pitched battle against God. He would be trapped here, forever, or forced to find greener pastures somewhere else. I didn't know enough about how it worked to know for sure. All I knew was that it would be enough to keep him from being as strong as he once was.

"Sarah," I said, letting go of Charis' hand and approaching her. I think she knew what I was thinking, because she nodded.

"It's okay, brother," she said. "I know what you have to do. I forgive you." She even tilted her neck, to make the killing stroke easier.

"What is she talking about?" Adam asked. Then he realized. "Landon, you can't."

"I have to," I said. "We lost."

"We haven't lost yet."

I turned to him. "No? How do you suppose we get through a million enemies with forty of us?"

"I can do it," Ulnyx said. It was a macho lie, and we both knew it.

"We don't need to get through them. Only the three of you do," he said.

"What's that supposed to mean?" Charis asked.

"We need to find a way to get the three of you to the Beast. The seraph can fly you there."

Vilya laughed. "You don't think he has demons waiting for you to try?"

"Do you have a better suggestion, demon?" Adam asked.

She stayed quiet.

I closed my eyes and focused, reaching upwards as far as I could. The demons were there. A lot of them. "She's right," I said. "It won't work."

There was silence for a moment.

"Landon, kill me," Sarah said. "Keep the Beast from taking everything. One world is better than all of creation."

I looked into her eyes. I saw the fear, and the sadness, and the strength.

She had stood up to Gervais, and had triumphed, overthrowing his power over her. For what? At least she hadn't been forced to kill me.

I felt my heart begin to race, and my breath caught in my throat. The realization hit my in the gut, and knocked the breath out of me. I turned and looked at Ulnyx, then Charis, then Sarah. There was one way to get the three of use there. It was scarier than anything I had ever imagined, but maybe it was just stupid enough to work. I took the sword and turned it, holding it out to Sarah.

"Sarah," I said. "You have to kill Charis and me."

"What?"

It was the same word, echoed by everyone there, except for Alichino.

"Yes," he said. "Yes. That's brilliant. Better than Averbakh-Spassky in '56."

"Landon, no," she said, her voice little more than a whisper. "I can't. You said I wouldn't have to. You said it wouldn't happen like that."

"You have to," I said. It was the only way.

"No no no no no no no," she cried, backing away. "I can't. Please, don't ask me to. I won't. I saw it, Landon. I saw it. I told you. You promised."

"Knock, knock," the voices said from outside. Something slammed into my wall, and the whole building shook.

"Sarah, we don't have time. Take the sword, and cut off my head." I couldn't believe I had said it, and meant it.

"Sarah, please," Charis said. "You have to."

"No," she screamed. She turned to run, but Vilya grabbed her.

"Let her go," Charis said. The demon complied.

"Sarah," I moved around in front of her. The wall got slammed again, and the building shook. "Your mother gave her life for me once, so that I could survive, and protect you. I'm giving my life to you, now, so that you can save everything else. All of those people out there, they don't belong to the Beast. They don't

292

deserve to be prevented from going to the next life, with God's grace in Heaven if that is their destiny."

She put her head down. "I'm sorry, I can't."

I looked back at Charis, and took a deep breath. I knew what I had to do, but it killed me to have to do it.

"Sarah. This is your fault. You caused this. Your selfishness, your desire. Melody is dead because of you. Thomas is dead because of you. Your mother is dead because of you. Izak is probably dead too."

Her head snapped up, her pain and agony obvious.

"You have a chance to redeem yourself, but you're still too selfish. You're still too concerned with what you want, instead of what will help everyone else. This whole time, you've been more worried about what you saw, the future you didn't want, then what might really happen, and what you might need to do."

I jabbed the sword at her feet, focusing to make sure it planted upright in the tile and cement floor. The walls shook again, and I could see them beginning to crumble.

Sarah was shaking, trying to contain all of the conflicting emotions that I knew would be racing through her. I had one more card to play. It was the last one in my hand.

"You're just like your father."

The growl that came from her was guttural and inhuman. I locked eyes with Charis, watching Sarah's reflection in them. I knew when she grabbed the sword and pulled it from the floor. I knew when she raised it up. I knew when she swung it at my head. It took a lot of effort to let her do it.

I died for a second time.

M.R. Forbes

CHAPTER THIRTY-ONE

Everything slowed. I felt my body, and the pain for only an instant, and then I felt nothing. I was floating weightless in the space I had just occupied, as though the air were water, and I could swim in it. There was a roar, like an ocean, or thunder, and in the distance I saw a small, round, black pinprick of emptiness that called out to me, ordering me to it.

I saw Sarah, standing there, her chest heaving, looking down on my body, on my head that had rolled a few feet away, and the volumes of blood pooling on the floor, so much that she had to step back to keep her freet out of it. I had no muscles to move, no brain to think. I was a soul, a form of light or darkness or maybe just plain grey. I had only the most primitive thought, and a single goal. Join with her. It was the thought I had died with, and it stayed with me.

I felt myself floating towards her, my momentum gathering but unable to be slowed, like a rocket in space. Her face grew in front of me, looming up, a massive visage of horror, pain, guilt, anger, sadness, and love. Her mouth was a black cave, and I flowed towards it, and then into it.

There was no sound, only feeling. First, it was empty, and then, it wasn't. I

could feel her soul. I could hear her heart. I could sense every hormone, blood
vessel, and muscle. There was a small white light, and I followed it. I fell on top
of it. I took hold of it, and wrapped myself into it. My own senses came alive. The
feel of air, the sound of the banging outside, the understanding of what Sarah was
feeling, of the damage I had intentionally done. I took it all in, and I held onto
it, and I forced it to be part of me. Sarah had no eyes to see with, but the world
lit up in shades and shapes and colors, senses that I didn't understand, and yet
suddenly found familiar. I was there, in Sarah's soul. I had access to her mind,
and her body. I could have wrested control, but I didn't. She needed to finish
this.

I felt her moving towards Charis. She didn't defend herself, and nobody tried
to stop it. Sarah brought the sword up again, still growling and whimpering, and
swung it hard. I pushed, just a little, guiding the blade to a cleaner cut. I
sensed her body fall, and I sensed the light of her soul. Sarah stood there,
panting, while she joined me.

"*Landon?*" her voice was ethereal, echoing, afraid.

"*I'm here,*" I replied. My confidence brought her comfort.

"*Brother,*" Sarah whispered in her head. "*Why did you make me do this?*" I
could feel her pain, I knew how much it hurt.

"*Your mother believed in sacrifice. You've done her the greatest honor you
could imagine,*" I replied.

"*I'm a murderer. An evil killer.*"

"*You're a hero. A savior. Tell Ulnyx he needs to take you to the Beast.*"

I didn't dwell too much on the fact that I was dead. I had already
technically been dead after all. The only thing I had lost was the freedom to move
about in a shell of my own. Now I was tied to Sarah's mortal body. Would I die for
real if she died? I didn't want to find out.

"*I never knew what to expect,*" Charis said. I couldn't see her, but I could feel her. I knew she was there with me.

"*I'm sorry this had to happen,*" I replied.

"*Don't be. If this is what it takes, so be it. I didn't spend all of these years preparing in order to lose.*"

"Ulnyx," Sarah said. The Great Were lifted his head and peered at her. "Landon wants you to bring me to the Beast."

The monster laughed. "Still alive in there, after all? You'll get used to it, meat."

"*Sarah, the Box is in my pants pocket,*" Charis said.

She stepped around the blood, leaned down and reached into the pocket, taking it out. She handed it to Ulnyx. "Do you know what to do?" she asked.

"Of course," he replied.

"Charis," Vilya said, stepping between the Were and Sarah. "Be careful."

The wall shook again, and the barrier began to crumble. The front line began crawling through the spaces, ignoring the deep cuts the jagged rock was making in their skin. Ulnyx reached out and took Sarah in a massive claw, tucking her under his arm, and backhanded Vilya. She flew away and rolled along the floor. With a grunt, the Were took off towards the rear of the building.

"What are you doing?" Sarah asked.

"It needs to look convincing," he said. "I didn't break the skin, she'll get over it."

We charged to the rear, where an angel was defending against the onslaught. Ulnyx ran him through on his claws and tossed him aside, then shoved through the undead.

"Change your mind?" the Beast asked through bodies the Were was mauling on his way by. He was clearly amused at the turn of events.

297

"I know a loss when I see one."

"I'll open a path for you. What are you terms?"

"Lylyx. That's all I want."

If he hadn't been helping us, I would have believed he wasn't helping us. It occurred to me that it could still be the case, but I was hoping our outing in Italy had been enough to convince him. It seemed oddly amusing that the fate of the universe had just fallen to the paws of a giant dog.

"Done," the Beast said. The mob spread apart around him, allowing him access straight to the building Dante had pointed out. The clouds were still there, but they had fallen into ruin. I could only imagine what he had done to the poet.

We reached him within two minutes, riding under the arms of the Were while he loped along. He didn't speak, and we didn't speak, all of us just waiting for the game to play out to its final move. We were down to the Hail Mary, but at least we had a killer quarterback.

The building the Beast had holed up in was a six story office that had earlier that day housed some kind of outsourcing firm. He had taken the liberty of hollowing it out, throwing the computers, desks, chairs, and other equipment out of the windows, and demolishing huge portions of the floors so that he had a tall ceiling above him. We entered at a slow walk, Ulnyx keeping his senses sharp for any kind of trick or trap. I had no doubt the Beast would betray him, and he probably knew as much too. The only question would be how and when.

We found him sitting on a throne of mortals, still alive but twisted by his will into a contorted mess of poses that gave him purchase to rest on their limbs. On his knees next to him on one side was Dante, his head bloody, his face more haggard then usual. On the other side was Izak. He was still alive, but he had a mark carved into his chest. Gervais' brand. The archfiend stood behind the demon, wearing a smug expression.

"No," Sarah said, seeing him there.

Ulnyx squeezed her tight, pushing the air from her. "Be quiet," he snarled.

"Now, now, Ulnyx," the Beast said. That sick smile spread across his face. "I need her alive."

Ulnyx put Sarah down and shifted, taking on the form of the big russian. "Here she is," he said, giving her a little push forward. "Go kill whatever, or whatever it is you do. Just get me Lylyx back."

He still held Avriel's Box in his hand, which was so large it concealed it completely.

"It's a wonder to me," the Beast said, rising to his feet and walking towards us. "I've never seen a Great Were who cared at all for anyone. Yet your heart's desire is to have a single bitch in return?"

"You have me," Sarah said. "Why don't you just do what you're going to do and shut up."

The Beast laughed. "Give me a few moments to enjoy this, won't you. Everything else is going to be a cake-walk compared to the crap that Landon put me through. Do you know, there was a minute there where I actually had the thought that I could potentially lose? It was only for a second, but it was there. That's more than I can say for anyone else." He walked past Sarah, getting right in the Were's face. "Well, Ulnyx? Is that really what you want?"

I could hear him breathing. I could feel his anger rising. He knew the Beast couldn't bring her back. If he hadn't, he'd realized it now.

"Yes," he said, holding his temper.

"Okay," the Beast said. "I can do that. There's just one thing." He leaned in close, his mouth only coming up to Ulnyx's bicep. "I know this is a trick," he whispered.

He held out his palm, and a flash of blackness hit Ulnyx right in the chest.

He fell to the ground in a heap.

"No!" All three of us said it at once. The Box fell from the Were's hand, coming to rest at our feet. Sarah bent down to grab it, but the Beast took her by the wrist.

"You think I'm stupid, don't you, kid," he said. "You think I wouldn't catch on to this? It was a ballsy move, and smart, I'll give you that. I haven't lived for eons just to be fooled by something so mundane."

He started tugging, the force pulling us away from the Box.

"You don't need that thing anymore," he said, "but I appreciate how much work you put into preparing it for me. It will make it much easier for me to reel in the Big Fish. I have to say, it was also pretty damn helpful how you wrapped up all of the power I need up into one big package. I mean, I was ready to let go of what you took from me, for the sake of the bigger picture, but this is going to work out better than I could have hoped. Gervais, the rift."

The archfiend and Izak both rose and walked to the rear of the human throne. There had to be a rift back there.

I found Sarah's consciousness. I pushed myself into it, aiming to take control. We had to break his grip, and get away from him. I found myself with muscle, bone, touch, and taste once again. I saw the way she saw, and I felt the pain of the Beast's grip. I planted my feet and pulled back, hard, focusing, finding my own power, finding Charis', finding Sarah's. I joined them all into the strength of her mortal arm, wrenching the Beast backwards, throwing him to the far wall.

I turned and saw the Box, ten feet away. I made a run for it.

Izak tackled us, knocking us to the ground and stealing the wind from our lungs. Even with my power, Sarah was still mortal. There was nothing I could do to make her body hold up as well as my Divine form could. I could make the muscles

300

stronger, but I couldn't make everything more resilient. Izak twisted our arm behind us, threatening to break it. I kept us struggling and fighting, but even one-handed he could hold her without much trouble. The Beast stood and dusted off his pinstriped suit.

"Full of surprises," he said. "I'm actually starting to think I'm going to miss you, kid. I don't even think God will be as much fun to play against as you've been."

"I'm not done yet," I said in Sarah's voice. I focused, taking all of the power again and willing the ground beneath him to open up. He stayed in position, floating over the gaping hole.

"No, not anywhere near good enough," he laughed.

I focused again, pulling the walls in on him, to crush him beneath the stone. He held out his hands, and it all crumbled to dust around him.

"Your power is my power, moron," he shouted. "Except, I have a lot more of it, if you haven't figured that out by now. There is nothing you can do to stop me. What?"

I didn't know what was happening behind us. What I did know was that Izak's hands were pulled from Sarah's body, and I heard a thump nearby. I would have loved to know what was going on, but there was no time. I focused, pulling the Box to our hand and then abandoning control, leaving Sarah standing there, holding it.

"No," the Beast said. "You're mine. You can't do this." He came running towards us, a sudden panic in his voice.

"*Sarah, do it,*" I said.

I felt her focusing, pulling at our souls. I felt the stream of energy pouring through me, from my Source to her. I felt Charis with me, within me, her being as raw and naked as my own. The Box began to glow in our senses, a red-gold hue that matched the color of Sarah's lost eyes.

301

"You can't do it," the Beast said. "His Box can't hold me."

"It can," Sarah said. She kept taking, and I started to feel dizzy and dry. It took her only seconds to suck every last bit of the Beast's power through our conduits to Purgatory, to steal it from our souls, and to mix it with her own, creating a perfect balance of strength.

The Beast reached us, and his hand grabbed for the Box. "I won't let it," he said.

The hand moved like it was in slow motion.

"You have no choice. Stop," she Commanded.

The power of it created a shockwave that shook the floor below us, and threatened to finish the collapse I had started. Outside, I heard a million cries of agony.

Inside, the Beast stopped.

The power kept growing, beginning to arc from the Box and swirl around us, catching us all in a maelstrom of energy.

"Get in the Box," she ordered.

The Beast reached forward and put his hand on the Box, and vanished.

He was in there. I knew it, because I could feel the change around us immediately. I heard shouting and confusion from the people outside. I felt the flames of the rift burst into existence behind us. Sarah held the Box, the power condensing on it, the Templar script glowing and flowing like the river of power that had contained the Beast once before.

Still she poured more into it.

"*It isn't enough,*" she said. "*Landon, it isn't enough.*"

I could feel it through her. Our power was almost used up. Hers was nearly gone. The Box was beginning to heat up and crack.

"You know what you have to do," Dante said, coming up next to us. He had been released when the Beast had gone in.

I did know, but I didn't want to just accept it. I had heard firsthand what had happened before. I knew that it would be forever. How could I do that? How could I just give everything for everyone else, and leave nothing for me? I was a nice guy, but I wasn't *that* nice.

"*You won't be alone*," Charis said. "*Landon, we have to.*"

The Box continued to get warmer, the cracks spreading.

"*Landon!*" Sarah cried.

Why couldn't I have just died, that day in the museum? Nothing that had happened since was worth this moment, and what I knew would come. Having Charis didn't make it better, it made it worse. She would be subjected to the same fate.

"Find a way," I said to Dante, taking hold of Sarah just long enough to speak to him. "Find a way to end this, forever. Just hiding the Box is too big of a risk. One day it will be found. It has to be over."

"I will, signore."

"*Sarah, stay strong. Your fate is your own, no matter what anyone says.*"

"*I will, brother.*"

I found Charis then, in Sarah's soul. She materialized in front of me, her nude form perfect in its radiance. She had tears in her eyes, and I'm sure I did too.

"I love you," I said. I didn't think I needed to say it, but I did anyway.

"I know," she replied. She didn't need to say it either.

I took her hand, and we stepped into the flood.

CHAPTER THIRTY-TWO

I saw it all, in a fog of emotions that made it hard to find the truth behind them. I watched him touch the box and disappear, after I took the weak, mortal form and used it to defy him. After I surprised the demon and pulled him away, giving them the precious seconds they needed. The other one had fled when he went in, his own power diminished by losing his master. He had taken his toy with him.

I saw it all. The Outcast approaching the girl, Sarah. Her words to him, not the girl's words but his. I knew what he was going to do. I knew what he had to do, for another had done it before. The Box had flashed in a vaporous blue light, the cracks had sealed, and she had been stricken with such grief, she had let it fall to the floor. It landed, bounced a few times, and sat alone in the darkness.

She had looked around then, confused, lost, and scared. The Outcast tried to speak to her, but she screeched at him and clawed at his face until he backed away, and vanished. She thought she was alone, but then other mortals started entering the building, confused, looking for answers. She had snatched up the Box and ran, pushing through them. Where was she headed?

The Were had fallen to the Beast's power, but the Beast was gone, and now he

304

woke. The mortals wouldn't remember him. He put his nose to the air, found the
scent, and gave chase.

I don't know how it had come to this. I don't know where most of these
emotions had been born. I could remember pain, and sadness, and anger, and
desperation. I could remember bright, white light, and finding myself outside of my
body, floating in the ether, a consciousness without form. I could recall the
change, the shift, the lust turning to love, the anger turning to compassion. I
didn't understand it, and I still couldn't, yet I felt its compulsion all the same.

Landon had been there, crouched over the Outcast, along with another like
him, and Sarah. He had looked towards me, with pain in his eyes. I had tried to go
to him, but I felt like I was floating, not running. I had flowed in his direction,
but there was no recognition in his eyes. They looked right through me. He couldn't
see.

I was caught in the energy. I could feel it running through me. I could see
the colors of it, the power of Purgatory, power that knew only one owner, that
could only have ever responded to one. It was a power I hadn't understood, but it
moved through me as though I were no more than energy myself. It swirled around me,
and then I was somewhere else. A field. They were still there.

Every part of me wanted to cry out, to tell him I was there, and that I loved
him. I knew I couldn't. I also knew my love had been no love at all. Lust, desire,
and hunger, but not love. Before, there had been no other meaning to the word. Now,
it was all clear. I could feel His touch, somehow. I could feel His warmth. How
could that be?

I watched him go, into the house with Sarah and the one I had known as the
Demon Queen. I didn't follow. There was so much between us. So much I had done that
couldn't be undone. If He willed it, one day I would have the chance to apologize.
For now, if I were to care for him, I could protect him. But how?

I stayed the night, right outside the house. I was there when the Beast arrived. I tried to stop him, but I had nothing in this form. Nothing but thought, emotion, and vision. I couldn't touch him, or hurt him. He didn't even know I was there. None of them did.

It wasn't until we reached Florence that I discovered I could gain physical form only through a mortal shell. Landon was being attacked, and I was desperate to help him. It was that emotion that drove me to a man sitting at a restaurant table. I felt my energy passing through him, and then I saw the light of his soul. I took hold of it, wrapped that desperation around it, and then I was looking through his eyes.

Mortals are weak, and they are slow. They are easily tired, easily destroyed. Their muscles are limited, a large majority of their bodies out of shape. In the past, I had held disdain for them. They were good only as a food source for the superior race. Now, even with those limitations, I found myself intrigued. I could see the man's memories. I could feel his emotions. I found respect for their complexity, and understanding for their plight. Maybe I knew Landon in a new way, then. Maybe I cared for him more. Either way, I had used the form to tackle one of the weres that chased him. It wasn't much, and the demon had killed my host with little effort, but it had slowed him down.

From there on, I had followed, always with him, or a step behind. I had seen the Beast's ambush on the train. I had pulled the brakes and stopped them short, giving him as much warning as I could. Being limited to controlling of mortals was difficult, for they rightly ran away from the Divine.

Then, in the depths of a warehouse in Japan, I had found my chance, my own true opportunity to try to reveal myself to him. To show him I was there where he couldn't reject me. I had taken the body of the girl, Elyse. I had fought him, with all the strength and fervor the mortal flesh would allow. I had played the role of the daughter well, and as he left I kissed him, hoping it would stir his memories,

and open his eyes to my true form.

He barely noticed.

It was the way he looked at her. He had never looked at me that way. There

had been lust, his as much as mine, but that was all. It was that lust that I had

believed was love, but he never knew me well enough to love me. Just as I didn't

know him well enough to truly love him. Yet, I cared. I cared that I had betrayed

him, that I had helped the Beast to escape, that I had caused him pain. I could see

in his eyes that he loved her. I could see when they looked at one another that

they *knew*. Even though they never directly showed it or said it. I couldn't compete

with that, and realized I didn't want to.

To truly cherish something is to do everything in your power to see it reach

its greatest potential.

Such thoughts had never been mine before. They'd been lost in a hunger for

control, a thirst for power, a desire of flesh and blood. They'd been buried

beneath the promises the Beast had made to me, promises that I had fooled myself

into believing would come to pass, right up until he plunged the sword into my

heart.

That was it, I knew. The sword. It had glowed with white heat, searing my

heart. Uncovering the layers of darkness and deceit, pulling them apart like petals

on a black rose. Beneath was a heart that could feel, all of the emotions He had

given His creations, though they had been twisted by his son's misunderstanding.

I followed, and I waited. I knew my time would come, my chance would come to

make good on my new heart's desire to atone for my sins, and to save the man who

had ignited the first spark of emotion within me.

It was that look. That final look he had given me before we left the prison.

Despite what I had done, he still cared. Forgiveness existed, if only I had the strength and will to look for it, and ask for it.

He had given me hope and catalyzed my redemption.

I would be his salvation.

Books By M.R. Forbes

The Divine

Balance

Betrayal

Broken

Tears of Blood

His Dark Empire

Thank You!

It is readers like you, who take a chance on self-published works that is what makes the very existence of such works possible. Thank you so very much for spending your hard-earned money, time, and energy on this work. It is my sincerest hope that you have enjoyed reading!

Independent authors could not continue to thrive without your support. If you have enjoyed this, or any other independently published work, please consider taking a moment to leave a review at the source of your purchase. Reviews have an immense impact on the overall commercial success of a given work, and your voice can help shape the future of the people whose efforts you have enjoyed.

Thank you again!

Shark Finning

10% of the royalties earned from sales of the copy of Broken will be donated to Sea Shepherd to help them raise awareness of the practice of shark finning.

Shark finning refers to the removal and retention of shark fins while the remainder of the living shark is discarded in the ocean. Sharks returned to the ocean without their fins are often still alive; unable to move effectively, they sink to the bottom of the ocean and die of suffocation or are eaten by other predators. * Wikipedia

You can read more about shark finning on Wikipedia here:

http://en.wikipedia.org/wiki/Shark_finning

You can read about Sea Shepherd's efforts to help sharks here:

http://www.seashepherd.org/operation-requiem/

About the Author

M.R. Forbes is a full-time nerd, and a part-time writer of fantasy novels. He's read at least three books, and has been trying to write them since he was nine. He's much better at it today than he was when he was nine. At least, that's what his wife says.

Have something to say? Want to be notified of new releases? Use the links below to make it happen.

Mailing List:

http://bit.ly/XRbZ5n

Website:

http://www.mrforbes.com/site/writing

Facebook:

http://www.facebook.com/mrforbes.author

Goodreads:

http://www.goodreads.com/author/show/6912725.M_R_Forbes

Twitter:

http://www.twitter.com/mrforbes

<<<<>>>>

CPSIA information can be obtained
at www.ICGtesting.com
Printed in the USA
LVOW10s1501260117
522286LV00010B/1120/P